Glass Slippers
and Champagne

Elena Djakonova

863 Production House
MIAMI, FLORIDA

Published by
863 Production House
Miami, Florida

Copyright © 2018 Elena Djakonova

ISBN: 978-0-69217-931-4

Edited by Carol Killman Rosenberg
www.carolkillmanrosenberg.com

Cover design by Dimitry Chamy
www.2urn.com

Cover Photography by Stacy O'Nell
www.sophotographyonline.com

Interior design by Gary A. Rosenberg
www.thebookcouple.com

To my muse, my husband. You lift me up and give me wings. You make me a better person and inspire me. Thank you for walking beside me every step of this journey.

Prologue

"**F**or someone who fixes people's hearts, you surprisingly lack one of your own—"

The sound of glass hitting the wall interrupted Andie's words. Sharp shards scattered all over the floor and glistened in the rays of the dying daylight. The door slammed shut with an explosive force, shaking all the windows and leaving her alone amidst the broken glass that resembled her relationship.

With trembling fingers, Andie speed-dialed a number on her phone, and the next thing she knew, she was seated on a couch across town, nursing a large margarita. Separated by a glass coffee table, in the chair opposite Andie, her best friend JoAnna, or "Jo," with an identical glass in front of her, sat texting with the determination and purpose that characterized everything she did. She had to cancel a promising date to deal with this red-hot mess. This was not the first time Andie and JC had fought, but this time it seemed like it was over for good. The shithead had the nerve to give Andie an "I-am-not-ready-for-this" speech—and that's after he had talked her into giving up her own place to move in with him!

"You know you are not homeless, right?" assured Jo, her gaze traveled through the open doorway into her bedroom, where Andie's crap was piled all over the place.

Andie nodded, and tears brimmed in her eyes. "I will have to drop out of grad school." The thought of giving up on her dream was almost more painful than the breakup itself.

"Let's not make any rash decisions, love. As I said, you can stay with my brother and me for as long as you need. You know Brian loves you like a sister."

"Thank you, but I can't sleep on your couch forever. I need to find a place to live and a job "job" to pay for it. That leaves no time for school and even less for the hundreds of counseling hours I need to get my license. This is a clusterfuck!"

Jo looked at the empty glass in Andie's hand and disappeared into the kitchen. A few moments later, she reemerged with a full pitcher. This was going to be a long night.

Chapter 1

Clair, a still attractive slender woman in her sixties with an auburn chin-length bob, locked the door to her office and rushed down the corridor. She needed to get out of the UM campus without a delay if she stood a chance to beat the traffic getting out of the Gables this late in the afternoon.

"Dr. Thompson!"

Here it goes, thought Clair as she turned around. A girl, one of her grad students, ran toward her.

"What is it, Andie?" prompted Clair without slowing her pace. "Walk with me."

The girl caught up and now walked beside her, following Clair out to the parking lot.

"Dr. Thompson, I was trying to sign up for your lecture next week on signs of post-traumatic stress disorder in preteens, but admission is restricted. They require your approval for any exceptions."

"Stop by tomorrow during my office hours, and I will sign off the admissions sheet. I am sorry, Andie, I have to run." Clair opened the door of her Lexus.

"Thank you! Have a good evening."

"You too, dear."

As Clair pulled out of the campus, her mind was still on the girl. She was a bright one; students like Andie were the reason she had chosen to teach almost twenty years ago.

She jumped onto the turnpike and was pleasantly surprised by the light traffic; it moved swiftly, and Clair made decent time navigating toward the beach. She had dinner plans at the home of her best and oldest friend, Evelyn Lindberg. A soft humming of the motor quieted her mind, turning her thoughts to the memories of their past. Clair drove over the bridge, reminiscing on how their life paths had diverged so dramatically from what they had dreamed of as girls.

Clair and Evelyn had grown up together, right here in Coral Gables. They had attended the same private school, their parents had moved in the same social circles, their lives had intertwined, mirroring each other's in almost every aspect until after high school graduation. To everyone's surprise, Clair had decided to study psychology and had gone to Princeton to pursue her degree, while Evelyn stayed in the Gables.

Evelyn had been young and beautiful, the belle of every ball when she met the dashing thirty-year-old multimillionaire Rick Lindberg, whom she had married after a whirlwind romance. Rick had built his young bride a stunning home where she hosted lavish parties and countless charity balls. As a matter of fact, Clair had met her future ex-husband at one of the Lindbergs' soirees.

Evelyn had given Rick two sons who grew up to be successful in their own right. The fairy tale did not have a happy ending; in real life, they rarely do. Even though Evelyn's world seemed enchanted looking in from the outside, in reality, it was a cold place.

The true heartbreak, however, was still on its way, when five years ago, Rick had suffered a heart attack while skiing in Switzerland and passed away abruptly and unexpectedly. Just two years later, Evelyn lost her eldest son and daughter-in-law. Still bewildered by grief, Evelyn suddenly became a caregiver to her then-four-year-old grandson.

The death of the boy's parents had a far-reaching effect on the child; he grew depressed and showed signs of regression, accompanied by bursts of anger. Almost three years after the tragedy, the child still displayed moderate symptoms of separation anxiety on the one hand and difficulty connecting with the people outside his immediate circle on the other. Despite countless hours of therapy, the boy was still withdrawn and irritable.

Clair pulled into the driveway of the Lindberg mansion. This place had always intimidated her with its size and stature.

Everyone has heard of Miami Beach, most have heard of the celebrity-rich Star Island, some even have heard of the exclusive and private Fisher Island, but only a few have heard of Indian Creek. Tucked away about fifteen minutes north of South Beach, this elite community hides the homes of the very rich and not so famous, though recently some highly private newcomers like Mr. and Mrs. Carter, better known as Jay-Z and Beyoncé, selected it as their residence of choice in South Florida. Here it is not uncommon to see the country's top politicians and future presidents promise the world—and the blood of their firstborn—to the wealthy and all-powerful few in exchange for their support.

Consuelo, the Lindberg's housekeeper of many years, opened the door and smiled in greeting at Evelyn's lifelong friend. Clair followed the petite, dark-haired woman into the grand room, the central entertainment area, an imposing space that stretched the entire width of the house. The French doors on both sides opened up to the front and backyard. The latter featured a magnificent 180-degree view of Biscayne Bay, an Olympic-sized pool, and manicured grounds.

A mahogany bar with intricate carvings, imported from somewhere in Ireland, stood in one corner of the room. Across from it, mounted on the wall, a majestic family portrait depicted Evelyn, surrounded by Rick and their young sons, Patrick and Erik. A grand piano and expensive, elegant furnishings dressed the rest of the space.

Consuelo poured Clair a glass of wine and offered her hors d'oeuvres on a silver tray. Clair took a sip of the excellent red Bordeaux, bit into a baked brie crostini with a hint of fig balsamic glaze, savoring its decadent flavors, and settled into a comfortable chair, relaxing her eyes on the picturesque views. She heard the light steps of her friend and turned around to greet her. Evelyn entered the room with her grandson, Christian, trailing unwillingly beside her. Consuelo fixed Evelyn a martini and ushered the boy away after a shy "Hi" to Clair.

"Nanny is off today?" asked Clair.

Evelyn took an anxious breath and a generous sip. "Quit. Another one just quit."

"I'm sorry to hear that! What happened?"

"Christian is not the easiest child. And nannies are in high demand."

"What did he do now?"

"Nothing in particular. You know how he can be. He does not listen, he throws things when he is upset. I think he just wore her out and she was not equipped to deal with a child like him."

"But you pay well, and they get their own room here at the estate . . ."

Evelyn shrugged her shoulders. "Everyone offers that here. All the nannies jump from one household to another. As I said, Christian can be difficult."

"How's his therapy?"

"It's a process. Some days he is well, just like any other kid. Other days he is quiet and withdrawn; other times he is kicking and screaming." Evelyn took a gulp. "Clair, I am not cut out for this. I am too old! Do you realize, we will be sixty-five next year? I just don't have the stamina! Kids are meant to be raised by young people. Christian needs someone who has the energy to chase after him! I can't deal with this any longer!"

"An au pair?" suggested Clair.

"They're usually too young and inexperienced. He needs someone who has more skills. A therapist on staff would be perfect." Evelyn chuckled bitterly. "I put the request with the agency. We'll see."

"I'll keep my eyes open as well." Clair felt helpless.

Consuelo quietly reentered the room. "Señora, are you ready for dinner?"

Evelyn nodded and got up. "Thank you, Consuelo."

The women walked into the cozy family dining room where the table was set for two. Phillippe, the chef and house manager, poked his head in through the doorway. "Wonderful to see you, Mrs. T. Do you ladies require anything else at the moment?"

"Thank you, Phillippe," responded Evelyn. "Is Christian eating upstairs?"

"Don't worry, ma'am. He's watching *Finding Dory* in the family room. I made him his favorite meatballs and mashed potatoes, and he's as happy as a clam." Phillippe chuckled at his play on words. "I'll be in my apartment upstairs. Howl if you need anything. I'll be back to take care of the dessert." Phillippe winked. "Mrs. T, I've made your favorite bread pudding."

Clair smiled. "You are spoiling me, Phillippe."

Evelyn chose medium-bodied Sangiovese to be served at dinner to complement the osso buco and mushroom risotto. A scrumptious meal and another glass of wine eased up the conversation. Both of the women loved to travel, and Evelyn spoke about the trip to Europe she was hoping to take the following year. It was too difficult to do now, but hopefully when Christian got a bit older . . .

Clair discussed an article she was writing for *Psychology Today* about habits of confident people, and the deadline she was trying to meet.

The conversation turned to Evelyn's younger son, Erik. He had spent most of the past few months between China and New York, working on some kind of acquisition, but Evelyn hoped he would make it to Florida to spend some time with her here in a month or so.

The women took their coffee on the veranda, a cool April breeze from the bay made it pleasant to be outside, and scarlet sunset lit the sky aflame. As promised, the dessert was in one of Phillippe's best traditions. After they parted, Evelyn felt better venting to her friend; Clair guilty about her inability to help. She tossed and turned in her bed that night, unable to sleep.

The next morning at the university brought the usual hustle Clair loved—the restlessness of youth, the noise, the overly dramatic talk in the corridors, and the smell of vanilla coffee in her to-go cup. She almost jumped when Andie knocked on her open office door.

"I am so sorry!" Andie gasped. "Did I startle you?"

Clair waved the girl in and pulled out her pen. She signed the paper the student handed her but paused before giving it back. Usually bright-eyed, this morning Andie looked like her light had been sucked out of her.

"Shut the door and sit down," Clair instructed. "What's going on with you?"

Reluctant at first, but with some encouragement Andie opened up. It was the same story: girl meets boy, boy is an asshole, now the girl needs a place to live and a job.

When Andie left, Clair picked up her phone. "Evelyn, it might be unorthodox, but I think I found you a nanny."

* * *

The following morning, a report with everything there was to know about Andrea Ellis and her twenty-six years of life arrived on Evelyn's desk.

Andie was born and raised in Northern California, about a forty-minute drive south of San Francisco. She was the only child of parents David, an architect, and Katy, a choreographer. She had played volleyball, captaining her high school team. She had been offered scholarships to several universities and had graduated from Stanford with a degree in psychology. After college, Andie had gone backpacking through Europe, and on her way back, she had stopped in Florida to visit with a high school friend. And voila! She was still in Florida a few years later. She had worked at a family counseling office under Dr. James Brice, PhD, but quit after enrolling in the graduate program in child psychology at UM. She now worked part-time at a coffee shop a few blocks away from the campus.

Evelyn took off her glasses and rubbed the corners of her eyes. It might just work; even Clair thought it might be the fresh start they all needed. At this point, she was willing to try anything. It was settled then; she would talk to this girl. Clair would set it up. *Friday. Yes, this Friday would be perfect.*

* * *

On Friday afternoon, Andie hopped into her sky-blue Mini Cooper and rushed off the campus. She had an interview with the Lindbergs—not the career opportunity of the lifetime, but beggars can't be choosers, she reminded herself.

Half an hour later, she drove onto the meticulously manicured grounds of the Lindberg compound.

"Holy shit!" she gasped as her car pulled into the driveway of the estate.

The mansion was nothing like what she had expected. *Do people really live like this?* She was not a scrub herself; she had grown up in Monterey, studied at Stanford, and lived in Miami. There had always been plenty of multimillion-dollar real estate around. But this place was like something from a reality TV show—or better yet, a Bruce Wayne stronghold. The property was grand, a two-story classic Mediterranean mansion with large terraces and a lush garden that framed the front of the estate. At the end of the driveway, to the right of the main building, stood a five-car garage with what looked like servants' apartments above.

Andie got out of the car and rang the doorbell. A diminutive woman in her fifties with a heavy Spanish accent opened the door and invited Andie into the imposing entrance, then guided the way past the grand stairwell and into an intimate and warm drawing room.

"Mrs. Lindberg will come soon," she said warmly.

Andie looked around. The richly upholstered walls were partially hidden behind shelves displaying tasteful antiques. Alongside the French doors that led into the front yard stood an ornate chaise lounge, and a petite satinwood desk was positioned in the middle of the room.

Andie heard footsteps in the hallway, and a tall, graceful woman with shoulder-length chestnut hair and blue eyes walked into the room.

"Miss Ellis, thank you for coming." Evelyn sat down behind the desk and gestured for Andie to take a seat. Evelyn gazed firmly at the young woman in front of her. *Pretty,* she thought, *Beautiful, actually.* Honey golden hair framed the heart-shaped face with high cheekbones; long dark eyelashes and confidently arched eyebrows accentuated her big blue eyes. Healthy glowing skin and a slender body suggested Andie was active and enjoyed the outdoors.

"Dr. Thompson is an old friend of mine," Evelyn explained, "and she recommended you highly. As you know, I am looking for a nanny for my grandson, Christian. This is not the direction I thought of taking, but I'm willing to give it a try. Do you have much experience with kids?"

"I worked as a babysitter through high school,"

Andie replied, "and I'm getting my master's in child psychology, but I agree this is a bit out of the box—"

"How long do you have left in your studies?"

"A little over a year, plus the counseling hours."

Evelyn nodded. "You're a young lady. As you know, I require the nanny to live here at the estate. I'm not inclined to entertain overnight guests." Evelyn lifted her hand to silence the words that seemed ready to escape Andie's mouth. "I can't stop you from living your life, but if I were to hire you, I really hope not to have to change the nanny a few months from now because you got swept off your feet. I hope I can count on you to be responsible and discreet."

Andie felt taken aback by the straightforwardness of the statement and paused before answering. "Of course," she replied carefully choosing her words. "As you mentioned, life goes on and there are no guarantees, but as of right now I am concentrating on getting my degree and moving forward, establishing my career. I can't promise I won't run away and marry a Prince Charming, but the probability of me finding one immediately is fairly low. Unfortunately."

"Very well." Evelyn watched the girl; she had a warmth about her, she was poised, her eyes intelligent. *This just might work.*

"Walk with me." Evelyn got up from behind the desk.

Andie followed her out of the room and up the grand staircase. The second floor opened to a rotunda-like foyer with the hallways leading in three opposite directions.

Evelyn pointed at the only door right across from the stairs.

"This is Christian's room," she said.

She led Andie down the hallway to the right, into a surprisingly casual and cozy family room complete with large bay windows, comfortable couches and armchairs, a fireplace, and, of course, a seventy-inch TV. On the floor in front of the TV, drawing in his coloring books, sat a small, slender boy with blond hair.

"Christian, honey, say 'hi' to Andrea," Evelyn said, interrupting his activity.

The boy lifted his pretty face and looked at the women with his big blue eyes. "Hello."
A knot tightened in Andie's stomach; the boy reminded her of Antoine de Saint-Exupéry's Little Prince. She stepped forward, got down on her knees next to Christian, and peeked into his coloring book.

"What are you coloring?"

"Spider-Man," replied the boy, turning his attention back to the page.

"Is he your favorite superhero?"

"I also like Wolverine," answered Christian without lifting his eyes from the page.

"I like Wolverine, too. Do you have any others in this book?"

"A few."

"Like who? Superman?"

"No. He's in my other book."

"I see. What about Batman? You like Batman?"

"He's okay."

"Cool. Who else do you have in there?"

"Hulk. But I don't like him."

"Why don't you like Hulk?"

"He's angry. He only gets his powers when he is angry. And he can't control them."

"So you like the heroes who are in control?"

"I dunno. And Flash. I like him, too. He's fast."

"I don't know much about him. Will you tell me his story sometime?"

Christian shrugged his shoulders. Andie got off her knees.

"It's nice to meet you Christian. See you soon?"

The boy nodded without lifting his head from his project.

Andie stepped back toward Evelyn, who had intently watched the interaction. The women turned to leave the room.

"Andie?" Christian called. He lifted his eyes and looked at the girl. "Will see you soon?"

Andie smiled. "Yeah."

They walked down the stairs and back into the drawing room. Evelyn pressed a button on a panel with an in-wall speaker, activating the house intercom system. "Phillippe."

A green light lit up and a man's voice answered. "I'll be right there, Mrs. Lindberg."

A minute or so later, a bald man in his mid-forties walked into the room; his brown eyes fixed on Andie.

He had a medium build, with fair, well-moisturized skin that suggested he did not indulge in sunbathing and paid special attention to his beauty routine. His dark eyebrows were meticulously groomed.

"Phillippe," Evelyn said, "this is Miss Andrea Ellis. Andrea, Phillippe is the manager of my household. He will take it from here. It was nice to meet you."

Realizing that her audience with the queen bee was over, Andie followed Phillippe across the hallway into the kitchen, which included a small office for Phillippe and a large butler's pantry. It was indeed a gourmet chef's dream kitchen, with a center island, state-of-the-art appliances, all the gadgets, and, to Andie's delight, an industrial-sized coffee machine. The glass doors opened onto a small porch with comfortable wicker chairs. In Andie's humble opinion, it offered the best view of the property, overlooking a tennis court to the right, a swimming pool to the left, and an unobstructed view of Biscayne Bay in front.

As if reading her mind, Phillippe smiled. "I know, this is the best seat in the house! I got this furniture not too long ago, so now every morning I start with a cup of tea and meditation. This is my oasis."

Andie politely smiled back at him. "I am sure Mrs. Lindberg enjoys this kitchen."

Phillippe laughed. "Honey, I have worked for the Lindbergs for over fifteen years, and I have never seen Mrs. Lindberg set foot in this kitchen! This is *my* domain!"

Andie contemplated the thought. Apparently, it was good to be the king—or the queen, for that matter. She followed Phillippe into a dark corridor off the kitchen to a room that Andie, if she was lucky, was to occupy. The room itself was cramped, but it fit a full-sized bed and a small desk, and it had a bathroom and a small closet. A window looked out onto the service entrance, driveway, and a garage building, with Phillippe's and Consuelo's apartments above it. Andie looked around. Not too shabby. It would work.

"It's not a master suite," acknowledged Phillippe, "but it'll do the job. Consuelo, the housemaid, and her husband, Javier, have the apartment to the right." Phillippe pointed through the window. "I have the smaller one to the left. But I only stay here when my partner, Greg, is away. He's a flight attendant. We have a cute cottage in Hollywood, but when he's away, it is easier for me to crash here. It's like my own man cave," he said proudly, while Andie politely smiled.

They walked back through the kitchen and into Phillippe's office. It seemed, all of a sudden, the man had realized he was being way too friendly and he switched to his all-important-sheriff-of-the-village role.

"If you were to get this position," he began, "we will do our best to accommodate your school schedule. You will also have one night off during the week, as well as Sunday afternoons, plus every other Saturday. You are free after eight p.m. when Christian goes to sleep. We will take care of your room and board. I would need a list of your food allergies, if any. If there are no extravagant requests, I am sure we will be able to accommodate your food preferences."

The man looked at Andie, expecting an acknowledgment of his terms and conditions. Andie nodded, and Phillippe continued, "Let us discuss this internally, and we will get back to you."

Chapter 2

SoHo House—the heartbeat of South Beach's vibrant social scene, the haven where socialites of both genders and all ages chill, sip craft cocktails, and emit bohemian vibes. An expensive and exclusive club obsessed with its nonconformist image, SoHo house draws world-class movie stars and fashion icons, along with "OMG, my fifteen minutes of fame are finally here" celebrities. Closed to the general public, the club opens its doors and offers its membership at a fraction of the cost to young trendsetters until they reach the ripe old age of twenty-seven. Beautiful people have a tendency to attract other beautiful people, so, dressed up in their overpriced understated styles, they all migrate to their mothership.

A balmy air had enveloped the city and the setting sun colored it orange. Nothing suggested the months of the upcoming inferno that was a South Florida summer, but the calendar reminded the locals it was on its way.

Stretched out on the couch, Jo and Andie enjoyed the last of the mild weather and a bottle of white wine at the members-only second-floor lounge.

"But I will never see you anymore!" complained Jo. "I am not sure I like the idea of you selling yourself into servitude!"

"It is hardly that bad," smiled Andie.

"Are you kidding me?" Jo made air quotes with her hands: "They will let you out for air one night a week and on Sundays. Is that even legal?"

"You forgot every other Saturday," chuckled Andie. "And I am allowed to get out during the day to go to school and back."

"Awesome! Are you expected to wear a bonnet and a maid's uniform? You know you don't have to do this shit, right? You can stay with Brian and me for as long as you need."

"Thank you. But I can't sleep on your couch indefinitely. This solves all of my issues for the next year. Plus, look at the bright side! I will get hands-on experience in my future career field, difficult kids, and all. What could beat that?"

"Be careful not to get too attached to the brat! Is he at least cute?"

Andie chuckled, Jo was never a sentimental type. "Yeah, he is cute. I don't think Mrs. Lindberg is a very warm person."

"Great! So they decided to hire him a mommy!"

"I don't think so," Andie answered thoughtfully evaluating the validity of Jo's point.

"Really? Because it very much looks like it to me."

Andie took a bite of the Manchego and a sip of the

Albariño, the peach and apple notes of the wine hitting her palate and complementing the nuttiness of the cheese. To be honest, she knew Jo was right. Admitting it was another matter entirely. "It will be fine. Don't you worry."

"Okay, if you say so. Light a candle in the north tower if you need us to rescue you."

Andie laughed. "They might chain me in the dungeon and not let me see the light of day."

"Well, then you are screwed," concluded Jo. "Why do they need a nanny anyway? Where the fuck are the parents? Did you Google them?"

"No, not yet. I wanted to make up my mind first."

"I can't believe you have not done your due diligence!" Jo's fingers were on it. She speed-typed "Lindbergs" into her iPhone. "Voila!" She scrolled down and scanned her search results. "Fuck me! Do you really want to get involved?"

She passed the phone to her friend. A *Miami Herald* announcement from three years earlier read, "An heir to the Lindberg fortune, Patrick Lindberg, and his wife, Lori Lindberg, were killed early on Sunday morning in a car crash. They are survived by their four-year-old son, Christian Lindberg."

Andie fought off a wave of nausea as tears began to roll down her cheeks. *Poor Little Prince. Poor Mrs. Lindberg.*

"Oh, great!" exclaimed Jo. "I really don't think you should take this job. It's way too much baggage, Andie.

It's not a babysitting gig where you can clock out and forget about it at the end of the night. You will be living with these people day in and day out. It's not just a difficult kid, it's a child who is probably majorly emotionally fucked-up. And so is that woman, as a matter of fact. You don't have enough experience dealing with that shit. Besides, I know you, you will get too emotionally involved."

Andie wiped her face, careful not to smudge her mascara. "It will be fine," she repeated. She changed the subject. "So what's the plan for my last weekend of freedom?"

"A good question! Let's see what Uncle Paul is up to." Jo, who had not put her phone down the entire conversation, typed a quick text message, and, a few moments later, her phone dinged, announcing an answer had arrived. "Want to go to LIV? He has his usual table."

"Sure. Who else is going?"

"Usual suspects." Jo's quick fingers were already typing the response. *"We are in."*

"I need the headcount. Who's going?" texted Uncle Paul.

"Just Tinkerbell and me," entered Jo.

A thumbs-up emoji indicated they were confirmed.

Uncle Paul was not at all related to either of the girls. Tall, dark, and Greek, in his late forties going on twenty—at least in his own mind—Paul enjoyed the company of fun, good-looking people, and his entourage reflected that. He had a particular soft spot for the tall, blond, vibrant Jo. His twenty-two-year-old girlfriend had less fondness for her.

"Let's see if he will take us out for dinner before the club," Jo suggested. Messages flew back and forth until the whole night was planned out, and with a sense of a job well done, Jo could finally put down her phone and finish her wine.

With Saturday night plans of Napoleonic proportions came the mission of getting ready. Back at Jo's cottage, relaxing on the bed, Andie watched her friend disappear into the closet and pull out different outfits, throwing occasional items to the middle of the floor. Jo's older brother and roommate, Brian, strolled in bearing two glasses of champagne and a beer for himself. He stretched out in the bed next to Andie and took a sip from the bottle.

Just two years apart, the siblings were nothing alike. Five-foot-ten, blond, green-eyed, and athletic, gifted with a larger-than-life personality and unlimited supplies of energy, Jo was the younger one of two. Brian, five-foot-seven, a bit overweight, with raven black hair and bright blue eyes, was laid-back and good-humored, which made him the perfect companion and partner in crime.

"I am just here to hold your purses," he would say every time they all went out.

As long as he could remember these two together, Brian had always gotten stuck covering for Jo and Andie with his strict mother, teachers, and coaches. It was like growing up with two sisters—incredibly cute, annoying sisters.

"I've got to take some of this shit to my mom's," announced Jo, throwing a box into the middle of the room. "This house is just too fucking small!"

Brian and Andie gave each other knowing looks and burst into laughter. Jo's "getting ready" routine always involved "shit going to mom's," only to end up back where it came from. Jo freed her closet of another going-to-mom's box.

"Are those our high-school pictures?" Andie jumped off the bed and pulled out the albums.

"Oh Lord!" laughed Brian as he opened the first page. "I didn't realize we even had them here. I thought they were either at Mom's or got lost or something. Look at your fucking hair! Andie, remember this moron?" Brian pointed to one of Jo's less desirable boyfriends from way back when.

He picked up an unglued picture of their mother, Mary. At five feet tall on a good day, the woman came up to Jo's shoulder but possessed as much spunk. Nicknamed Mary Poppins for her domestic talents, she ran a tight ship raising two young kids by herself. The last year of Jo's high school, Mary's job had relocated her to Fort Lauderdale, and the family had moved, breaking up the gang.

Brian handed Andie another picture.

"Okay, sorry to interrupt your trip down the memory lane, but can we, please, concentrate on important things now? Like what I am wearing tonight?!" demanded Jo.

She held out a dress on a hanger and pressed it against her body.

"Not sure," answered Andie. "Got to see it on. Is it new? Have I seen it before?"

"Yeah, at Jersey's birthday," reminded Jo. She squeezed into the dress and motioned to Andie to zip her up.

"Ah, that's right. Yeah, that looks great on you."

"Thanks. What are you wearing?"

Andie pointed toward the bathroom, where an azure Herve Leger signature bandage-style number hung from the door.

"Oh, hot!" approved Jo. "Love it!"

Brian took a chug of his beer and got off the bed. "Going out with Uncle Paul?"

"Yep!" Jo nodded as she applied pink lip gloss.

"Where to?"

"Mr. Chow, then LIV," answered Andie.

"Nice. Wish I was a chick. I would never pay for shit!"

Jo laughed. "We can put some heels on you, spike up your hair, some lipstick . . . you might pass—"

"*Pass* is the correct word," chuckled Brian.

"Hey, don't say we didn't offer. What do you have planned?" asked Andie.

"Meeting the guys for some beer and bowling at Lucky Strike."

"Have fun!"

"Yeah, you too. I will make myself scarce and let you get ready in peace."

"Say 'hi' to the guys from us." Andie smiled.

"Will do. See you tomorrow."

Andie slipped into her minidress and five-inch high heels. The girls looked at each other and smiled; they constituted a fierce duo. In a city full of beautiful women and manipulative men, they managed to hold their own.

"Let's do it!" they said in unison.

* * *

The tart smell of fresh-cut white lilies filled the air at the trendy and fabulous Mr. Chow. The restaurant, a vast white hall with tall ceilings and minimalistic décor in the heart of South Beach, occupied the entire west wing of the posh W hotel.

Jean-Pierre, a long-standing maître d', greeted the girls as if they were his most honorable guests. Flamboyant and feminine, he made everyone feel important, in particular, if they were a beautiful woman or a wealthy patron. And when a beautiful woman was accompanied by a wealthy patron, the sky was the limit. He recognized the girls, of course; it was his job to remember repeat clients. He knew the remaining part of the group was on the way, and they were generous spenders. Right on cue, Uncle Paul, his girlfriend in tow, surrounded by his entourage, strolled through the doors.

"Hello, honeys." His Greek accent was still detectable, even after decades of living in Florida.

The usual table awaited, and the drinks appeared like magic. An array of Asian fusion dishes teased the senses with bold flavors and appetizing aromas. Laughter and the clinking of glasses enveloped the table, and the promise of a fun evening ahead set a lighthearted tone, fueled by free-flowing champagne and good food.

From Mr. Chow, the road led straight to Fontainebleau. First, drinks at the Bleau Bar in the lobby, then, past the velvet robes to a table at LIV. The quintessential South Beach hotspot, LIV was already jam-packed with masses of people enjoying themselves alongside VIPs and celebrities, dancing to thumping electronic dance music. A colossal, lavishly decorated, multilevel space with private tables and a sexy second-floor lounge, LIV redefined what the nightlife experience should be. Its massive central dome, often referred to as "The Spider," outfitted with hundreds of individual screens, was programmed to create an unforgettable light show that danced along to the beat. Beautiful people, blasting music, drinking, kissing, laughing—the night slowly turned into a blur.

* * *

"Rise and shine!" Brian chirped.

Cruel morning light pierced Andie's consciousness and brought her back to reality. Her mouth felt like the Sahara Desert. She cautiously opened her eyes and growled. Brian handed her a tall glass of water and two Advil.

"Fuck me!" Jo appeared in the doorway of her bedroom wearing boy shorts and a tank top. She collapsed on the couch by Andie's feet.

Brian chuckled. "May I say, ladies, you look lovely this morning!"

Jo glared at her inappropriately cheerful brother. "Scratch that! Fuck *you*!"

Brian laughed. "Fun night, huh?"

"I need food!" declared Andie. "Preferably something greasy and disgusting!"

"Big Pink?" suggested Brian. "I will drive. Let's get going. You still have to move today."

Andie growled again and unwillingly removed herself from the couch; the need for food took precedence over the need for sleep.

After breakfast, with her belly and her car full, Andie took off for the Lindbergs' world. It was only a twenty-minute drive, but she felt like she was leaving everything she knew behind.

The Mini Cooper pulled in through the imposing gates. Andie parked in the driveway in front of the garage and cautiously walked through the service entrance into the kitchen. Phillippe, wearing thin-rimmed glasses, moved around the room with an iPad in hand, ordering groceries and supplies for the week. He lifted his eyes over his glasses and greeted her with a nod.

Andie nodded back and sheepishly pointed toward her car. "Is it okay if I park there?"

Phillippe nodded again. "I will call Javier to help you with your things."

"Thank you! That would be great."

Phillippe pressed a button on the intercom, and a few minutes later a stocky man in his fifties with a bright smile walked into the kitchen.

"Javier, *esta* Andie," Phillippe said. "*Por favor, ayuda a la chica a traer sus cosas del auto.*" *Please help the girl to bring her things out of the car.* Phillippe turned to Andie. "Javier is Consuelo's husband. He takes care of the cars and repairs around the estate. If you ever need anything, he is your guy. Ah, he does not speak much English."

With a smile, Javier waved Andie to follow him. He grabbed two of her bags and brought them into her room. He left and reappeared within a few moments, carrying a box.

"Gracias, Señor."

Javier smiled again, nodded, and left. Andie sank down on the bed and looked around the small room. What was she supposed to do now? She walked back into the kitchen as Phillippe finished up with the ordering and put down his iPad.

"Have everything you need?" he asked.

"Yes, I think so."

Phillippe grinned. "Would you like to see the house?"

Shocked at the unexpected friendliness, Andie looked at the man as he continued, "C'mon, Mrs. Lindberg is not here. I'll give you the grand tour."

The Lindbergs' estate sat on over an acre of water-front property, across the street from an eighteen-hole, world-class championship golf course. The monstrosity of a house was designed for year-round, indoor-outdoor entertainment, with large terraces that overlooked the front lawn and a backyard with a pool and an outdoor kitchen.

They started at the main entrance, from which a marble hallway led past the kitchen to the right and Evelyn's drawing room to the left, past the imposing staircase and into the grand room. They strolled through it into another corridor and past several guest suits into an awe-inspiring library.

The library was a two-story piece of architectural art, partially open to both levels. A statement red-wood stair-case led up to the loft that housed rows of bookshelves. Evelyn, a passionate collector, had built an impressive bibliotheca. There a bay window, with cozy cushions for comfortable reading, overlooked the front lawn and offered a peek down to the office.

In the office an antique mahogany desk sat facing the door and the staircase. The wall behind it was uphol-stered in cream-colored calf leather embellished with decorative nails. To the right of the desk, a set of French doors looked out to the pool and the grounds, and to the left a sitting room, where a leather couch and chairs faced the fireplace and the TV. In the corner of the room stood an elegant bar cart, fully stocked with top-shelf liquor; behind it, an ice fridge camouflaged as a console.

Andie was in awe of the handsomely masculine room. Phillippe led her out of the library and up the stairs into the more private quarters of the estate. She recognized the bright and comfortable family room where she had met Christian several days earlier. A hallway to the left led into Mrs. Lindberg's quarters. According to Phillippe, it contained an elegant bedroom with neutral pastel tones, a sitting room, a grand master en suite, and a butler's elevator connected to the kitchen, so he could send up the coffee and the paper in the morning without disturbing Evelyn. Next to Evelyn's suite was Christian's room.

On the opposite side on the same floor was a second master suite, which was occupied by Mrs. Lindberg's younger son when he stayed in Florida.

They walked back downstairs. Phillippe opened and closed several doors in a row, revealing the various rooms.

"Media room." Phillippe introduced the theater-style space. "Formal dining room, informal dining room," he continued, opening and closing the doors.

The tour ended back in the kitchen.

"Mrs. Lindberg and Christian are at their house in Palm Beach," Phillippe explained. "They visit there every few weeks. Consuelo goes with them. They are coming back tomorrow, closer to the end of the day. This will give you time to settle in. I am staying here tonight, so if you need anything, let me know. Help yourself to whatever you want to eat. I am going to finish the menu for the week, so let me know if you need anything specific. Yogurt? Cereal?" He pointed to the fridge and the pantry.

"Thank you," Andie replied. "I think I am okay. I just need coffee in the morning. Do you have any tea?"

Phillippe's serious expression melted into a smile. He opened a cabinet full of rare and exotic teas.

"This is an impressive collection!" acknowledged Andie.

"Thank you. Erik brings me different fabulous teas from everywhere he travels."

"Erik?"

"Mrs. Lindberg's son." Phillippe corrected himself, "Younger son. In any case . . . if you need anything, just buzz me." He showed Andie the appropriate button that rang at his apartment over the garage.

"Does every room have an intercom?"

"Most. Yours does. Also, Christian's room has a camera, so Mrs. Lindberg can see him on her phone. You will have to download the app to your phone as well."

"Of course."

Phillippe walked into the office nook to finish his business for the day, and Andie went back to her room to unpack. It had already been a long day. Overwhelmed, she slowly tried to organize her new home and her thoughts. The light outside the window started to dim, along with her mood. She crawled into bed and took a deep calming breath. Sadness and grief over the relationship that could have been but was no more overpowered her in an overflow of angst. An image of JC, with his crazy, curly black hair and boyish grin, had haunted her since the day they broke up. His lust for life and his "live and let live" attitude had become a part of her own philosophy. She'd learned so much about herself from him; their relationship had become a part of her identity. Without it, she felt lost and disoriented.

Everything happened for a reason. Was this strange place a part of her rediscovery? Only time would tell, she decided.

Chapter 3

They met at the March of Dimes Gala a year earlier, where JC was being honored for his work as a heart surgeon for prematurely born babies. Jo's real estate firm sponsored a table, and Andie volunteered at the check-in desk.

New to Miami, she was eager to meet people. Jo had introduced her to a circle of her friends, including Jersey, who had an extra room at her cottage at the time and needed a roommate.

Jersey—Melissa by birth—was, as the name suggests, from New Jersey. She worked as a hairdresser at a trendy salon in the Design District and was renowned among Miami's socialites for her magical highlights. Her claim to fame, however, was a *Playboy* centerfold she had appeared in a few years earlier. Reasonable rent and a discount on hair services were enough reasons for Andie to move into Jersey's spare bedroom. A job at the doctor's office paid the bills, and volunteering at fund-raisers gave her a glimpse of and access to Florida's who's who.

The Annual March of Dimes Gala traditionally took

place at the bright and shiny JW Marriott Marquis in downtown Miami. Hordes of Miami's elite poured in to show their support. A popular cause, the event was the right place to be seen at.

Newly arrived JC gave his name at the check-in desk and paused when he noticed a beautiful girl at the other end of the table. He put his phone and credit card inside his pocket and approached her.

"Can I help you to register, sir?" Andie looked at him with a polite smile.

"Sir?! Do I look *sir* age already?!" exclaimed JC.

"Not at all. But you look very distinguished in your tuxedo," assured Andie with an approving look.

"Well, thank you. I've just registered, but I could not help but notice how lovely you look. I'm sorry; that came out cheesy. You must be busy . . . there are a lot of people. Good turnout tonight, I see."

Andie nodded. "People need to find a cause to feel good about. Babies are a safe choice. And why are you here, may I ask?"

"Just another guest."

"Enjoy!"

Andie smiled and watched him walk away. *He's hot,* she thought, *and did he just try to flirt? Whatever that was?*

After the registration hour ended, Andie found herself released of her duties. She looked around. The hot guy disappeared, but Jo came across her radar.

"All done?" asked Jo. "Come, we need to get you a drink and a date to Jersey's birthday."

Andie chuckled. "Important things first. A glass of champagne, please." She smiled at the bartender.

"Make it two," corrected Jo. "Are you looking for someone?" she asked, noticing her friend scanning the room.

"Yeah, I checked in this cute guy, and now I can't find him. I hoped to casually bump into him."

"Hmm. That sucks. Maybe after the dinner."

The girls walked to the table where Jo's colleagues and clients had already taken their seats. The emcee, Miami Heat's Shane Battier, started the program with nominations and honors. When JC came onstage as an honoree, Andie jumped in her seat. She pushed Jo with her elbow. "That's the guy!"

"Dr. Cortez is your 'lost boy'?"

"You know him?"

"Not personally. I saw his name on the program and heard my boss talk about him. Hmmm . . . I imagined him much older."

"How old do you think he is?"

"Thirty-six, thirty-seven? Maybe forty?"

"Yeah, that's what I kinda figured."

"He is cute. Why don't you talk to him after dinner?"

Andie grinned. "I fully intend to. Do you know if he's married? I didn't notice a ring."

"Dunno, hopefully not." Jo winked.

A hum of conversation and the sound of the emcee's voice gave way to a live band performance. Jo followed her boss to make the rounds and shake some important hands.

Andie, left to her own devices, walked over to the bar to grab another champagne. She paused to see if she could track the elusive "lost boy" when the "lost boy" found her.

"Are you off duty?" He materialized from nowhere, and startled Andie into spilling her drink. "I am sorry! I didn't mean to sneak up on you," apologized JC. He grabbed a napkin from the bar and patted her dress.

"I think you did." Andie smirked.

"You're right. It's my trick to get to second base without having to buy dinner first."

"Hmmm . . . very smart. What other tricks do you have up your sleeve?"

A sly smiled emerged on the man's face. "Wouldn't you like to know?"

"I would indeed."

"Would you like to check out the dance floor first?"

"Sure." Andie put down her glass and followed him into the crowd.

JC steered her by the waist with his right hand, leading her through the passionate sounds of salsa. Their hips swayed in response to the music, synchronized to the three-step, forward-backward motion. His fingers on her back directed their footsteps. Hypnotized by the rhythm and the movement of their bodies, carried away by the sensual nature of the dance, they moved on the floor, enthralled by each other's energy. With the last notes, JC spun her around and pulled her into his arms.

"Nice moves," she complimented. "Looks like you've done this once or twice before."

JC grinned. "Of course, *amor*. I am Latin!" He kissed her hand and wrapped her arm around his neck. "Want to get out of here?"

Andie's eyes met his. "Yeah, let's do that."

They giggled with the mischief of teenagers cutting class and rushed down the escalator into the brightly lit lobby. Unwilling to wait for an Uber and anxious not to be noticed, they grabbed a cab.

"Let's go to Seaspice," suggested JC as he gave the directions to the driver.

Tires screeched, and the bright streets lined with tall, glass buildings gave way to the dark roads and drawbridges of the Miami River district. Amidst an urban neighborhood forgotten for decades, with no more than a few rusted riverboats and their inhabitants, the local institutions had been joined by a trendy newcomer—Seaspice. A chic lounge with maritime blue and white décor, yachts parked at the dock, and a distant view of the downtown skyline, Seaspice was rumored in its past life to have been a seaplane hangar for the eccentric billionaire Howard Hughes. It had since been reimagined into one of Miami's prettiest hidden spots.

By the time they arrived, a dinner rush had given way to a lounge-y vibe with live music under the stars.

"I guess we are a bit overdressed for the occasion," JC observed. He took off the tuxedo jacket and unbuttoned the collar of his shirt as they parked on the couch by the bar. "Are you from Florida originally?"

"No, California. You?"

"Nicaragua. How did you end up in Miami?"

"I traveled around Europe for a few months after college and stopped in Miami on the way back to visit with a friend. I really liked it here, so I've stayed."

"You had nothing holding you back in California?"

"No. I was lucky to find a job quickly, so it was an easy transition."

"What do you do?"

"I work at a doctor's office."

"That's refreshing. So you don't have a portfolio book and a waitressing job while you wait to be discovered?"

Andie smiled. "You are not too bad yourself. 'I am just another guest.'"

"I don't like to ring my own bell."

"You prefer others do that for you?"

"Exactly. Much more effective."

Andie lifted her brow. "But in all seriousness, heart surgery! At your age! Very impressive. I feel unproductive."

"What do you want to do? It does not look like you are a girl who is happy working as a doctor's help."

"Yeah . . . I want to get my master's eventually."

"You have preferences in the field?" asked JC, playing with her hair.

"Child psychology. Start from the root, you know?"

"Do you have a boyfriend?"

"That's a change of subject if I ever heard one!" laughed Andie.

"And?"

"No. I just moved here a few months ago."

"Oh, so you are interviewing right now?" JC winked.

"Exactly." Andie grinned. "You?"

"I don't have a boyfriend either."

"Ha-ha! Very funny." Andie crinkled her nose and stuck out her tongue.

"I thought so. No, I don't have a girlfriend. I was seeing someone for about a year, but we broke up a few weeks ago."

Andie chuckled. "Hey, I am all for the rebounds! It's just usually I am the one who is on it!"

"I am not on a rebound," protested JC. "It was a short-term relationship that lasted longer than it should have."

"Would she have agreed with this evaluation?"

"Are you going all shrink on me?"

"Don't worry, I won't charge you," teased Andie.

"And yet somehow, I feel, I will pay for this dearly." He stroked her arm with the back of his hand.

Andie sipped her champagne, gazing at the murky water of Miami River. She turned to JC and smiled at feeling his touch. He cradled her face in his hands and brushed her lips with a kiss that sent a jolt of lightning through her stomach. Their bodies drew closer, she ran her hand through his curls and inhaled his scent. Andie's heart pounded like a drumbeat announcing capitulation. Her eyes grew darker, and a rush of passion colored her cheeks.

"Oh, don't look at me with those eyes," JC breathed out, and pulled her back in for another kiss.

They made out on the back seat of their ride all the way to JC's place in South Beach. Andie walked into a minimalistic bachelor apartment that opened to the view of the ocean. She stepped out onto the balcony, leaned over the railing, and gazed at the golden moonwalk over the dark flat water.

JC followed her out and put his arms around her waist. He pressed his body against hers, pushing her against the bars. He pulled her hair to the side and slowly kissed her neck. He traced her bare back with his fingers, found the zipper, and freed her of her dress. It cascaded down to her feet, unmasking her statuesque, seductive body. He spun her around, speechless at the sight of her, as the moonlight shined through her hair, her skin glimmering in the soft golden glow. Overcome, he pulled her back into his arms and covered her lips with his.

A moment later, he steered her into the bedroom and gently pushed her onto the bed. He looked down at the girl in front of him, her long blond hair wild on his sheets, her full lips swollen from his kisses, her eyes dark with desire, her sensual body yearning for his.

"You are so beautiful," he whispered.

* * *

The next morning, Andie woke up in an empty bed. The aroma of the freshly brewed coffee filled the apartment and made her crave a hot bittersweet sip. She showered, wrapped herself in a towel, and walked out into the living room. JC lay on the couch, reading on his iPad. He grinned at her and took off his glasses.

"Hmmmm." Andie smiled in response and slid on top of him. "You are an old man, after all."

JC unwrapped her towel and flipped her on her back. "You might regret saying that after I am done with you."

Andie giggled. "Stop, stop! I need coffee!"

"Coffee will have to wait. I must take care of your more primal needs first."

* * *

When she made it home late in the afternoon, still dressed in her sequined cocktail dress from the night before, Jersey burst into laughter: "Looks like someone had an eventful night!"

Andie changed into a jumpsuit and planted herself on the couch with the remote control. Her phone made a chirping sound, and she looked at the text message: *"Have dinner with me tonight. JC."*

"Who is it?" asked Jersey seeing her friend's wistful smile.

"JC. He wants to have dinner."

"When?"

"Tonight."

"You just saw him this morning!"

"Ah-ha." Andie nodded and typed, "*Yes.*"

"That's tran," concluded Jersey and flipped the channel.

When she called Uber at the end of the evening, JC insisted on dropping her off and again they made out all the way to the cottage. The next day, he had a work dinner in the neighborhood and stopped by for a drink afterward. Jersey's birthday celebration fell on the following weekend, and he went as her date. JC had an invitation to a friend's wedding, the weekend after, and she went as his. There were more dinners and parties. He liked to kitesurf; she liked to play volleyball. They had exchanged dreams and ideas, they had talked about the meaning of life and about starting a family together. She stayed over at his apartment more than she stayed at the cottage, so when Jersey's cousin decided to relocate to Florida, JC suggested she move in with him.

"No reason for you to pay rent," he said over coffee one Sunday. "You are here most nights anyway. Besides, have you looked into the grad program? If you don't have rent to worry about, you can go back to school. Life is too short. You need to do what makes you happy."

Andie was beyond excited. It seemed like all of her dreams were about to come true. JC had taken their relationship to the next level, and she was going after her goal.

"Do you think he is the one?" asked Jo, after Andie told her the news.

"He is!" She was sure of it; they would be engaged by Christmas. She would make an excellent wife for him.

Andie had thrown all of her energy into getting into UM, and in September, they celebrated her first day of school. Christmas came and went. They talked about getting married, but it seemed JC always pointed out something that needed to happen first. She needed to learn to be more responsible, they needed to communicate better, he needed to start his own practice, she needed to finish school—the list was endless. Andie grew resentful, JC annoyed. There were more and more boys' nights out. Andie grew annoyed, JC resentful. By mid-March the relationship resembled a car wreck filmed in slow motion.

After finishing a twelve-hour shift at the hospital, JC met a friend for a beer. "Show me a beautiful woman, and I will show you the man who is sick of fucking her," he confided. "Between medical school, fellowship, and residency, there has never been the time or the money to do anything fun. And now, when I've got both, I am stuck! I live in South Beach with all of the hot girls and the models, and I can't even fuck around. Andie is fun and open-minded, but she wants to get married and have kids!"

"Most of the girls do. Come to Vegas with us. It will be fun."

* * *

"What am I doing wrong?" Andie exclaimed, searching Jo's eyes in desperation. "I try to be patient! I try to look good for him! I take care of him! What happened?"

"I am sorry, love,"

"Guys are just tran," offered Jersey, "You never know what the fuck they need. You can have a pussy made of gold and they want one made of silver. They're just lame."

Jo laughed. "Tinkerbell does not have a golden pussy, she has pussy dust! So go, spread it around! You know you can have any guy you want! Fuck JC!"

"You two are vile," laughed Andie.

"At least we made you laugh!" Jersey pointed out.

Andie finished her drink and headed home to find JC packing a bag.

"Hey, you had fun with the girls?" he asked, hearing her come in.

"Yeah, are you going somewhere?"

"Vegas, with the guys for the weekend." He looked at her defiantly. "You mind?"

"Ah, when were you planning to tell me?" Andie asked, trying to remain calm and not sound accusatory.

"I am telling you now."

"Seriously?"

JC was clearly looking for a fight. "Yes, Andie, seriously! Last I checked, I didn't need anyone's permission!"

"You don't, but it would have been nice to have been given advanced notice. That's what people do when they live together. I would have made my own plans with the girls."

"It was a last-minute thing. Get over it."

"Oh, go screw yourself!" She walked out onto the balcony, unable to restrain the tears.

"Nag, nag, nag! All you do is nag!"

Brought to her breaking point, Andie screamed, "What the fuck do you want from me?! I can never please you!"

"It's too much, Andie! Okay?! I am fucking suffocating! I've never wanted a fucking wife! I feel trapped!"

"For someone who fixes people's hearts, you surprisingly lack one of your own—"

JC smashed the glass he was holding against the wall. With an ear-piercing sound, it shattered into thousands of pieces and scattered over the floor. Amidst the deafening silence that followed, JC grabbed his bag and stomped out. The windows shook from the explosive force of the slamming door.

Andie sunk into the couch, dumbstruck, and stared at the wall. Slowly coming to her senses, she looked at the broken glass and, with trembling fingers, dialed Jo's number. Sobs burst out of her chest before she could speak.

"Come down here," said Jo. "Do you need me to get you?"

"I'll drive."

Andie tossed her belongings into her suitcases; whatever she left behind was not worth packing.

Moments later, she was parked on Jo's blue suede couch, holding a large margarita.

Chapter 4

Spending the first night at the Lindberg's mansion alone gave Andie an eerie feeling. Silence enveloped the room, every inch of it filled with darkness; the walls seemed to be closing in on her. Her heartbeat pounding in her ears and the sound of her anxious breaths were the only things that broke the deafening quiet. Entombed inside the empty house, she lay in bed motionless, staring into the blackness around her. She welcomed the first glimpses of morning light, relieved the night was over.

Free to explore the estate, Andie wandered into the library. She admired the old-world masculinity of the room with the musty smell of books and the beautiful woodwork. She drifted into the grand room, light and airy, with its high ceilings and a carefully curated collection of artwork. Among the paintings of Impressionists and modern artists, a family portrait in a massive frame took center stage, drawing Andie's attention. She examined the faces, frozen for eternity on the soulless canvas. Evelyn, young and regal, sat in the armchair, while a man with strong features exuding power towered over her. Andie analyzed the depiction of Evelyn's husband, fascinated by his commanding presence. She shifted her attention to their two young sons. They resembled their father, but with softer, prettier features. There was a hint of Evelyn in them, just a whisper. Their steel blue eyes, however, were unmistakably Lindberg. She saw Christian in them.

Her heart grew heavy for the family that was no more. Rick Lindberg, dead of a heart attack. Patrick, killed in a car crash along with his wife, leaving Christian an orphan and Evelyn, cold and distant, as his caretaker. Had Evelyn always been cold and distant?

Andie heard steps and turned around as Phillippe entered the room. He walked around the bar counter to stock the wine fridge.

"What were they like?" asked Andie, instantly realizing she had crossed the line.

"Excuse me?" Phillippe lifted his eyebrow.

"I am sorry. I will go change before Mrs. Lindberg and Christian come back." She hurried out of the room.

"Good idea," Phillippe breathed out, pausing in front of the portrait he had seen many times.

He knew the whole story; Rick had told it to him once. The rest had happened in front of his eyes.

* * *

Rick had been born to Albert and Abigale Lindberg on a stormy winter night in the palatial home of his grandparents, in Stockholm, in the prestigious district of Ostermalm. Rick's grandparents, Otto and Elsa, were not at all thrilled when twenty-two-year-old Albert, an heir to the Lindberg name and the family fortune, had married nineteen-year-old Boston socialite Abigale, the only daughter of John Vanderwoodsen. Abigale's father had come from humble beginnings; a self-made man, he had built his wealth in the retail business, starting as a clerk at a woman's department store and working his way up. After years of hard work and with the help of a few influential friends, he had opened his first store-front. By the time John had married Abigale's young and beautiful mother, he was a fifty-year-old bachelor who owned a chain of retail stores throughout the American Northeast.

When Albert had met Abigale, she was the apple of her father's eye and had never heard the word "no." The Lindbergs, whose family lineage was long rooted in Sweden's rich and noble history, were furious. But after huffing and puffing, they were left with no choice but to accept Albert's peculiar choice in a wife.

Rick's birth was a consolation prize for his grand-parents' misery. Strong-willed and intelligent, the child took after the patriarch, melting the old man's heart. And when his younger sister, Gertrude, was born, Abigale was forgiven for being an American.

All was well in Lindberg-land until Albert received an invitation from his father-in-law, John, to move to Boston to take over the company. Albert was exhilarated, John relieved, Abigale excited, the Lindbergs, once more, furious. Once again, they got their consolation prize; Rick stayed behind in Sweden's Sigtuna Boarding School, the same one then-crown prince Carl Gustav attended.

A talented entrepreneur, Albert had grown the business and, after John's death, sold it to a national retailer. The Lindbergs' piggy bank increased exponentially. Albert added a hefty pile of cash to the family fortune, and to Rick's and Gertrude's already substantial inheritance.

Back in Sweden, Rick grew up under the watchful eye of his grandfather Otto with little connection to his parents. Sure, he saw them during the holidays and received expensive guilt-gifts, but his true identity was formed by the influence of the stoic Lindberg patriarch. Failure was not an option; there was only one winner. Second place belonged to the guy who had lost. Light-hearted Abigale could not relate to her willful and spirited son, and Albert did not care to try. The boy was his grandfather's creation, with one drastic difference: though not traditionally handsome, Rick was endlessly charming, and he artfully used his gifts to achieve what he desired.

At boarding school, Rick had become close to Marcus Petersson, an heir to a prominent banking dynasty. A few years older, Marcus had grown to be somewhat of a big brother to the boy. Rick had often joined the Peterssons on their yacht. They had cruised together in the Greek Isles, and the Mediterranean, the Baltic, and the Adriatic; they had skied in Switzerland and hunted in Africa; they had vacationed in the French Riviera and had hiked Machu Picchu.

After graduation, Rick chose Yale as his alma mater. He had thrown his endless energy into his studies and had graduated with degrees in law and economics and the hunger to prove himself. A child of two worlds, he moved back and forth between Europe and the U.S. in search of his place in the sun. While attending a party during a ski trip to St. Moritz, Rick had reconnected with his classmate, the crown prince Carl Gustav, and his friend Marcus. Marcus had approached Rick with a business proposition: the Peterssons were raising capital to invest in an old, failing communications enterprise. Despite his father's protest, young Rick persuaded his grandfather to let him put a portion of his future inheritance into Marcus's venture. The old man was not convinced by the business concept but was impressed by Rick's excitement, due diligence, and determination, so he allowed his grandson an opportunity to gamble. Plus, even if the deal was a loss, Otto thought, it might keep Rick in Sweden for at least a few years longer.

After much effort, the company had been saved from bankruptcy and closure with the help of Swedish banks controlled by the Petersson family, government backing, and a selected group of handpicked private investors, with a significant chunk of cash coming from the Lindbergs. Marcus and Rick had put all of their energy and family influence behind the effort to rebuild the company financially; the brand was restored. It did not just survive—it exploded. Rick had earned his stripes with the family. Better yet, he had become the guy with the Midas touch. To the old man's dismay, this enterprise did not keep Rick close to home for long—quite the opposite. Rick had set his sights on conquering New York.

The success of his first big win did not go to Rick's head. He took several apprentice positions in top investment banks, built his network, watched, and learned. After a few years, much research, and shrewd negotiations, he joined one of New York's most prestigious investment firms, Turner & Smith. By his late twenties, Rick had become the youngest associate ever to make partner.

Life was good. Rick was young, healthy, not bad looking, and filthy rich. The doors of every high society party and private club, no matter how exclusive and prestigious, were open to New York's latest golden boy. He enjoyed his status, dated a few socialites, and was connected to an actress or two, but his passion was business. The excitement of the hunt—finding the right deal, piecing it together, the triumph of closing it, and ultimately getting his reward—was intoxicating. No drug or pair of long legs, no matter how perfect, could compare to the thrill of the win.

As Rick approached the "big three-oh" milestone, not without pressure from his grandfather, he started to think about the future, in particular about starting a family. Sure, there were plenty of willing candidates, but Rick was not accepting applications from any of the women he had met so far.

In the late fall of 1973, Rick's mentor and a founding partner of Turner & Smith, Theo Turner, had invited the young man to attend his seventieth birthday celebration. Theo threw his black-tie extravaganza at his estate in Coral Gables. Rick flew into Miami and checked into a suite at the iconic Biltmore Hotel.

Of course, Rick had heard of Miami, but he had not been aware of its thriving social life. Influential families and heads of corporations chose this piece of paradise as their secret hideaway. The Gables was a Holy Grail of affluence and power. Rick recognized his misjudgment and the wealth of missed opportunities—a mistake he was not about to repeat.

He had embraced the break from the New York scene, where it seemed he knew everyone worth knowing, and everyone recognized him before he had a chance to finish his first drink.

At the party, Rick had masterfully navigated through the crowd, made connections, asked for introductions. Theo knew what he was doing when he had offered Rick a full partnership; "the boy" did have a golden touch. Rick was intelligent, charming, and driven. Florida's high society, it seemed, was willing to eat up whatever he cared to serve. Theo watched him work the room with supreme confidence.

"You fit right in, my boy," Theo said and patted Rick on the back.

Rick plucked a glass of champagne from the tray of a passing waiter and followed Theo out to the terrace. Seemingly relaxed, both of the men had business on their mind, watching, calculating, prospecting.

"I am meeting your friend over there when we get back to New York." Rick pointed his glass at a heavyset bald man. "He is not our client. Why?"

Theo nodded his approval without answering the question. "I have chosen my successor wisely."

"Have you? Chosen your successor?"

"All in due time, my boy, all in due time."

Rick's eyes traveled through the crowd, identifying and analyzing, when his gaze stumbled on the face of a young woman. Her graceful demeanor radiated quiet confidence and poise. Tall, with bright blue eyes and chestnut hair, she stood next to her parents and their friends with a polite, "I-am-bored-to-death" smile on her face.

"Beautiful, isn't she?" winked Theo.

"Exquisite."

"Evelyn Hurley, daughter of Scott and Jane Hurley, dear friends of mine. Would you like me to introduce you?"

"Please," muttered Rick, enthralled by the striking creature.

Theo walked the young man over and, after accepting birthday well-wishes, made an introduction. "Meet Rick Lindberg. Rick just made partner. One thing I know for sure, I can spot talent when I see it, and I can tell you, this boy is *it*!"

Rick hated when Theo patronizingly called him "the boy," but he gallantly smiled. "Thank you, Theodor, you are too kind."

After the initial small talk, the conversation returned to its due course: investments, Florida weather, who had died lately, and who was about to get married. The distraction of the chatter afforded Rick the chance to move closer to Evelyn, who looked ever more bored.

He leaned over and whispered, "I know I don't have a white horse, but are you in need of rescuing?"

Used to attention from the opposite sex, Evelyn glanced at the man Uncle Theo gushed about: "Either that, or a clean and painless death would do."

"May I offer you a glass of champagne instead?"

"You may."

Rick waved over the waiter and handed the young woman a glass. She smiled and extended her hand for a handshake. "Evelyn Hurley."

"Delighted." He raised her delicate fingers to his lips. "Rick Lindberg."

"It is a pleasure to meet you, Rick. I've heard of you from Uncle Theo."

"I am flattered my name is mentioned at the dinner table. All good things, I hope?"

"Unfortunately. You are his 'boy with the golden touch'—good family, most eligible bachelor." Rick cringed, and Evelyn continued, "You are the talk of New York! You spend your time chasing beautiful and . . . oh, not-so-well-mannered women."

"Well, let's be clear here on who chases whom—"

"Oh, so you are a victim?" Evelyn lifted her eyebrow.

"I would not call myself a victim, no. I just sit back as they fly into my web."

"You are a spider then?"

"Hmph, I don't really like that comparison either," protested Rick.

"Well, there is no pleasing you." Evelyn smirked.

"You are most unfair," Rick complained with a smile. "Maybe I am just a bachelor ready to be tamed."

"It is a truth universally acknowledged that a single man in possession of a good fortune must be in want of a wife," she quoted.

"You are a fan of Jane Austen?"

"I've read *Pride and Prejudice* once or twice," she smiled. "In any case, Uncle Theo wishes you would settle down."

"Would you do me the honor?"

"Of what?"

"Of settling me down."

Evelyn laughed her mellifluous laughter. "You would have to work much harder for that!"

"How much harder are we talking?"

"You have no idea, Mr. Lindberg! But you can start by offering me another glass of champagne."

"That can be arranged." Rick snatched two glasses off a passing tray, "And while we are at it, would you do me the honor of dining with me?"

Evelyn smiled and lifted her hand, pointing to her ring finger. "You do recognize I am an engaged woman, don't you?"

"None of us is perfect, but I do forgive you for your bad judgment. After all, you hadn't met me when you made that silly promise."

"Huh! Silly is it?"

"Well, for one, I do not see your betrothed by your side."

"He is away in school," explained Evelyn.

"A schoolboy?!" Rick exclaimed, aghast. "You have promised yourself to a schoolboy?! Hardly an appropriate choice for a prized jewel like you!"

"First I am silly," laughed Evelyn, "and now I am a jewel—a cold, soulless thing? Keep insulting me, Mr. Lindberg! See what happens!"

"I do think you are a jewel, radiant and bright. It was not meant as an insult but as a compliment. I would never dream of offending you. It would make for a miserable start to the marriage!"

Evelyn giggled. "Mr. Lindberg, you think yourself a charming man. And you very well may be. But I have to excuse myself. I've promised this dance to my father."

Rick was not kidding; right then and there, he had decided Evelyn Hurley would be the future Mrs. Lindberg. The fact that she was already engaged to some poor chap did not bother him a bit; a young man who had the misfortune of falling in love with the woman Rick

Lindberg had set his mind on for his future wife was about to have his heart broken. Oh, well. Worse things could happen to a man.

Rick had approached this challenge with the same energy he had dedicated to any other business transactions. He extended his stay at the Biltmore indefinitely and gave the matter his full attention. The very next morning, Evelyn Hurley received an embarrassing display of exquisite white flowers. And the next day. And the day after that. The visits from the florist continued for several weeks before Rick called on Evelyn's father and met him for a round of golf. They chatted about business, investments, and weather, on and on, until the old man invited Rick for dinner. At dinner, Rick had charmed Mrs. Hurley, hardly paying any attention to Evelyn. More flowers followed the next day—one arrangement for Mrs. Hurley as a thank-you for a lovely evening, the other one for Evelyn. And the next day. And the day after. First, Evelyn was flattered, then annoyed, then intrigued.

Evelyn kept hearing of Mr. Lindberg from her parents, her parents' friends, her own friends. He surely got around. She ran into him at a store; he bumped into her at a café. He was always gallant, stylish, and charming, but never engaging. One by one, her girlfriends developed crushes on him. He still had not called on her.

Finally, the word of inappropriate behavior reached Evelyn's fiancé at Princeton, and he rushed back to Florida to confront her. He was furious. This public display of admiration was unsuitable, to say the least. What was she doing to encourage this man to so openly pursue her?

He yelled. She looked at him, bored. Finally, she grew tired of his rant and asked him to leave and take his ring with him. He did. She would regret her insolence—he was sure of it!

Word of the breakup spread fast. The next day, Rick Lindberg called on Evelyn.

They wed that May at the Biltmore Hotel. Evelyn had planned the entire wedding herself and enjoyed every minute of it. The whole Lindberg clan had gathered for the grand affair. The old patriarch, now widowed, was pleased by his grandson's appropriate choice. Rick's parents, Albert and Abigale, had flown in from Boston, and his sister, Gertrude, had debuted her boyfriend, viscount Moretti. Rick took an instant dislike to him. Handsome and idle, the man was a clichéd example of a hanger-on. He had a title, a sense of self-importance, and no money. He raced cars and drank champagne. It infuriated Rick to see that his sister had chosen so poorly. It infuriated Gertrude that the family disliked her choice so blatantly.

"I'm afraid we pushed her right into this marriage," said Otto to Rick six months later, after receiving the news Gertrude had eloped.

Rick and Evelyn's wedding was the talk of the town for years. No expense had been spared for the celebration. With one move, Rick had firmly placed himself on the social map of Florida society. Evelyn would reign supreme as a grand hostess, and invitations to the Lindbergs' would be sought by all.

They honeymooned in the French Riviera at the exquisite Chateaux Ezza in Ezze, a four-hundred-year-old chateaux and former winter residence of a Swedish prince—an appropriate backdrop for the Lindberg heir—located along the coast from Cap Roux to the Cabuel. Nestled at the top of a thousand-year-old village between Monte Carlo and Nice, its splendid views of the azure waters and sun-kissed horizons of the Mediterranean Sea transported Evelyn into the pages of a fairy tale. Rick spoiled his bride with extravagance and pure indulgence—a Royal Suite with a private terrace and an endless wine cellar full of exquisite wines, trips to Monte Carlo, dancing the nights away in Nice. Evelyn, who had not ventured far from Florida before, became enamored with the glamor of her new lifestyle and the sophisticated charm of Old Europe.

Upon their return, they settled into a grand estate in the heart of Coral Gables. Evelyn had been given the reins—and the checkbook—to redecorate. The nesting exercise kept her entertained for several years. Meanwhile, Rick resumed his duties in New York. He returned to Florida for the weekends and whenever Evelyn hosted a party. Eager to please her husband and entice him back home, Evelyn had thrown one social affair after another. She sought to invite politicians and leaders of the community, along with aspiring entertainers and artists. Rick was grateful; he felt proud of his wife and the home she had built for him.

When Clair, Evelyn's childhood friend, returned from Princeton, she had become a permanent fixture at the Lindbergs. Pleased that his wife had a suitable companion, Rick encouraged their friendship. At one of the parties, he introduced Clair to a young lawyer, Michael Thomson. Rick had met the man during one of his business transactions. At the time, Michael represented the other side. As soon as the deal went through, Rick hired Michael as his own legal counsel.

It was Clair's turn to walk down the aisle.

Phillippe remembered seeing a photograph of her in her wedding gown, and of Evelyn as the maid of honor in a pretty lavender chiffon dress. Both women looked so happy and young. He wished he had known them then.

Chapter 5

By his early thirties, Rick had achieved almost all he desired. Now he needed a son. His grandfather's health began to fail, and the old patriarch hoped he wouldn't die without knowing that the family name lived on.

Evelyn had difficulties conceiving, but after a few years of conscious trying, she finally got pregnant. The pregnancy was a difficult one but she carried to term and, on a sweltering hot summer's afternoon, she gave birth to a girl.

To Evelyn's devastation, the child died three weeks later from a congenital heart defect. She was inconsolable. Rick, after a few days by his wife's side, flew back to New York to close on his current deal.

Before his plane took off from Miami airport, he called Clair. "My wife is distressed. Do me a favor; check on her."

Despite being pregnant herself, Clair rushed to Evelyn's side. The situation was worse than she anticipated. Late in the afternoon Evelyn still wore a bathrobe over her silk nightgown. Heavy black shadows framed her red eyes; her stare was unfocused and bewildered.

"Why are you here?" she asked Clair.

"To check on you,"

"Why?" repeated Evelyn sharply.

"I am concerned for you and so is your husband."

"My husband?" laughed Evelyn bitterly. "You mean Rick? Oh, don't be a fool! He doesn't care about me. He doesn't care about his wife! All he needs is a working womb!"

She grabbed their wedding picture in its heavy silver frame from the top of the dresser and thrust it to the floor. It crashed with a thud, cracking the glass. Evelyn sank onto the unmade double bed and began to sob.

Clair pulled her into a hug, holding her until she calmed down. The following day Clair stopped by again. Evelyn sat on the porch and stared unseeing into the distance, her arms protectively crossed over her chest, she rocked the baby that was not there.

For the next several months Clair's routine included daily visits to the Lindberg house to comfort her friend. She used all of her training as a psychotherapist to walk Evelyn through the bottomless pit of depression.

Clair, unlike Evelyn, had an easy pregnancy and, in September, delivered a healthy baby boy, Sean. A doting godmother, Evelyn smothered the child with affection and gifts. She showered all of her unspent love on her godson. To everyone's joy, when Sean turned six months old, Evelyn discovered she was pregnant again.

In December of 1976, newborn Patrick made his appearance right on time and with much fuss. Rick could not have been more proud. The excitement was short-lived, however; a week later, the old patriarch passed away, and Rick flew to Sweden to attend the funeral. The Lindberg clan gathered to pay their final respects to the head of the family. To Rick's infinite annoyance, his sister, Gertrude, showed up with her playboy husband, viscount Moretti. To add insult to injury, Gertrude was seven months pregnant.

To everyone's surprise and delight, Evelyn got pregnant again a few months after giving birth, and in March of 1978, the family welcomed their second child, Erik. Rick got an heir and a spare. He felt unstoppable.

In contrast, exhausted from back-to-back pregnancies, Evelyn succumbed to deep postpartum depression. Her distress fell on Rick's unsympathetic ear. He hired a nanny to take care of the kids and additional help around the house. When his practical solutions did not work, annoyed by his wife's endless tears and anxiety, he spent more and more time in New York.

"I plan to file for divorce," Evelyn announced to Clair over a martini, as they watched their boys play in the care of a nanny.

Clair did not pretend to be surprised. In the beginning, Evelyn found excuses for Rick's absentee-husband behavior, but the reality was hard to ignore: Rick would never be the type of husband Evelyn dreamed of. The romantic notion of happily-ever-after collided with the actuality of their relationship. Clair could not disagree, but, at the same time, she knew that Evelyn was not in a state of mind to make such a life-changing decision. She advised her to wait.

After a long struggle with depression, with Clair's help and counsel, Evelyn eventually started to feel like herself again. However, it was not her old self; part of her died with the child she buried. She loved her sons, but in her heart of hearts was forced to admit she never felt the fullness of motherly affection she felt for her firstborn.

Moreover, there was the conundrum of her marriage. Again, she contemplated divorce. However, Rick appealed to her rational side: What was she to gain from that? Staying married to him had many benefits: status, influence, a blank checkbook, and a fair amount of freedom. No other man could have given her those things. Besides, they did love each other in their own way and, through the years, had developed a sense of friendship and partnership. After careful deliberation, Evelyn made her choice. Now that she better understood the dynamics of her marriage she felt confident and empowered. She was Mrs. Evelyn Lindberg, wife of one of the wealthiest men in the country and mistress of her estate.

Graciously she stepped back into the role of a perfect wife and hostess. The Lindberg Coral Gables estate again filled with laughter and the cheerful noise of lively get-togethers and elegant dinner parties.

Crisis averted, Rick returned his full attention to

business. Managing partner of a successful private equity firm, he bought and sold companies, turned around failing enterprises, and relished every moment of it. The Lindbergs played host to many influential guests and, through it, gained both financial and political clout.

Rick was grateful for and proud of Evelyn. He possessed enough self-awareness to recognize her sacrifice. He tried to repay her in every way he could. He never cheated on her—not with a woman, that is; his mistress was his work. So when his wife took to traveling, Rick was relieved she had found a hobby that took him out of the equation. He made sure to afford her all of the comforts and financial resources she required and dutifully listened to stories of her escapades upon her return.

When at home, Evelyn endeavored to give her boys a sense of family and belonging, especially during the holidays. Every year, she made an effort to bring the whole family together for Christmas. Her parents had always been a part of the children's lives, as had Clair and her husband, Michael, and their son, Sean. The Lindberg side, however, was absent most of the time. Evelyn put effort into changing that situation. Once a year, she insisted, in addition to her parents and Clair's family, on hosting the Lindbergs. Everyone complied. Rick's parents, Albert and Abigale, dutifully appeared in late December, bearing countless gifts for all of the kids. Rick's sister, Gertrude, with her husband and their son, Jonathan, flew from Stockholm and spent the better part of winter in Florida. Rick still detested the viscount but behaved cordially, not willing to risk his wife's displeasure. The four boys, Sean, Jonathan, Patrick, and Erik, reveled in the festivities and one another's company and together found endless ways to get themselves into trouble.

Despite an initial awkwardness, the Christmases at the Lindbergs were enchanted. Everyone played their roles perfectly. Evelyn would not have it any other way.

After the holidays, Evelyn took off to ski in Switzerland, where the European beau monde flocked for the season of glamorous parties and fun on the slopes. Evelyn found the European high society quite different from the one she knew in Florida. She reveled in the sophistication of the aristocracy, their elegance and depth of education. She cherished the fact that she was accepted into this exclusive club. Rick guarded his independence in New York and refused to introduce his wife to the society in the Northeast, a situation Evelyn grew to resent. Her admission into the realms of European elite put a Band-Aid on her bruised vanity.

Evelyn fell in love with the mountains and the snow, with the freedom, and in the winter of 1986 with her skiing instructor. Young and athletic, with dark hair and hazel eyes, the man was eager to please. Starved of male attention, Evelyn capitulated with little resistance. He spoke a few words of English; she knew a little French, so most of their communication was conducted by touch. After several weeks of nonstop sex, Evelyn returned home in a good mood and with a healthy glow.

The affair continued into the spring when she met him in Prague. A few months later she planned a rendezvous in London. Rick, who had never taken an eye off Evelyn, was entertained by the idea of his proper wife having a fling. His curiosity got the best of him, so on his way to Stockholm, he stopped for a layover in London and checked into the same hotel, arriving the day before Evelyn was due. In the evening, he went downstairs to the bar for a drink. He relaxed, sipped his Blue Label, and waited. When the young man walked into the bar, Rick paid attention. He studied Evelyn's choice from afar and in the end, shrugged his shoulders; his wife had good taste. The man was well-built, with a handsome face unburdened by any signs of intellect. Satisfied with his research, Rick retired to his suite and got a solid night of sleep. The next morning, he flew to Stockholm to close on the deal he has been working on for a year. He had his fun; Evelyn was entitled to have hers.

However, by the end of summer, Rick decided it was time to intervene. A casual affair was healthy for a young woman; a long-lasting extramarital relationship, on the other hand, was not.

In early September, Rick surprised his wife with a trip to Venice. He booked a suite at Hotel Danieli. The opulent Palazzo Dandolo was built at the end of the fourteenth century by a patrician family and is situated on the embankment of the Venetian Lagoon, steps away from the famed Bridge of Sighs and the Piazza San Marco. The pink Byzantine Gothic façade, with its marble columns and pointed arches, looks more like a palatial residence than a hotel, having been built as such. Frequented by artists, musicians, and writers throughout its centuries-long history, Danieli has been featured in movies like *Moonraker* and *The Tourist.*

Rick and Evelyn arrived by private jet at Venice's Marco Polo Airport and were picked up by the hotel's water taxi. Cruising through the stunning Venetian lagoon, Rick smiled, as he admired his wife's beauty in this fairytale setting. He wrapped his hand around her shoulder. "I'm sorry I allowed it to be so long since we traveled together."

Like a child, Evelyn laughed, the sun in her face, the wind playing with her long chestnut hair.

"I'll make it up to you," he promised and kissed her on the temple.

As soon as their Riva motorboat pulled up at the hotel entrance, the bellman rushed to greet them and to help with their luggage.

They stepped inside the richly embellished four-storied courtyard, topped by a stained-glass ceiling. The natural light bathed them in a soft glow as Evelyn spun around to take in every inch of magnificent interior. At the center of it all, a grand "Golden Staircase," with intricately carved balustrades, framed by Byzantine-style pointed arches, led to the opulent guest quarters of the original Palazzo.

While Rick checked them in, Evelyn strode out of the stately foyer into a majestic grand room adorned with

Murano glass chandeliers, massive hand-carved stone fireplaces, and original Baroque furnishings.

Determined to romance his wife, Rick checked them into the Doge Dandolo Royal Suite. Shadowed by a bellman, they entered the hotel's most luxurious accommodations, dedicated to the Republic's forty-first Doge, Enrique Dandolo. Portraits by nineteenth-century artist Ermolao Paoletti adorned the walls of the main salon, and antique Persian rugs and golden silk curtains framed the extravagant apartment.

Tired from the long transatlantic flight, Evelyn retreated into the comfort of the lavishly decorated bedroom. She lay in bed, unable to close her eyes, admiring an original ceiling fresco by famous eighteenth-century artist Jacopo Guarana, the silk-upholstered walls, and the iconic Venetian detailing. Leaving her to rest, Rick kicked off his shoes, pulled out a cigar, and walked outside to the oversized balcony with its 180-degree views of the Riva degli Schiavoni. He breathed out the tart aroma of his Montecristo. *Majestic!* They should vacation more often.

Their first stop the next morning—Caffé Florian on the Piazza San Marco.

"Did you know," chirped Evelyn, who had prepared for their trip by reading as much about Venice as she could get her hands on. "This is the oldest café in Europe. It is claimed, the hot chocolate here is so good that the infamous Casanova stopped by here to have his last cup after he escaped from prison. He then fled to France, forever leaving his beloved Venice." She finished her story in the exaggeratedly dramatic tone of a storyteller.

Rick picked up the menu and read out loud: "Cioccolata Casanova. Hot chocolate, mint cream, and chocolate shavings. That's what I must have, then."

Evelyn continued with her history lesson: "Casanova is said to be the only prisoner to walk the Bridge of Sighs both ways!"

After breakfast, they aimlessly strolled the streets, marveling at the wilting beauty of the "Bride of the Adriatic," drawn back into the piazza at the first signs of the dying daylight when the Byzantine-style basilica looks its most dramatic. They sipped bellinis at Harry's Bar and ate grilled razor clams at a local five-table restaurant. They explored the breathtaking interior of Basilica San Marco and Palazzo Ducale. They crossed the Bridge of Sighs and shopped on the island of Murano. They admired handcrafted Venetian masks and ate pistachio gelato.

On the last night of the trip, over dinner at the Terrazza Danieli, overlooking the lagoon and the red brick bell towers of the city, Rick asked his wife to end the affair.

Evelyn, who by then had grown bored of her "boy-toy" and needed a reason to break off the affair, was given an excuse to do just that. In addition, she had been handed the perfect opportunity to bargain with her husband.

She took her time answering him. When the appetizer

of Vitello Tonnato arrived, she savored its decadent flavor and her moment. By the end of dinner, they reached a deal: Evelyn gained a house in the Hamptons, and an introduction to New York society, Rick—new-found respect for his wife. They came back to Florida hand in hand, pleased with each other and themselves.

One late afternoon, a few weeks after their return, Rick walked into Evelyn's study, pulled a chair up in front of the chaise where she reclined reading, and sat down facing her.

"I've learned of an opportunity to buy a unique property in Indian Creek," he informed her in his business tone. "The house is a teardown, but the land is magnificent. We would have to build from the ground up. Are we game?"

Evelyn put down her book and glared at her husband. "Are you suggesting I am to get a shed in Florida instead of the house promised me in the Hamptons?"

Rick smiled. "I would not dream of it. You are to get both. As you should."

Rick had never consulted Evelyn in his business dealings before, and now she felt flattered that he asked her opinion. A guarantee of her Hampton house secured, she jumped at the challenge to build her dream home, and Rick—at the prospect of keeping his wife happily occupied for several years.

They demolished the old structure and hired Miami's leading architectural firm to head the construction. Evelyn insisted she would oversee the project herself; she met with the engineers, architects, designers, landscapers, and craftsmen. She picked the finishes and searched for the antique pieces for both properties. To her surprise, Rick took an interest in one of the wings of the house. Still, under the spell of Venice and enchanted by the open stairwell at Hotel Danieli, he pored over blueprints for his office-slash-library. Evelyn had never before seen her husband pay such keen attention to matters unrelated to his business. Rick scrutinized every detail and drew the renderings. He designed the balustrade and hired the best artisans money could buy to re-create his vision. Evelyn did not question or interfere, but seeing the finishes and craftsmanship, she estimated her husband spent north of a million dollars on the room. To him, it was worth it. The unique, multistory space, reminiscent of the Byzantine-Gothic style of Venice, was his magnum opus.

But then there was another matter entirely. Family drama began to unfold on a scale worthy of a Parisian salon when Rick's sister's marriage came to an unsavory end. Gertrude's husband, viscount Moretti, had run off with his boyfriend and a significant portion of her inheritance. Rick was furious in his impotence, Gertrude—inconsolable. Neither of them appreciated the impact this event had on young Jonathan. He withdrew into himself and blamed both his mother and especially his uncle for his father's disappearance. Always polite and proper, he never spoke of it, harboring his resentment and letting it fester.

In the midst of it all, it became Evelyn's turn to console her best friend. Without prior warning signs, Clair's marriage fell apart after Michael met Caroline, a new paralegal at his law firm. The news of the affair hit Clair like a ton of bricks. While counseling her patients on their relationships, she had failed to see the coming of her own crisis. News of the affair quickly spread, and she could not ignore the facts. She filed for divorce, and, as soon as it was finalized, Michael married Caroline. Clair hated the song "Sweet Caroline" from there on.

Clair focused all her energy on making sure to give Sean the tools to cope with his parents' separation. To keep his mind occupied, she enrolled him in multiple activities—soccer, swimming, math. More than ever, the two of them spent the weekends and holidays with the Lindbergs.

Evelyn enrolled her boys into the same groups. Along with Sean, they attended math studies, soccer lessons, and a swimming camp.

A competition marked the last day of camp. Dutifully, if not willingly, Evelyn showed up to watch her sons swim. In the seat next to her, Clair cheered for Sean. Eight-year-old Erik came in first place.

After the competition, the coach approached Evelyn. "Erik is a natural athlete. He has potential. Consider continuing with the lessons."

Evelyn paid little attention to the man's comments and had forgotten all about them by the time she had the first sip of her martini that evening.

Erik did not forget. He marched into his father's office and demanded to continue with the training.

"Make your case." Rick challenged him.

He listened to his son's spirited speech with rapt attention. When the boy finished, Rick shook his hand and set out to hire Erik the best swim coaches money could buy. Going forward, he would make sure his son had everything he needed to pursue his career. Erik trained at the best facilities in the country and, in his first high school year, earned a place on the U.S. national team. He received scholarship offers from several Ivy League schools and chose Harvard as his alma mater. In his sophomore year, during intensive training for the Olympic trials, at the Training Center in Colorado Springs, he tore his rotator cuff. The injury was serious enough to require surgery and rehabilitation. The treatment repaired the damage, but time was lost. The trials went on without him, shattering his Olympic ambitions.

Rick took the news in stride. He suppressed his disappointment and stepped up to support his son. He saw Erik's internal struggle. His life goal crushed, Erik did not complain about the unfairness of it. Instead, he redirected his anger and frustration on his future career. He enrolled in extra curriculum classes and zeroed in on potential employers. Despite Rick's offers to help him with introductions, Erik had set his mind on getting his foot in the door without using his family's connections. It was in this year, in his father's eyes, the boy became a man.

Unlike his brother, Patrick had grown up cerebral and more interested in academic achievement than sports. He joined Sean and Jonathan at Princeton, and all three graduated in the same class.

Evelyn threw a grandiose graduation party for them at the Island Creek estate. Addressing the boys and the guests in a toast, Rick raised his glass. "To my sons! I could not be more proud of you both. I eagerly await to see what your future holds and all you will achieve. The world is yours for the taking! Carpe Diem, my boys!"

Chapter 6

Andie set the laptop down on the pillow next to her. She had stared at the screen for hours, and her eyes started to burn. She shut her lids and rested for a few moments. The school report she'd been working on for weeks was almost written, and whatever was left of it she could finish during Christian's piano lesson the following day.

Andie got out of bed, stretched her neck and shoulders, and walked to the kitchen. She knew the house would be empty this late at night, so she did not bother to throw anything over her Eberjey chemise. She opened the cupboard and raided Phillippe's tea stash. She brewed an aromatic cup, sat down at the kitchen island, and flipped on the TV. One of the Kardashians was whining about her man again; Andie changed the channel. She needed to unwind; sleep had eluded her for the past few weeks, ever since she had moved into the mansion. The grad school program demanded her best efforts. At the same time, learning to interact with everyone in the Lindberg household was a delicate dance and presented a challenge of its own. The only moments she found for herself were late at night when she would brew a cup of tea and watch some mindless TV and early in the morning when she would go for a run before the start of her day. At times, she felt her sanity starting to slip away.

Andie took a last sip, turned off the TV, and rinsed off her cup. She prayed for a good night's sleep.

* * *

"I should be so disciplined," commented Phillippe when Andie walked into the kitchen the following morning, still panting from her run.

She poured a tall glass of water and chugged it down in one gulp.

"Good run?"

Andie nodded without parting her lips from the glass. Phillippe set a silver pot of coffee, a porcelain cup, and a warm croissant on the silver tray, laid down the morning's paper, and sent it up in the butler's elevator to Mrs. Lindberg's room. He then brewed two more cups and handed one to Andie. She gratefully accepted it and followed him outside to the veranda.

"I am not sure if Mrs. Lindberg has told you, but she is having friends over for dinner tonight. You need to have Christian ready by five thirty. The nanny usually joins in as well."

Andie nodded in acknowledgment.

"But I think you will enjoy it," encouraged Phillippe. "Lucy will be there, too."

"Where will Lucy be?" asked Lucy, Mrs. Lindberg's personal assistant, as she walked out and sat down in an empty seat.

"I was just telling Andie about Mrs. Lindberg's dinner tonight."

"Ah, yes, the dinner."

"You are here early this morning," Andie pointed out.

Lucy, a pretty Filipino woman in her thirties, nodded. "Mrs. Lindberg's accountant is coming today. I had to prepare some info for them to review."

Andie wondered what Lucy's life story was because Lucy looked like she had an interesting one. No time to ruminate, however; she needed to change and get on with her morning.

Christian woke up in a foul mood, which promised a stressful day ahead. A threat of an alien invasion and the need to save the city got the child out of pajamas and into his pants; a dying battery in his imaginary supersuit forced him to eat a few bites of food. Before the afternoon heat made the backyard uninhabitable, Andie took the boy outside to play, hoping to rid him of the negative energy and to release some endorphins. By the time his piano teacher arrived, Christian's drama meter had gone down from a bright red to a medium yellow. Andie handed the boy off, relieved to have an hour break.

After the piano teacher departed, it was time again to save the world. As the afternoon drew to an end, so did the limits of Andie's imagination. Batman always dressed up for the cocktail hour; as his apprentice, it would behoove Christian to do the same. Andie lay out the boy's clothes and ran to her room to change into a sensible outfit. Pants for dinner were out of the question; Mrs. Lindberg would not stand for it. Andie briefly wondered what the woman would say to a pair of jeans at the table. Instead, she put on a proper (read: boring) navy blue dress from Anne Taylor; she bought a few of them when she took the job. This unfortunate event made Jo proclaim, "Winter is coming,"[1] as she firmly refused to go shopping with her in protest.

Andie rushed upstairs to check on Christian and, to her surprise, found the boy neatly dressed, his blond hair brushed to the side. Under his arm, he held a chess set.

"Dr. Knight needs to practice," he announced when Andie asked him why.

They peeked into Mrs. Lindberg's study before going to the grand room.

Lucy raised her eyes over her glasses and smiled. "Be there in a minute. Almost done. I think I hear Dr. Knight's voice," she pointed out to Christian.

Andie followed the boy into the grand room. Evelyn and Clair were sipping martinis in the company of a man in his sixties, his hair too dark for his age, his clothes too contemporary. He stood up to greet Andie and bowed slightly. "James Knight," he introduced himself, flashing a dazzling white smile. "It's a pleasure. Pleasure! Oh, yes, thank you," he said, accepting a drink from Consuelo before returning his attention to Andie. "Please, please, sit down!" Light on his feet, Dr. Knight pulled over a chair. "Well, my friend," he addressed Christian, "are you ready for a spirited game of chess?"

The boy nodded and sunk to his knees to set up the board on the coffee table in front of them.

"I can just feel it!" exclaimed Dr. Knight rubbing his hands together. "Today will be my lucky day when I snatch victory from you!" He took two pawns—one white, one black—from the board and hid them behind his back. "Young man, make your choice!"

Christian picked a hand and ended up with the black figurine.

"I hear you are a scholar of psychology," acknowledged Dr. Knight and glanced at Andie over the board as he made his first move. "Pawn to d4. I am also a doctor of psychology, you see."

"Dr. Knight is well respected in his field," Clair pointed out with a smile.

"Bianca is running late," announced Lucy as she entered the room. With a purposeful stride, she walked over to the bar and poured herself a generous glass of wine. She took a sip and sat down next to Andie. "You not drinking, love? It's okay," she reassured her. "Mrs. Lindberg really does not mind." Lucy waited for Mrs. Lindberg to acknowledge her statement and then got up to pour Andie a drink. "Oh, Bianca just pulled in."

A moment later, a tall woman in her fifties with straight dark hair glided in. She wore loose white pants and a white linen blouson with bell sleeves and a deep

V-neck. A coral multilayer necklace covered her décolleté; gold hoop earrings and golden and leather bangles stacked on both wrists completed her ensemble.

"I am sorry! You have not waited for me long, have you? Oh, it is so nice to meet you, sweetie pie!" She kissed Andie on both cheeks. "I've heard lovely things about you! I am sorry again. I got held up with the curator. We are opening an exhibit in a few weeks! It's going to be fabulous!"

"Bianca owns a gallery," explained Lucy.

"We are bringing in this artist," continued Bianca. "Oh! She is just beyond! Very powerful! So feminist! So erotic!" She took a sip from the glass Lucy handed her. "Oh, girls!" she chirped, looking at Andie and Lucy, "You must come for the opening night! It will be heavenly! You see, in the art world, it is accepted that painting eroticism is reserved for the male artists. She is breaking all of the barriers! Her nudes are just beyond!"

"I won!" Christian jumped to his feet and threw his hands in the air. "I won! I won!"

"Ugh! Darn it!" Dr. Knight feigned exasperation. "I can't believe I have lost again!"

"You need to practice more, that is all!" encouraged Christian.

Consuelo came around with a silver tray. She collected empty glasses and replaced them with fresh drinks—martinis for Evelyn and Clair, scotch for Dr. Knight, wine for the rest.

"She is also a Reiki." Lucy pointed her glass at Bianca.

"I have the gift," acknowledged the woman. "It's not just Reiki. I work with energy and stones and the chakras. Whatever my *friends* tell me the body needs." She raised her hand to the sky. "Andie, you should come see me sometime! I can help you release the tension you are harboring in your chi."

Andie smiled at the woman and nodded her agreement. "That would be nice. Thank you. I will take any help I can get."

"Good. Some people are so closed-minded to these things! And the energy flow is so important—"

"So, Andie!" Dr. Knight changed the subject, adjusting his seat to better see her. "There is a little game we play. Name three persons, dead or alive, whom you would invite for dinner."

"Beware, dear," warned Clair, "you will have to justify your choice."

"Your time starts now," Dr. Knight announced.

"Oscar Wilde," Andie said without thinking, counting off on one finger. Then she paused for a few seconds. "Leonardo Da Vinci," she counted the next finger. "Umm . . . Hatshepsut?"

Dr. Knight rubbed his chin, evaluating her pick. "I am surprised, as a student of psychology you have not invited Sigmund Freud or Dr. Jung."

"I figured either you or Dr. Thompson would have already invited them, so I did not want to waste a seat," responded Andie with a smile.

"Wise," agreed Evelyn.

Dr. Knight pointed his index finger at her. "Explain."

"Well, Oscar Wilde is easy. He is my favorite writer, and he would be an amazing conversationalist." She paused. "Leonardo . . . I don't know who wouldn't want to have dinner with him—the Renaissance man personified."

"And then, there is the question of Queen Hatshepsut," reminded Dr. Knight.

Andie made victory signs with her fingers. "The original *girl power?*"

"I don't know what to say there, Evelyn," Dr. Knight said with a grin.

"Well, that's a first," teased Bianca.

"You got a smart one," affirmed Dr. Knight.

Andie saw Evelyn give a faint nod of approval. Apparently, she had passed the test.

Chapter 7

Erik was in that delicious state of consciousness when one is not yet entirely awake, but already, the memories of the pleasant night before start to flood the brain. He vaguely heard the sound of running water in the shower, and a faint morning light in the room hinted at the time. He extended his arm, and it landed on the silky-soft skin of the body next to him. He affectionately caressed what he could only identify as the rounds of a perfectly formed butt. The owner of the butt moaned and moved, apparently waking up herself. Erik took a deep, satisfying breath, spreading it through his well-rested body into his core, and slowly opened his eyes. The girl next to him stretched, rolled onto her back, and pulled the sheet over herself in a lazy daze.

Erik turned his head toward the sound of water just as it stopped, and a slim, tanned silhouette emerged from his oversized shower. The slender body with small, perky breasts grabbed a towel and mercilessly rattled her short hair. Then, still covered in droplets of water and nothing else, Natalie stepped into the room and studied the figure in the bed. Erik was a marvelous male specimen, with his long, toned limbs, steel blue eyes, blond hair, and self-assured casual attitude. He was sexy as hell, and the motherfucker knew it.

Just as the "motherfucker's" hand was fondling her friend's breasts, he grinned, pulled the sheets off his naked body, and pointed at his hard-on. "Want to take care of this?"

Natalie's friend sat up, glanced at her watch, and sprang out of bed. "Holy shit! I got to pick my boyfriend up from the airport!"

Natalie did not break eye contact with Erik as her friend frantically collected her belongings and dressed.

"Hey, Erik, do you have a toothbrush by chance?" asked the girl buttoning up her blouse.

"Bottom left drawer," answered Natalie, and deliberately she slowly mounted Erik. He moaned with pleasure as she forced herself up and down in the manner and rhythm she knew he liked best. They both failed to acknowledge the sound of the shutting door.

"Why the fuck would anyone pick up anyone from the airport anymore?" Natalie wondered aloud.

"Beats me," chuckled Erik and flipped the girl on her back, spreading her on the sheets.

Hovering over her, he propped himself up on his elbow, his fingers fondling her nipple, rolling it between his fingers almost to the point of aching. He moved his hips with a deliberate motion, delivering the precise level of pressure and depth until he succeeded in pleasing her and she arched her back, gasped, and dug her nails into his ass.

Natalie enjoyed their fuck-sessions. The boy was a damn good lay. They'd been hooking up for years, keeping it casual, the status quo Natalie had begun to question. They had fun outside of the bed as well. They went out together or ran into each other while they were out with other people. A few times, Erik had invited her to fly with him to hot spots like Ibiza or Mykonos or to join him at wild parties in Europe. *Eyes Wide Shut? Oh, please!* Erik had introduced Natalie to *Madam "O" Society*, a private club with the members spread all over the world, with its sex masquerades and swinger bashes in castles and villas around the globe. Madam O had created an enchanted world of fantasy and erotica, an adult playground designed to shock and delight one's senses. Oh, and the "O" stood for Oscar, and he was no fucking Madam.

Erik followed her into the shower. "Round two?" he asked with a cocky grin.

Natalie shrugged her shoulders and grabbed him by his balls. "I'll call your bluff."

"Bitch," Erik playfully pinched her nipple, shook the water out of his hair, and got out.

"Do you have time to grab breakfast?" Natalie asked as she briskly dried herself.

"Sure. Has to be a quick one, though. I am flying to Miami in a few hours. You okay with the diner on the corner?"

"Yeah, that's fine." She put on the sexy outfit she'd worn the night before. "Ah, can I borrow a pullover or something?"

Erik chuckled, pulled a light cashmere sweater out of the dresser, and tossed it to her.

"I look like a scarecrow," Natalie commented, rolling up the sleeves of the sweater that was too big for her five-foot-six frame.

They took the elevator down to the lobby of the posh New York high-rise and crossed the street. A slew of people waited outside the diner for a table. A hostess Erik had never seen before welcomed them with a polite smile. "It will be about forty-five minutes," she announced.

"Thank you," nodded Erik and waved to the manager.

"Mr. Lindberg! Always a pleasure, right this way please!" The potbellied man showed them to the window table.

They sat down at the booth across from each other, displaying no signs of affection. Natalie opened the menu and apathetically scanned the page.

"Morning, folks. What can I get ya to drink?" A middle-aged woman with visible traces of wear and tear appeared in front of their table ready to do them a favor and not spit in their food.

"Good morning, Marge. You look lovelier than usual today. Is it a fresh hairdo or do you have a new air of condescension about you?"

"No, it's just my sparkling personality and a

good-natured disposition that throws you off today. Now, what d'ya want to drink?"

"We are ready to order, too." Natalie handed the woman her menu.

"Aren't I lucky!" Marge turned her attention to Natalie. "So . . . ?"

"May I please have a mimosa, scrambled eggs, sliced tomatoes, no toast, no potatoes?"

Marge scrabbled down the order and turned to Erik.

"I will have that piss water you call coffee and blueberry pancakes. Please."

Marge read the order back. "Walk-of-shame special, no carbs, piss water, and pancakes. Got it!"

As she disappeared into the madness of the rush hour, Erik grinned at Natalie. "Love that woman!"

Natalie rolled her eyes and prayed for a mimosa. "For how long are you going to Miami?"

"Not sure. Sean came across an opportunity he wanted me to look at."

"Cool. How's he doing?"

"He's good. I haven't seen him in a while. Look forward to catching up. Are you working on anything fun?"

"Yeah, waiting for a callback to do the makeup for a movie my friend got a part in." She pushed her eggs around on the plate and reached over to steal a bite of pancakes from Erik's plate.

"Very cool. Here?"

Natalie nodded. "Yeah, and Paris." She finished her mimosa and looked at her phone. "Let's catch up when you are back in New York. I've got to run." She got up and kissed Erik good-bye.

"Good luck with the movie," he offered, following her outside.

It was time to get out of here. The Lindberg jet waited at Teterboro airport, ready for the short flight to Florida. As soon as he boarded, a smiling flight attendant offered him a drink before preparing for takeoff.

"Just a Pellegrino," he said, and she fixed his water the way she knew he took it.

Erik leaned back in the plush chair and rested his eyes. He hadn't gotten much sleep the night before, what with running into Natalie and her friend at the nightclub. The party had turned into the after-party at his place. Erik smiled.

As the plane took off, his thoughts turned to Miami. He had not spent much time in Florida in the past few years since Patrick's death. The place brought back too many memories. It was hard to see his mother, who could never express her emotions and looked as put together and manicured as ever. He felt even more uncomfortable around his nephew. The guilt that the boy's parents had died, while Erik had survived, overwhelmed him. He had missed Christian's and Evelyn's birthdays, and Christmas. Of course, he had sent expensive gifts, thoughtfully picked out by his assistant, Jeanne. He knew the drill; he had been given those his entire life.

Jeanne . . . she was awesome. Born in Jamaica, she was raised in New York by a single mother and a much older sister. Brought up by two strong women, she grew up to be one. Jeanne had followed Patrick from the firm he had worked for before opening the fund with Erik. In her late forties, intelligent and loyal, she took care of the boys ever since. Erik's life ran smoothly largely thanks to her. She took care of everything, his schedule, his reservations, she managed the office, and made sure he had all the documents he needed before going into any meeting. He would bring her to Miami if he were to spend more time there. He did not know how he would get along without her. She was a lifesaver—sometimes literally. When Jeanne had threatened to quit if he did not see a shrink to deal with his grief and survivor guilt, he had protested, but she was dead serious, and now he was almost ready to move on. He missed Miami and his friends. They all met up in New York and Vegas from time to time, but it was not the same as running around South Beach together. It was time to go home. It was time for him to be a part of his own life again, instead of watching it go by.

Erik intended to buy a place in Miami, but he was not in a rush. He had his eye on a few specific buildings in the heart of South Beach. Until an apartment came up for sale in one of them, he would stay at the mansion. God knew the place was large enough to accommodate the population of a small nation.

Erik thought of his mother and what she had gone through with Christian over the past few years. That reminded him that Evelyn had hired a new nanny. Erik pulled out his laptop and opened the report his private investigator had sent him. One could never be too careful these days.

Andrea Ellis, he scanned down the page. *Born in California, captain of high school volleyball team, boring, blah, blah . . . Stanford, backpacking in Europe, blah, blah, Miami, worked at the doctor's office, enrolled in the psychology grad program at UM, boring, boring, blah, blah . . . aha! Places seen: SoHo House, LIV, Story, Hyde Beach—we have a party girl.* Erik smiled. *Favorite drinks: champagne, Albariño, gin and tonic, no food allergies, blah, blah . . .*

Erik looked out the window at the skyline of Miami, just as the captain announced they had started their descent.

Javier greeted him on the tarmac, grabbed the bags, and dropped them into the trunk of the Maybach, and they were on their way to Indian Creek. Erik took a deep breath as they pulled into the gates of the mansion.

* * *

Christian heard the motor of the car first. Despite the protests of his piano teacher, he jumped off the bench and ran out into the hallway.

"Hey!" Andie, who was studying in the large comfortable chair in the opposite corner of the room, trotted behind him. "Where do you think you are going?"

"Uncle Erik is here!"

Evelyn heard the commotion and walked out to greet her son as soon as the young man walked in the door.

Andie noticed that Evelyn had summoned the wealth of her affection, while Christian dove into the man's arms.

"What's up, buddy? How have you been?" Erik tossed the boy up in the air and set him down to kiss Evelyn.

Christian pulled the man by his hand. "Uncle Erik, you have not said 'hi' to Andie yet!"

Erik turned his head and nodded his acknowledgment. "Jane Eyre."

Andie chuckled at his reference to the character of Charlotte Brontë's novel. "It's nice to meet you, too."

Phillippe appeared in the doorway, and his ear-to-ear grin said it all. Erik smiled back and affectionately patted the man on the shoulder.

"So good to have you home!" Phillippe gushed. "I am making your favorite for the dinner party tonight."

"Mom? Dinner party? I just got in."

Evelyn shrugged. "Just us, the Thompsons, and Dr. Knight. I thought you might want to invite Matt as well."

"I'll text him."

"Seven o'clock," confirmed Evelyn.

Erik pulled an exotic-looking box out of his briefcase and handed it to Phillippe. "This one is from Sri Lanka. I got it in Singapore. It'd better be good, or I'll kick the guy's ass for robbing me."

Phillippe lovingly looked at the newest addition to his tea collection. Andie was surprised to see an emotional side of him. He blushed and nodded his appreciation. Without a word, he turned around and went back into the kitchen to finish the feast he had planned for his favorite Lindberg. With the music lesson at the point of no return, Andie led Christian away to change him into his swimming trunks and take him to the pool.

Erik followed his mother into the study and stretched out on the chaise. "How's this situation working out?"

"Surprisingly well."

"Christian looks happy. How are you doing?"

"I am fine, thank you. Finishing up the details for the fund-raiser I am hosting for Senator Wells. I've told you about it."

Erik nodded. "Lucy is helping you with that?"

"Yes, she is a gem."

"Remind me, when is it?"

"A week from Saturday. I expect you will be here?"

Erik nodded again.

"It's a black-tie event. See if you can get your friends to attend. We need to get more young people involved. The senator is a very promising politician; he will do well, I am sure of it."

"Mom, it's a political fund-raiser. I am sure the guys have better things to do on a Saturday night. As a matter of fact, I would've, too."

"Well, thank you for your sacrifice. After missing my birthday and Christmas, this is a small price to pay."

"Mom," chided Erik, getting up, "you know guilt does not work on me. I will see you at dinner. Oh, by the way, Matt said he will be delighted to join us tonight."

"Lovely. Please let Phillippe know."

Erik crossed the hallway into the kitchen. He sat

down behind the counter, turned on the TV, and looked at Phillippe, watching him peel and chop onions, carrots, and celery.

"Matt is joining us tonight as well," said Erik.

"Great!"

Phillippe poured the vegetables into hot oil in his frying pan. He added salt to release the juices. The smell of what is known to chefs as a "holy trinity" filled the kitchen. "The more, the merrier," he said with a smile and crushed two gloves of garlic with the flat of his knife.

Erik grabbed a beer from the fridge, curious to see how long Phillippe could go without spilling all the gossip. Phillippe did not make him wait for long. Soon, Erik knew all of the comings and goings of everyone, which were not very exciting—except for those of the new addition to the family, namely Andie. Finally, there was someone in this mill pond who had a life worth hearing about.

Satisfied with his entertainment for the afternoon and caught up on everyone's business, Erik made his way into his office inside the library.

The room was the only imprint his father had left on the mansion. Rick, who had never taken an interest in anything home-related, had spent months on the designs. He had worked with the architects and hired craftsman from all over the world to build the exquisite staircase. As with everything he had touched, Rick had spared neither expense nor time to make sure his vision came together just the way he had intended it.

Erik sat down behind an ornate redwood desk, plugged in his laptop, and pulled a stack of folders out of his briefcase. He threw his hands behind his head, leaned back in the chair, and looked out the French doors into the backyard, observing Christian and Andie playing in the pool. The scene made him smile. It seemed like his mother had finally found the winning formula; it looked like the girl did make the kid happy.

The doors swung open, and Sean, texting on his Samsung, barged in. "Bro!" he exclaimed with laughter and threw his arms open to embrace his friend. "Finally! I thought I would never see the sight of you in this house again! Matt just texted me. I guess he is coming tonight? Is he coming by himself?"

"I think so. Why? Is there a new development?"

"Oh, yeah! He is full on with the teacher."

"The brunette?" specified Erik.

"Yes, Susie." Sean walked over and leaned against the French doors. "Wait, is that your new nanny?"

Erik chuckled. "Not mine, technically."

"Man, why didn't our nanny ever look like that?"

"Christian is a lucky man," concurred Erik.

At six-foot-two, Sean stood a few inches shorter than Erik. He was well-built and fit. His pleasing features and the contrast of brown hair and green eyes usually drew approving looks from the opposite sex. A successful venture capital business secured him second dates.

As Miami natives, they had become a permanent part of the social scene. Patrick, his high-school friend Matt, and Jonathan—Erik's cousin, whom he did not like to think about anymore—were Miami's golden boys. A winning combination of Black American Express cards and an intimate knowledge of all the hot spots, their owners, and their bouncers guaranteed them entry and the best tables. The party had gone on until the music suddenly stopped. The death of Patrick and Lori had turned all of their worlds upside down, especially Erik's. He had exiled himself to New York, Jonathan had gone rogue, and then, it was just Sean and Matt left. Life had continued, but it was not the same. The two friends looked at each other for a long moment without saying a word.

Erik broke the silence. "It's good to see you, man."

He walked over to his desk and picked up one of the folders. "Here," he said as he handed it to Sean. "I signed the non-disclosure agreement."

"Thanks, man. I will send you the PowerPoint deck tomorrow. You have time to get on a call with my partners in Argentina in the next few days?"

"Yeah, I'm around. Just send me a few options. CC Jeanne."

"Will do." Sean walked over to the bar and grabbed himself a beer. "Matt texted. He's on his way."

Erik nodded. "He texted me, too."

"Is Dr. Knight coming?"

"What'd ya think?"

"He is a character," chuckled Sean. "How old is he now? By my calculations, he should be like a hundred."

"His pants have been getting tighter and his hair darker every year," agreed Erik, turning the TV on to CNBC.

"What's the market closing at?" asked Sean rhetorically, coming closer to the TV to take a look. "Hmmm. DOW is up. Are you still mostly invested in Berkshire?"

"Yeah. You know, it's basically a mutual fund. Buffet's invested in everything."

Sean nodded. "Warren is the man. I think Matt is here."

They strode from the library into the grand room just as Matt walked in.

"Hey, my brother! Long time, no see!" Matt gave Erik a hug and a friendly punch on the shoulder. "Are you sticking around or what?"

"At least for a little bit," assured Erik. "What are you drinking?" Erik walked behind the bar counter and opened the fridge. "Beer, wine, whiskey?"

"I'll have a beer, thanks."

Erik handed Matt a bottle and opened another one for himself. Evelyn, accompanied by Lucy, strolled into the room, ready to start the happy hour.

"What can I get you, ladies?" asked Erik, "Mom, a martini?"

"Thank you, dear," nodded Evelyn. "Consuelo should be here any moment to help with the drinks."

"I don't mind." He fixed his mother a drink and poured a glass of wine for Lucy.

"Sean," Evelyn began, turning to the young man, "is Clair coming from the university?"

"Not sure. I haven't spoken to her in a few days. Probably."

Evelyn sat down on the terrace that overlooked the front lawn, enjoying her martini, watching Lucy laugh with the boys. Christian, in his big boy outfit, followed by Andie, ran into the room. She heard Dr. Knight's voice as Consuelo greeted him at the front door. Life was returning to the grand house. They all needed that.

"You look well," Erik said as he shook hands with the older man.

Dr. Knight smiled, proud of his lean physique. He wore tight white jeans and a dark blue linen shirt, his tresses not showing a single gray hair. "Thank you, so do you. You staying for long?"

"Not sure yet."

Dr. Knight nodded, took a deep sigh, shook his head, and turned around to greet Evelyn. "Where is your chess board, young man?" he exclaimed, glaring at Christian.

"Um . . . it's upstairs. I will bring it." The boy ran back up and returned with the box. He set the board on the coffee table and organized the pieces.

With Clair's arrival a few minutes later, Evelyn felt at peace. Everything was going according to her dinner schedule. "Ask the boys about next Saturday," she reminded Erik from the terrace.

"What about next Saturday?" Sean reacted, worried he would be pulled into a mandatory outing.

"Mother would like to invite you to the black-tie fund-raiser for Senator Wells, who is, and I quote, 'a very promising young politician, and he will go far, I am sure of it.'"

"I can hear you, dear," laughed Evelyn, sipping on her cocktail.

Sean shook his head "I would, literally, rather have a root canal—"

"Let me ask Susie," Matt replied at the same time.

"Dude." Sean raised his eyebrows at Matt. "Are you serious?"

"What? She likes that type of thing."

"Great!" Erik tapped Matt's shoulder. "I won't have to suffer alone."

"I said I would ask—" Matt said hastily hoping to reserve the right to back off.

"Afraid it's too late. Mother heard you. Lucy will send you the details. Right, Lucy?"

"Absolutely! Looking forward to having you and Susie!"

"Man." Matt chuckled and shook his head in disbelief.

"Immature!" Sean teased.

"That's how we do it!" Erik said with a grin. "Come for dinner, stay for the fund-raiser."

Chapter 8

Summer had unmistakably arrived, and it did so with a vengeance. The heat and humidity made the air thick and sticky, but Andie hoped to squeeze in a few more weeks of running outside. Covered in sweat and out of breath, she hobbled into the air-conditioned oasis of the kitchen and chugged down a tall glass of water. As she did every morning, Andie brewed herself a coffee and stepped out onto the patio, where Phillippe was enjoying a cup of his own.

"Ah, Andie, perfect timing." He grinned and patted the seat next to him.

As he spoke, Erik strode out of the house, with a towel casually thrown over his bare torso. He sauntered down to the pool and stripped out of his board shorts. Wearing just a Speedo, he dove into the pool, his long, muscular body breaking the water without so much as a splash, his powerful arms propelling him forward with confident strokes.

"I told you, this is the best spot in the house," Phillippe said, winking.

"Impressive," smiled Andie, admiring Erik's physique.

Lucy rushed out and cozied up on the couch. "Did I miss it?"

"Just in time." Phillippe smirked, then swore in response to the sound of the doorbell at the delivery entrance. He rose to answer it.

Done with his laps, Erik got out of the pool, wrapped the towel around his hips, and strode onto the patio. He sat down in the seat vacated by Phillippe and shook his hair, splattering drops of water all around. "Lucy. Jane Eyre."

"Hey, I see the parallel, but you really need to stop calling me that," protested Andie with a chuckle.

"As you wish," complied the man.

Phillippe rushed back with a glass of water for Erik. "Can I get you some coffee?"

"Thank you." He sank deeper into the chair. "Did you go for a run this morning?" he asked as he turned to Andie.

"Yeah, it's miserable."

Erik nodded in agreement and got up. "Lucy, pleasure as usual. I will see you later, Miss Ellis." He winked at them and strode inside.

Lucy laughed and fanned herself with her hand. "It's getting hot in here," she sang as she strode into the house.

Andie inhaled hot air. A few more minutes of peace and silence before she had to change, get Christian ready for school, and drive to the university. Just a few more minutes. She felt her gut tighten, courtesy of her mind's endless loop of anxious thoughts and memories and "what ifs," sadness about the past, worry about the future. A sharp pain in her eyes forecast that waterworks might be on the way. She shook off the upcoming wave of emotions. *Deep breath from the bottom of the belly,* she thought, *bring the thoughts to the present.*

And right now, she needed to get Christian ready for school. Later, she had the night off and a date. Josh-the-stockbroker—not the most exciting companion, but she needed to start somewhere. Not that it would go anywhere, but good enough for a dinner or two. Determined to have a good day, Andie got up, ready to take on Christian, whatever mood he woke up in.

Showered and dressed, she ran up the stairs only to find that Christian was not in his room. Andie followed the sound of the TV into the family room and discovered the boy on Erik's lap, watching CNBC.

"Andie, great news: the market is up. We are making money today," announced the child.

"That is great news!" Andie smiled. Apparently, Erik had everyone in the house under his spell. "Come, let's change you out of those pajamas."

As they exited, Erik looked at his empty coffee mug. *Ugh, this house is a monstrosity. It's a hike just to get another cup.* He personally preferred condos—all one level, the maintenance is taken care of, turnkey, come and go as you please. He craved the simplicity. *Speaking of condos* . . . He looked at his phone; the realtor had sent him a couple of listings for the ones he might be interested in.

Erik got up and sauntered downstairs into the library, opened his computer, and clicked on the attachments. He looked at his empty mug and growled.

"Hey, Phillippe, could you please get me another cup of coffee?" he requested over the house intercom system. There was a benefit to this house after all.

Erik's phone lit up with group text messages about dinner plans. He was jonesing for a steak, and there was only one place where he liked to eat his in Miami: Prime 112. He suggested they meet at the Smith & Wollensky for happy hour and then walk over to Prime. Thumbs-up emojis all around.

He emailed the realtor to schedule a showing for an hour prior. The condo was a two-minute walk from their meeting spot in the exact building he coveted, the unit—a disappointment. He arrived at Smith & Wollensky early, grabbed a high-top table by the bar, and ordered a pitcher of margaritas. The restaurant, a bit tired and outdated, occupied the best spot on South Beach to watch the sunset. The last rays burned behind the outline of Miami, coloring the waters of Biscayne Bay. A cruise ship passed by, taking excited passengers on new journey. Erik felt he was finally ready for his— the journey, that is, not a cruise.

Sean arrived just as a bartender brought out the pitcher and the glasses. "Hey, man," he greeted Erik with a high-five handshake. "My timing is impeccable, I see."

Both of their phones lit up with a message: *We r here.*

Erik shrugged his shoulders. "I guess Matt is bringing Susie."

"Get used to it, bro," warned Sean with a good-natured smirk and got up to greet the approaching couple.

At five-foot-four, Susie seemed tiny next to the three men. But what she lacked in height, she made up for in personality. Smiling, she climbed into a tall chair and accepted a glass with the enthusiasm of a person who is forced to deal with others day in and day out.

"Mmmm." She puckered her lips in a drinkgasm and melted in her seat. "So what's new in the zoo?"

The pitcher did not stand a chance against their thirst, and the second one made its appearance shortly thereafter. The happy hour crowd began to thin out as the street lamps lit up with changing colors.

"Guys, I'm hungry," announced Susie. "Where are we going to eat?"

"Prime 112."

"Ugh, we'll never get in. Do you have a reservation?"

Matt smiled. "Watch and learn."

They crossed the street and walked into the cramped, dark entrance of a deceptively small yellow house.

"Hi, guys! Long time, no see!" exclaimed the hostess. "Four of you today?"

"It is," confirmed Sean, leaning against the stand with a charming grin. "Do you have our usual table?"

"Not right this second, but they will be done soon. Just wait at the bar, and I will come get you when it is ready."

"Thank you, darling, you are the best!" Sean replied.

They squeezed into the tight bar and ordered a bottle of wine. Susie picked a slice of thick smoky bacon from a crystal glass on the counter. Bar nuts are so passé. The bottle appeared in the blink of an eye.

"I have never been served this fast here before!" Susie exclaimed in disbelief.

"Stick with me, kiddo," Matt said as he wrapped his arm around her waist and pulled her closer.

"I intend to," she remarked with a wink.

"Is that Andie?" Sean asked, pointing toward a table in the dining room.

"I know her!" exclaimed Susie. "I met her at a fundraiser for our school. She is friends with a girlfriend of mine, Jo."

Erik squinted his eyes and confirmed. "Hmm, I guess she is on a date . . ."

"He's cute," noted Susie.

"Whatever." Sean shrugged his shoulders dismissively.

"He looks pretty clean-cut," Matt added approvingly.

"Is it just me, or is she hot?" probed Sean.

"No, she is pretty hot," agreed Susie.

Erik waved in the bartender and nodded. "Please, send that table two glasses of Veuve on me."

"If you are going to do something, why don't you send them a bottle?" asked Susie.

Erik smiled. "It's a school night."

Andie turned around, looking for the benefactor of

her champagne. She nodded her thank-you to Erik, and excitedly waved to Susie, recognizing her.

"We should crash their date," suggested Sean.

"I don't think so," interfered Erik.

A young hostess appeared from behind them. "Miss, gentlemen, right this way. Please watch your steps."

"I can't believe it!" Susie gaped. "I have waited here for over an hour, even with a reservation!"

Matt laughed. "It's because of slackers like us."

"From now on, I only go out with you people."

"You got it!" Matt smiled affectionately, kissing Susie on the temple.

Sean rolled his eyes and laughed.

* * *

On the day of the fund-raiser for Senator Wells, the craziness started in early morning. The caterers had occupied the kitchen hall on the north side of the house that was reserved for large events. People bounced in and out, stocking the bars and setting up cocktail tables inside the grand room and out on the front lawn.

Usually even-keeled, Lucy looked rattled as she bossed around the staff and stressed over every detail. She barked out orders and checked things off on her iPad. Andie hadn't seen this side of the woman before and, out of a sense of sheer self-preservation, vowed never to get under her skin in the future. It was impossible to stay out of everyone's way cooped up inside the house, so she packed Christian into her Mini Cooper and they took off to Jungle Island. They spent a good part of the day playing with the animals and swimming at the beach, then met Jo for lunch and walked around Lincoln Road. They got back home in time for dinner.

When they returned, the house buzzed with anticipation. The valets had already taken their places, ready to receive influential guests. Lucy seemed calmer, and Evelyn looked elegant and poised. Andie caught a glimpse of Dr. Knight having drinks by the bar with Erik and Matt; all three dressed in tuxedos.

Tiring Christian paid off. He climbed into his bed early and asked to watch cartoons. Andie settled him in and turned on the TV. "I will come check on you in a few," she said.

She changed into a pair of cut-off shorts and an oversized cardigan, grabbed her books and laptop, and sneaked into the library. She cozied up on the cushy bench in front of the bay window in the loft that overlooked the party outside.

One after another expensive car pulled into the driveway, letting out sophisticatedly dressed guests. The walkway decorated with shimmering lights led them down to the meticulously manicured lawn, carefully concealed speakers emitted the sounds of soft music, and high-top cocktail tables adorned with flowers and candles enhanced the ambiance. This was a completely different world from the one Andie knew. This was something out of *The Great Gatsby*—it was not real, at least not to 99 percent of the population. She had always wondered what it would be like to be a part of this world of privilege and inexhaustible wealth. On the other hand, the concept of "a front seat and a back seat and a window in between" was outdated.[2] Erik and she were a part of the same circle, they went to the same clubs and ate at the same restaurants. Guys like him dated girls like her, and no one found it unsuitable anymore. Not that she would ever date Erik. It would be totally inappropriate under the circumstances.

Andie forced herself to return to her studies. She tore her attention away from the party and stared at an empty page of her unwritten paper. She put aside her laptop and picked up a textbook and a yellow marker. She scanned a few pages and highlighted the key ideas for her report. Analyzing what she just read, Andie shifted her gaze from the book into the empty space in front of her, looking down at the desk and a large leather couch. She mouthed the first sentence of her essay before typing it.

Andie was fully immersed in her work when the sound of the shutting door jolted her out of her thoughts. She heard muted voices, and a second later, Erik and a red-haired woman emerged in her line of sight. Andie opened her mouth to make her presence known, but before she could utter a sound, the woman pushed Erik down onto the sofa. He pulled her over, and she climbed on top of him, covering his mouth with her lips. His bow tie flew onto the floor as the woman struggled to unbutton his shirt. Erik grabbed the redhead by her hair and yanked her head back. He brought his mouth to her neck, with his free hand, he pulled up her dress, and squeezed her thighs with his fingers. The woman moaned when Erik freed her breasts and drew her nipple into his mouth, sucking on it and roughly caressing the other with his fingers. She leaned over him, biting his neck, and reached down to his pants to fondle him. Erik growled, gently pushed the woman off, and got up, steadying her on her feet.

"You should go back," he said quietly in a hoarse voice. "I will come out in a few minutes."

Reluctant, the woman headed toward the door.

"Hey!" Erik called after her. "You should fix your lipstick. Stop by the bathroom. It's on the right, as soon as you walk out."

Andie heard the door close. Erik grabbed a napkin from the bar cart, wiped the lipstick off his lips, and poured himself a drink.

"Gin and tonic, Miss Ellis?" he asked.

Andie's heart jumped into her throat. "Yes, please," she forced out.

A moment later, Erik ascended the stairs and appeared in front of her. He handed Andie the drink, pulled over a chair, and sat down facing her.

"Cheers." He clinked his glass against Andie's.

"How long did you know I was here?" she asked feigning composure.

"From the beginning," answered Erik.

"Why didn't you stop?"

"It turned me on."

"Are you an exhibitionist, Mr. Lindberg?"

"Aren't we all?" countered Erik.

"Did you care that she was unaware of it?"

"No."

"So if your girlfriend had known, you think she wouldn't have minded?"

A momentary look of confusion ran across Erik's face, then he gestured with his head toward the downstairs. "You mean Vicky? No, not a girlfriend; that's the senator's wife."

Andie raised her eyebrow. "Lovely."

"She is, isn't she? You don't approve?"

"Of extramarital affairs?"

"It's not an affair. I've only met her a few hours ago."

"Are you a philanderer, then, Mr. Lindberg?"

"I am." Erik's teasing eyes were permanently fixed on Andie, and to her despair, it made her blush.

"You are proud of it?"

"Neither proud nor ashamed. I don't pass judgment on who I am. And you, Miss Ellis, should not either."

"You are insolent."

"And you are petulant," he countered. "Now that we have established that both of us are in command of our vocabulary, please tell me, are you always this direct?"

"Only when traumatized, after being forced to watch my boss pretty much have sex in front of me."

"Did you enjoy it?" Erik took a sip of his drink, his eyes locked on her face.

"I tried not to pay attention."

"Liar." Erik traced Andie's bare leg with his finger, cold from holding the ice-filled glass, sending shivers through her body.

"This is wildly inappropriate," Andie uttered, trying not to meet his glare.

"Most of the exciting things in life are."

"Do you always kiss and tell?"

"I did not. You spied on us."

"I—what? Ugh! I most definitely did not!" protested Andie.

"You could have made your presence known," suggested Erik.

"I . . . what? Shouldn't you be going back down to your guests?"

Erik took the last sip of his drink and stood up. Towering over her, he reached out with his hand and lifted Andie's chin, forcing her eyes to meet his. Holding her face in place, he brushed her lips with his thumb.

"You know you're turned on," he said in a coarse, quiet voice and left the room.

Andie took a gulp of her drink and, with a shaking hand, put the glass down. He was not wrong; she was incredibly turned on. Another thing she now knew was that Erik Lindberg was a dangerous man, and she needed to steer clear of him.

Chapter 9

Just one final exam separated Andie from summer break. She had studied all day and now felt incapable of holding another piece of information inside her brain. She cozied up in bed, flipping through TV channels, pausing at the programs that caught her attention but not enough to watch them. During a commercial break, she got out of bed and crossed the dark hallway separating her room from the rest of the house.

She regretted walking barefoot as soon as her toes touched the cold kitchen tile. Unwilling to do anything about it, she proceeded on her tiptoes, turned on the kettle, and picked a tea from Phillippe's collection. She opened the box, breathing in the delicate aroma, and jumped up, startled, when the door into the kitchen swung open and Erik, dressed only in his pajama pants, walked in.

"Jesus Christ!" cried Andie, her heart still pounding in her throat. "What are you doing here?!"

"It's my house. I live here." Erik pulled out a box of Cheerios from the cupboard.

"Of course." She retreated and continued in a calmer

voice. "I am sorry. Um . . . it's just Mrs. Lindberg never comes into the kitchen."

"That is correct, she does not," confirmed Erik, as he poured the milk over his cereal and sat down at the island. "Are you making tea? Can I have some?"

"Sure." Andie poured Erik a cup and set it in front of him. "Good night," she said, and tiptoed toward the door.

"Keep me company while I eat? Please."

"Um . . . I am practically naked."

"You were practically naked five minutes ago," reasoned Erik.

It was a valid point. Andie sat down on the opposite end of the island. "Midnight snack?"

"Uh-huh. Ready for your exam?"

"I think so."

"I'm sure you'll do just fine."

"Of course I will! I'm on track to get an A for the course. I need to do better than 'just fine' tomorrow!"

"Well, pardon moi, Miss Ellis." Erik smirked. "How's Josh-the-stockbroker?"

"Do you and Phillippe have nothing better to do than gossip about me?"

"We really don't," affirmed Erik. "I've heard that stockbrokers are boring in bed."

Andie chuckled. "I wouldn't know, but based on the dinner conversation, I believe it."

"Haven't you just broken up with a boyfriend or something?"

Andie nodded.

"Any reason?"

"It turned out we wanted different things, I guess."

A pained expression ran across her face. As fleeting as it was, Erik noticed it and did not pry further. "You just need to have some fun," he encouraged.

"Yeah, I fully intend to. I'm done with school in about a week. Then, I can have something that resembles a life. The girls are going to Vegas at the end of June—"

"Are you going?"

"Not sure. It might be too soon to ask for the time off."

"I think you should. It sounds like fun. Let me know if you need hookups. I have a few good contacts at the clubs and for the pool parties."

"Thank you. We might. Though my girlfriend, Jersey, is flying there for a *Playboy* reunion, so they are putting her up in a hotel, and she has a bunch of invites to private parties and clubs, and stuff."

"Sounds like you are better connected than me," Erik said with a smile. "Maybe the next time I go, I will ask you for the intros."

Andie changed the subject. "That girl, Susie—"

"What about her?"

"Is she Matt's girlfriend?"

Erik nodded.

"She is nice."

"Uh-huh," agreed Erik.

"Have you ever had a girlfriend?"

"Yeah. I had a few."

"Why did you break up with the last one?"

"She cheated on me," Erik answered dispassionately.

"Oh, sorry!"

"Don't be. It wasn't going anywhere."

"Did you love her?"

"No."

"Why did you date her, then?" Andie pried.

"I wanted to be with someone. Patrick had Lori, and I wanted what they had. Liz seemed nice enough. She wasn't really pretty, like the other girls I've dated, so I thought, somehow, because of that, she would be nice. I thought by being with her I was growing as a person or becoming less shallow . . . but all it really was, was me wanting to imitate my brother's relationship. Then after Patrick died, she claimed she felt neglected . . . and I really was not in any shape to be with someone at that point anyway."

"She cheated on you after your brother's death?"

"Yep."

"Oh, that is so wrong on so many levels!"

"I thought so," agreed Erik calmly.

"And since then?"

"And since then, I've refused to settle for 'nice enough.' Well, Miss Ellis, you really are in the right field. Are you practicing for your exam on me?"

Andie blushed. "I'm sorry. I did not mean to be nosy. It's just, um, after JC and I broke up . . . um, I just don't get it anymore. I am trying to understand . . ."

"There is nothing to *get*. You have to kiss a whole bunch of frogs before you find your Prince Charming, Miss Ellis. Look at me, I am on a mission!" Erik grinned.

"To find a Prince Charming?" laughed Andie.

"No. To kiss."

Andie got up and put the cups and the cereal bowl into the dishwasher. "Thank you, Erik. It was really nice talking to you," she said softly.

"You are very welcome, Miss Ellis. Thank you for keeping me company. Despite your being practically naked."

Andie threw a dishtowel at him and stuck out her tongue before tiptoeing toward the door.

"Hey, Andie," Erik called out.

"Hmm?"

"Break a leg. You will do great!"

She smiled, nodded, and walked out of the kitchen. She *would* do great tomorrow. She knew it.

* * *

Andie put down her pencil, handed her work to the professor, and left the classroom. She breathed a sigh of relief; the first year of her grad program had come to a successful end. She dialed Jo.

"Hey, girlie. All done?" asked Jo in a cheerful voice.

"Done and done!"

"How do you think you did?"

Andie beamed. "I honestly think I did well. I totally overstudied for this test."

"Great. Congratulations! What time do you want to meet at Baoli?"

"Around ten? I will put Christian to bed and Uber over as soon as I am ready."

"Sounds good, love. I will text Jersey and let her know."

* * *

Anyone in South Beach with an inkling of social trends knows where to go on any given day of the week. Nobody would want to make a rooky mistake and choose the wrong venue, as every hotspot has its own happening night. Wednesdays belong to Baoli and its "My Boyfriend Is out of Town" party. An elegant restaurant that magically morphs into a club, Baoli fuses the styles of the French Rivera and South Beach. A stunning interior flows into an Alice-in-Wonderland–like inner courtyard. Crystal chandeliers, plush red bar stools, and candlelit tables add to a sophisticated ambiance and sexy vibe. The locals and in-the-know jet-setters flock there to play and flirt to the music by the best DJs.

Erik knew his Wednesday night date, Beatrix, loved Le Baoli in Cannes, so its South Beach counterpart was a good place to take her after dinner. Besides, there was nothing else happening that night. He sipped rich French wine and smiled at the woman across the table. Stunning in her feline beauty, with long, straight black hair and blue eyes, she reminded him of a young Monica

Bellucci. He had become infatuated with her the moment he saw her, a few years back at her Champs-Élysées flat. Erik's friend had invited him to what happened to be her fortieth birthday party. The moment their eyes met, before they had gotten a chance to exchange pleasantries, they both knew Erik would be spending the night. Their meeting of minds had been as powerful as their sexual attraction. They both enjoyed the libertine lifestyle and Madam O parties.

Beatrix had married young to an overcontrolling older man. She had suppressed her personality for the sake of marriage until she could not stand it any longer. Her divorce was her coming-out party. She had bloomed like a wildflower, robust and sensual. The single lifestyle suited her; the freedom to choose and play with whomever she chose empowered her.

A few months earlier, Erik had invited Natalie to join them at a soiree at the chateaux, and the three of them had partaken in each other's fantasies. He saw Beatrix every time he went to Paris and had been pleasantly surprised when she told him she was planning to visit Miami for a few days.

Sean met them for a drink after dinner at Setai, and together they strolled down to Baoli. The music was pumping as they walked out to the patio.

"Is that . . ?" Sean was not quite sure how to finish his sentence.

Erik looked in the direction Sean pointed and laughed. Half a dozen people were dancing on the top of the neon-lit bar. Among them he saw Andie, surrounded by two other girls, he presumed to be Jo and Jersey.

"Oy! They break their necks!" exclaimed Beatrix in her slight French accent.

"Mmmm . . . she has a wild side. Me like!" grinned Sean and waved.

Andie noticed them and waved back with excitement. The song ended, and Sean picked Andie up from the bar top and set her on the ground, holding her while she steadied herself.

"That was inspiring!" he effused, kissing the girls hello.

"Melissa." Jersey extended her hand.

"Jo." Jo exchanged kisses with the newcomers.

"Beatrix," Erik replied, introducing his date.

Andie looked with admiration at the beauty and style of the woman in front of them.

Beatrix smiled. "It is nice to meet you," she said. Her voice was deep and melodic.

Erik waved to the bartender, anxious to order a drink. "Bottle of Veuve and two Patrons on the rocks with extra lime." When the drinks arrived, he raised his glass to Andie's. "Congratulations. To a job well done!"

Andie lifted her arms in a victorious gesture a la Rocky and, like a child, jumped up and down. "I am free!"

Sean took a sip of his Patron. How come he had never run into her before? They clearly went to the same clubs. From head to toes, she was his type: sexy, fun, intelligent. Should he ask her out like Susie had suggested or should he wait? He got closer to her, standing right behind her, enjoying her warmth and the smell of her perfume. She smiled at him, sweetly, like she smiled at everyone. She flirted with him without realizing she was doing it. She made everyone she paid attention to feel special. Like with most beautiful women, it came natural to her. He poured her another glass and put his hand on her waist, urging her to dance with him. They swayed together for a moment, and she broke away from him to dance with her friends. The three girls moved to the music, familiar and comfortable with each other's motions. Sean watched.

So did Erik. He knew his friend well. He suspected what Sean was thinking, and he did not like it one bit. Sean's track record with women left much to be desired. If he were to hook up with Andie, Erik would be in the front-row seat when the shit hit the fan. With Sean being a part of the family and Andie being Christian's nanny, the situation was about to get awkward. Erik ran his fingers through his hair, an unconscious movement he made when he was annoyed.

Andie noticed the gesture. She wondered what had agitated him now.

"Hey," said Sean quietly to his friend, "I am thinking about asking Andie out. What do you think?"

Not willing to appear unsupportive, Erik shrugged his shoulders. "Go for it."

Sean nodded. When the music changed and the girls

stopped dancing, he poured Andie another glass. "So, what are you up to this summer?"

She smiled. "Just going to try to have some fun."

"Don't try—do, or do not," said Sean, channeling his best Yoda.

"Oh my God," Andie laughed. "You are such a dork!"

"Maybe I can take you out for dinner sometime?"

Andie looked into his eyes. "I'm sorry, Sean. It's really not a good idea in this situation."

"What are you talking about? It's a great idea. Erik would not mind!"

"Still. I am sorry. It would be inappropriate."

"Are you sure?"

"Positive." Andie smiled and kissed him on the cheek.

"Flirt," Sean said accusingly, playfully pinching her arm.

Erik, who had watched the exchange from the other side of the bar, breathed a sigh of relief. It looked like his nanny possessed more common sense than his friend.

Beatrix put her hand on Erik's cheek. "Let's go from here."

Erik kissed her. "Okay."

He reached over to Andie. "You are not driving, are you?"

"No, I Ubered."

Erik nodded. "Good girl. Have fun." He paid the tab and followed Beatrix outside.

"Are you okay to walk, *ma chére?*" asked Erik pointing at her high heels.

"No, I prefer you carry me, my Erik?" cooed the woman.

Erik picked her up and spun around as Beatrix laughed in that velvety voice of hers. He gently put her down and gave her a kiss full of desire and promise.

They crossed the street to the W Hotel where Beatrix always stayed and walked into the stylish contemporary lobby. Erik could recognize a W Hotel anywhere in the world with his eyes closed simply by the distinct smell of modern sophistication.

They rode the elevator to the top floor and walked into a contemporary suite with an oversized wrap-around balcony. Erik opened the sliding glass doors and stepped outside. The vast abyss of the night-darkened ocean, with the sound of waves rhythmically splashing on the beach, lay in front of him.

"Erik, I brought you present."

Erik turned around, just as Beatrix walked onto the balcony wearing only her five-inch Louboutin's and a Hermes tie. She handed him a glass of champagne and traced the curve of his neck with the tip of her tongue. She then strode back into the room and spread herself on the bed, caressing her body with her fingers. Erik pulled his shirt over his head, threw it on the floor, and followed her inside.

Standing over her, Erik looked down at the woman

yearning for him. He took a sip from the crystal glass and poured the rest of his champagne over her naked body. She shuddered at the cold and the delicate tingle of bubbles, he leaned down and licked it off her luxurious skin. His tongue traveled up from her navel to her breasts, tasting the sweetness of the champagne and the salt of her skin. He sucked her nipple into his mouth, softly biting it, making her moan. Erik pulled the tie off her neck and tied it around her eyes.

"Now, about that present," he whispered, gently wrapping his fingers around her neck and pressing inside her.

Chapter 10

One date with Josh-the-stockbroker was enough, but he kept texting and calling almost on a daily basis. Unimpressed and disinterested, Andie found excuse after excuse to blow him off. She knew she should cut him loose, but hoped he would get the hint. He did not. Finally, in a moment of weakness, she agreed to a low-key afternoon of pizza and a movie at his house. Determined to get it out of the way on Friday, she looked forward to the free weekend to go out with Jo and Jersey.

Mrs. Lindberg and Christian left for Palm Beach, which they did several times a month. Consuelo and Javier accompanied them, and the house turned empty and quiet, affording Andie time for herself.

She picked up a bottle of white wine and drove her Mini Cooper to Josh's cottage in North Miami Beach. Josh, beaming from ear to ear, opened the door and ushered her in.

"Let's get the important stuff out of the way," he urged. "What do you like on your pizza?"

Andie smiled. "Hmmm . . . what are my choices?"

Maybe she should give him another look. He seemed nice.

They ordered from Lucali—the only pizza in Miami worth the calories. In anticipation of the sinful, carb-laden indulgence, Andie reclined on the couch and took a sip of the Albariño. Josh settled next to her, casually threw his arm around her shoulder, and picked the remote. They studied the list of on-demand movies and chose one of the Marvel flicks.

Josh grinned and raised his glass. "I guess we need to toast to the summer! Congratulations on your finals. I look forward to getting to know you better."

"Thank you." Andie set her glass down on the coffee table. *He is nice,* she thought.

The movie, a mindless escape with a good-looking cast, offered the perfect background for the get-to-know-you-better date. Josh brought out some grapes and cheese while they waited for the pizza. Eager to please, he poured Andie some more wine. Grateful for his effort, she smiled and patted his knee. He took the gesture as an encouragement and moved closer, his hand awkwardly fondling her fingers.

"You know," he said, "you are one of the most beautiful women I've dated, since my wife."

Not true, thought Andie. *I saw a photo of your ex-wife, and I am way prettier.* "You are too sweet," she said politely.

"You really are."

Without warning, he kissed her. His tongue moved

mercilessly inside her mouth, and Andie felt like she was in a sci-fi flick getting her face sucked off her skull by an alien. *Oy!* she thought. *Someone needs to teach this guy the basics.*

She was not that "someone." A vision of a summer spent faking orgasms flashed in front of her eyes. Nice is nice, but orgasms were sacred. She gently freed herself. He sprung back like a puppy being scolded. His puppy eyes looked back at her, in hopes of positive feedback.

Andie smiled, trying to appear casual. "When do you think the pizza is getting here?"

"You know, it is our third date," Josh said slyly and slid his hand up her leg.

He leaned toward her lips again. Trapped in his arms, Andie endured another assault on her mouth.

"Good to know," she muttered as she softly moved his hand and shifted away from him.

Josh moved closer, nuzzled his face into her neck and walked his fingers up her inner thigh. Andie stood up, forcing him off her. He bounced to his feet.

"What's wrong, baby?" He caught her waist and pulled her into his arms for another kiss.

She stepped back. "Josh, wait. How about we take it slow—?"

"Seriously?" He reached over, catching her wrists, while Andie put out her hands, defining her space. "Are you really going to play hard to get?"

"I'm sorry, I am not playing anything. It's just . . . this is a bit much."

"Are you kidding me?" Josh started to get aggravated, and Andie took another step back. "Hey! What the fuck?!" He tightened the grip on her wrists.

"Josh, you need to let go," Andie said with a calmness she did not feel. "You are hurting me."

He pulled her closer. Should she call for help? Would anyone hear?

"I am sorry, but I have to go."

She turned around, eyeing the exit. Josh grabbed her arm and roughly spun her to face him. "Don't turn your fucking back on me!"

Now seriously frightened, Andie jerked away from his grip. He wobbled and caught her shirt.

"You bitch!"

Andie pushed him away with full force. Enraged, he slapped her across the face, his class ring slicing the skin on her cheekbone. Andie lost her balance and tumbled to the floor, unwillingly pulling Josh down. He crashed next to her. Cursing, he grabbed her ankle, slid her underneath him and pinned her down with his weight. She felt his hands crudely fondling her breasts, his breath getting heavier and louder. She felt his teeth on her neck and his fingers clasping her hair.

In a frantic attempt to free herself, Andie drove her elbow into his chest. Gaining an inch of freedom, she snatched the wine glass from the table, slammed it against the floor, and pointed the jagged edge of the broken stem at her attacker. Taken aback, Josh loosened his grip and retreated for a brief moment. With the little strength she had left in her, Andie shoved him off and jumped to her feet.

"Get away from me, you fucking asshole!" she cried out, still threatening Josh with sharp glass.

"You fucking psycho-kitty," he yelled, stepping back but still trying to catch her wrists.

"You are fucking right! Take another step, and I will fucking cut you!" Andie screamed, grabbed her purse, and dashed to the door. She flung it open before Josh could stop her and ran outside. Out in the driveway, she jumped into the car, locked the doors, and raced away to safety.

Andie stopped at the traffic light and surveyed herself. Her wrists and thighs showed blue fingerprint bruises, her hands were shaking, and her face throbbing. She touched her cheek and saw traces of blood on her fingertips. She flipped down the visor mirror.

"Fuck!" The bruise had already darkened. "Fuck!" she barked again and slammed her fist against the wheel. "Ouch!" She sucked on her now-painful knuckle. A wave of nausea washed over her as a flood of tears poured down her face, stinging the cut even more.

She felt more alone than ever. With no other place to go, Andie drove back to the mansion and prayed no one was home. Pulling into the gates, she cursed out loud when she saw Erik, barefoot and wearing only his board shorts low on his hips, washing his favorite Aston Martin. He waved her in and pointed the hose away so as not to splash her.

Andie got out of the car and put her head down, hoping to slip inside without a conversation.

"Well, hello to you, too," chuckled Erik, playfully spraying her.

Reacting, Andie glanced back. "Oh, fuck off!" she swore under her breath, turned away to hide her face, and briskly headed up the driveway.

Erik's jaw tightened as he dropped the hose. In two strides, he caught up with the girl, grabbed her shoulder, and swung her around.

"Fuck off!" she screamed out loud, trying to shake off the iron grip of his fingers. He held her in place. With his free hand, Erik clenched her chin and turned her cheek toward him so he could clearly see it. He forced her to meet his eyes; they were dark with fury.

"Let go of me!" she cried out, trying to escape.

He pulled her into his arms, holding her tight. She hid her face in his chest and started to sob.

He felt her heart pounding as her body spasmodically convulsed against his. Erik's skin was wet with her tears, he felt utterly helpless against her distress. He softly patted her head and kissed her hair. He let her calm down before he took a step back and gently held her away at arm's length to examine her face.

Embarrassed, Andie tried to hide her bruise, but Erik's hand tightly clasped her chin in place, so she finally gave in and lifted her eyes. His handsome face was still distorted with anger. For her sake, he tried to control it.

"Come." He led her into the kitchen and, as if she

were a small child, picked her up and set her down on top of the counter. He walked over to the freezer, pulled out a bag of frozen vegetables, wrapped it in a towel, and pressed it against Andie's cheek. He looked at her black and blue wrists and clenched his jaw.

"Is it bad?" she asked.

"You have a bruise," he answered calmly, and pulled the bag away from her face to look at it again. "Good news, you don't need stitches."

"My God, what am I going to tell Mrs. Lindberg?" she cried out. "This is so white trash!"

"Just tell her you got carried away in the kickboxing class!"

"She is not stupid!"

"That she is not," he agreed. "She won't be home for a few days. By then you should be able to cover it up with makeup." Erik now paced in front of her, running his fingers through his hair. He finally braved the question. "Did—?"

Andie shook her head. "No, no . . . nothing happened. He . . . no."

Erik nodded, relieved. He had a strong urge to punch something but restrained himself to avoid traumatizing the girl further.

Her phone rang. She looked at the number and instinctively pulled away. Noticing her panic, Erik answered the phone.

"Who the fuck is this?" barked the man on the other end of the line.

"This is Erik Lindberg. If you ever call this number again or come anywhere near her, I will bury you. Am I clear?"

"Are you threatening me, you asshole?"

"You fucking bet it! Google me. I am not joking. I will destroy you."

Erik hung up, blocked the number, and glared at Andie. She shook her head and threw her hands up in the air. "I am not self-destructive."

"Good!" he nodded.

Andie put down the ice bag and jumped off the counter. "Okay if I lie down?"

"Yeah, of course. I will check up on you later, okay?"

Andie nodded and headed toward the door. "Erik . . ." She turned around and threw herself into his arms for a hug. "Thank you."

He wrapped his arms around her and kissed the top of her head. "I am so sorry, sweet pea. I will never let anything bad happen to you again."

She raised her face to him, and Erik felt her eyes pierce him down to his soul.

* * *

Andie climbed into bed, finding comfort in her old stuffed bear. She must have dozed off because a soft knock on the door made her jump.

"Yeah?"

Erik stepped into her room and handed her a cocktail. He looked around, realizing he had never been in this part of the house before. He looked down on Andie, who was still clinging to her teddy bear. "Come, it's the sunset."

They walked out on the terrace to watch the sun kiss the waters of Biscayne Bay good-bye. Erik took a sip of his twenty-year-old Macallan and breathed in the sultry summer air.

Andie watched him, still feeling guilty for the trouble she had caused. "I am sorry."

"For what?" he asked without emotion, not taking his eyes off the water.

"It was my fault . . ."

Erik slowly turned his head to face her. She saw his jaw clench again, as he rushed the fingers through his hair. "It was not," he replied coldly.

"I shouldn't have—"

"There is nothing in what happened that was or is your fault," he interrupted, speaking deliberately and slowly. "As a future shrink, you should know that."

"Okay."

"Look at me!" he ordered, and Andie nervously lifted her eyes to meet his. "Did you hear what I just said?"

"Yes . . ."

Erik nodded trying to let go of his anger. "Are you hungry? Do you want me to take you out for dinner somewhere?" he asked.

"It's a Friday night," she reminded him. "You don't have to babysit me. I'm sure you'd rather go out with the boys—"

"I appreciate your consideration, but I am laying low tonight."

"That woman, on Wednesday, she was beautiful," Andie observed.

"She is," agreed Erik.

"Is she French?"

Erik nodded.

"For how long is she visiting?"

"For a week. I am taking her out tomorrow, to answer your next question."

"How long have you known each other?"

"A few years. You are being nosy again, Miss Ellis," teased Erik.

Andie chuckled. "Sorry. Do you want to call in delivery and watch a movie?"

"Sounds like a plan."

They ordered some greasy Chinese food and turned on reruns of *Game of Thrones*. Erik sipped his scotch and stretched out on the comfortable couch in the family room, while Andie sat next to him, her leg crossed and her foot tucked under her knee. He smiled, amused by how animated she became watching the show, rooting for her favorite characters. When they had had enough drama, they played a game of Go Fish, and she jumped for joy at each round she won. Erik could not remember the last time he had enjoyed himself just hanging out with a woman he had no intention of having sex with.

Chapter 11

Andie did not mind the hectic hustle of the airport; if she was in the midst of it, it meant she was about to travel. Today's destination: Las Vegas!

Since the incident, she had not seen much of Erik during the day, but whenever they ran into each other in the kitchen for a midnight snack, their interaction became casually friendly. So when Mrs. Lindberg had agreed to give her a few extra days off, Andie wandered if Erik had said something to her to make it happen.

Andie arrived at Miami Airport early and strolled down the terminal, looking at the knickknacks in the stores. She was delighted to find a bar in front of her gate. Jo showed up next, ready, willing, and able to party in Sin City. To make the five-hour flight bearable, the girls ordered mimosas and poured them into their sports bottles. Just as the flight attendant announced boarding, they spotted Jersey walking leisurely toward them.

"Hey, girlie," Jo said kissing her friend on the cheek. "We are ready to board, but do you want to grab a mimosa to go? We are all fueled up."

"I don't drink on planes," announced Jersey. "It's dehydrating."

"Who are you—?"

"Are you serious?" Jo and Andie exclaimed in one voice.

Jersey shrugged her shoulders, dismissing them both. As soon as the plane took off, she put an eye mask on her face and reclined her chair.

Andie shook her head and sipped from her bottle. "This is a whole new, unattractive side of her I have never seen before!"

"And you think you know someone," sighed Jo.

"You two are so tran!" murmured Jersey as she wrapped herself in a Louis Vuitton pashmina. "I can hear you but choose not to acknowledge your hatefulness."

Andie and Jo giggled and looked around, trying to guess for what purpose all of the other passengers were flying to Vegas.

The dry, hot air hit their faces the moment they walked out of the air-conditioned belly of the airport. They looked at the long, serpentine taxi line and cursed. Jo and Andie, who after the mimosas had switched to doing shots with the neighbors in the row next to them who were flying to Vegas for a bachelor party, giggled, while Jersey, stone cold sober and looking like the only adult in the group, was getting aggravated. Finally came their turn to get into a cab, thus enjoying air conditioning and the sights, they made it to their hotel without too much of a hassle.

"Sober up, you two trannies!" barked Jersey as soon as she marched into their room at Aria. "We have a party to make an appearance at and then an all-paid table at Omnia."

Andie stuck out her tongue and hopped into the shower. A short nap was in order.

"Okay, sexy bitches!" sang Jersey, twerking in front of the mirror as they finished getting ready. "Let's blow this joint!" She smoothed out her emerald minidress, which emphasized her dark chestnut hair and green eyes. One of *Playboy's* few dark-haired centerfolds, she looked exotic in a sex-forward kind of way. Petite, with large breasts, pouty lips, and doll-like features, she embodied the fantasy.

Jo turned off the flat iron and ran her fingers through her hair for the last time. She rubbed bronzer on her long, toned legs and arms, dusted herself with luminous powder, and dabbed on her favorite perfume, Chanel Chance. "I am ready!"

"Finally," sighed Andie and put on her heels.

They checked each other out, looking fierce as they walked out of the hotel and into the night ahead.

* * *

The Playboy Bunny Penthouse Suite at the Palms swirled with excitement. Cocktail waitresses dressed in the famous bunny outfits passed around champagne, while half-naked guests splashed in the glass pool over-hanging the Strip.

"So many beautiful women, and not one cute single guy in sight," complained Jo.

"What about him?" Jersey pointed at a man in the corner.

"He is with someone," sighed Jo. "And that one over there is also."

Andie nodded. "Let's get out of this land of bubbleheads and selfies. What time do we need to be at the club?"

"Doesn't matter," replied Jersey. "I just have to take a picture with the rest of the girls, and then we can go. Afrojack is DJing tonight, but I don't think he is coming on 'til two." She disappeared to join the rest of the models for a photo before making her way back to her friends. "This party sucks! Let's get out of here," announced Jersey as soon as the moment allowed.

Ready for the next adventure, Jo and Andie followed their well-connected leader to Omnia at Caesar's Palace. The line into the club extended out through the lobby and down to the entrance of the hotel. Jersey marched past the crowds and straight to the men who guarded the velvet ropes. As much as they tried to ignore her, she commanded the attention of one of the bouncers. "What can I do for you?" he asked lazily.

"We have friends waiting for us at the table inside."

He remained unimpressed. "Everyone does."

Jersey pulled out the text on her phone and shoved it into the man's smug face.

He waved them in. "Just the three of you, ladies?"

"Yes, please," she answered sweetly, and, victorious, they paraded into the club.

They pushed their way through to the second floor's VIP section and past another roped-off area. Magnum bottles of vodka and champagne chilled in the tub-like buckets. Apparently, the man was celebrating his thirtieth birthday in style, surrounded by a few dozen of his closest friends.

"Hey, Nick! Happy birthday, trannie! These are Andie and Jo!" Jersey hugged the birthday boy.

"Nice to meet you, ladies. Welcome! Please." Nick gestured toward the tables. "What can I make you?"

Jersey vanished into the crowd amid the welcomes of people she apparently knew. Andie and Jo surveyed the scene. A cast member from a popular reality TV show partied at the table to the right. Some big-deal teen pop idol, not old enough to be up so late on a school night, was dancing on the table in the opposite corner.

The music was blasting, the drinks flowing, and Andie's feet were killing her. She sunk down onto the golden leather couch. The bliss of taking her high heels off, known only to women, spread through her body. She took in the feeling of the moment—a complete assault on the senses, an incredible combination of a light show and live entertainment.

Nick appeared out of nowhere and parked next to her. "You are not fading on us, are you?"

Andie smiled. "No, not yet! Just resting my feet."

Nick reached down and commenced massaging her soles. "How's this?"

"Awkward."

Nick laughed. His brown eyes sparkled, catching the lights, as he caressed her back with the tips of his fingers.

He's cute, Andie thought. He was, not tall, but well-built with thick dark hair and playful eyes.

"You are beautiful," he murmured.

Jo appeared, grabbed Andie's hand, and pulled her up to dance. The three girls, each one beautiful in her own way, provocatively danced to the electric beats. Andie's and Jo's lips met in a playful kiss.

Nick shook his head and inserted himself in between them. He put his hands around Andie's waist and pulled her close. "You are messing with my head, you know that?"

"Oh, I am sorry," Andie said innocently, gazing at him with her big blue eyes. "Would you like me to stop?"

Nick moaned and drew her closer, going for a kiss. Andie blocked his lips with her fingers.

"You are a cruel creature!" he exclaimed.

"'I've never said I was kind," teased Andie.

"It's my birthday," bargained Nick.

"Well, if you are going to pull out the 'B' card—"

"Really?"

"No."

"Ugh!" Nick exclaimed. "Why are you doing this to me?" He laughed and walked away.

"Fucking pussy dust never fails," giggled Jersey into Jo's ear.

Unable to stay away for long, Nick came back and grabbed Andie by the hand. "Come!"

Curious, she followed him down the stairs. Pushing through the crowds, he steered her to the DJ booth. The bouncer nodded, recognizing him, and invited them in. Andie found herself inside the DJ section, with famous Afrojack spinning in front of her. The DJ put down his earpiece and turned around. He saw Nick and gave him a bro-hug. "What's up, dog?"

Mesmerized, Andie looked into the club; the entire place pulsated to the beat that tapped into something primal within all, becoming one entity, following the music and the lights. The euphoric feeling took over her body. *We have not come as far as we think we have from the age of the shaman dances and tribal rituals.*

Nick caught her in his arms and kissed her. She did not resist this time but allowed herself to get carried away in the sensation. When the DJ changed they returned to the table. Andie reunited with her friends.

"You look like an angel," she smiled at Jo, joining her in a dance.

"Thank you, love," Jo replied, and kissed her deeply on the mouth. They laughed when the music changed and sunk onto the couch, exhausted.

"I think I am ready to go," announced Jersey as she crashed next to them.

"Yep, me too," agreed Andie.

They snuck out of the club, so as not to make a fuss, leaving the blasting music behind. The lobby of the hotel was quiet and empty with the exception of a few stranglers returning from a night out on the town.

"Food?" asked Jersey.

"Yeah, let's get pizza or something." Andie moved toward the inviting lights of a twenty-four-hour restaurant.

Satisfied with an early morning snack, exhausted, and drunk, they returned to the hotel room and crashed onto their beds only to wake up and repeat a few hours later. The superpower of the young is their ability to rally.

* * *

Andie pulled the eye mask off her face and looked around. Glimpses of daylight broke through the blackout curtains. Jersey lay texting, and Jo sat in bed scrolling through Facebook on her phone.

"Hey, Tinkerbell," Jersey called out, "Nick has been texting me since we left. He wants your number, and also they have a cabana at the Marquee. Do we want to go?"

"Yeah, I am all for that. Do we need to be there at a specific time?"

"He said they were heading out there in about an hour, but we can go whenever we are ready."

"Cool. What do you think? He is cute, no?" asked Andie.

"Totally cute," agreed Jo. She set down her phone and headed for the shower.

Andie got up, wrapped herself in a plush hotel robe,

and walked into the bathroom to brush her teeth. Her phone rang. She ran back out to grab it and, seeing Consuelo's number, turned on Video chat.

"Miss Andrea, sorry to bother you," said the woman on the other end. Through her screen, Andie could see into the upstairs living room with Christian screaming in the background. "Christian is difficult, upset. He don't listen to me or señora. Can you talk to him?" Consuelo handed the phone to the child.

"Christian, what is happening?" asked Andie in a stern voice.

"Consuelo is stupid! She doesn't let me play my video games! I hate her!"

Andie acknowledged his feelings. "Oh, I am sorry! You must be disappointed!"

"Yes, I am!"

"Bummer! I wish we played video games on Sunday afternoon, right?"

"Right!" agreed Christian.

"Do we?"

"Yes!" insisted the boy.

"Really?"

"No," whimpered the child.

"Okay. So do you really hate Consuelo, or are you just upset she is strict with you? You are angry with her actions, not her. Right?"

"No, I hate her! She is stupid!"

"Christian! You know Consuelo loves you, and it hurts her feelings when people call her names. Is it kind?"

"No."

"Well, I know you are a good and kind boy. Even though you are upset, you don't stop loving someone. And you don't call them names."

"Yes, but . . . I want to play, and she does not let me!"

"Christian, what time is it?"

"I don't know!"

"Yes, you do," Andie insisted. "You know how to read time, so please, look at the clock behind you and tell me, what time is it?"

"Four thirty p.m."

"Do we usually play video games at four thirty p.m. on Sunday?"

"Yes we do!" insisted the child stubbornly.

"Really?" Andie lifted her eyebrow. "Is this your final answer?"

Christian sulked. "We don't."

"So did you lose control like Hulk because you got angry about not getting what you wanted?"

Christian crinkled his nose.

"Christian, you know you are wrong. What do we do when we are wrong?"

"I am not going to apologize!"

"Okay. I will let your conscience dictate what you do. Just remember: you hurt the feelings of someone who loves you very much. I have faith that you will do the right thing."

"When are you coming back?" Christian pouted.

"Tomorrow, late. You miss me?"

"No!"

"Too bad because I miss you. Will you be a good boy and not give Consuelo any more grief?"

Christian nodded.

"Okay, Monkey. You will be asleep when I get in tomorrow, but I will talk to you before I get on the plane."

Consuelo took the phone from Christian. "Thank you, Miss Andrea. He acting bad since you go."

"Thank you so much, Consuelo, for watching him."

"Have a good time, miss."

Andie hung up her phone. Jo, who had watched their exchange, stared her down.

"What?" Andie exclaimed and rushed to take a shower to avoid the confrontation.

"Andrea Elizabeth Ellis, don't you turn your back on me! What the fuck was that?!"

"What? I am just doing my job," answered Andie, walking into the bathroom.

"Bullshit! You are way too involved! He is not your fucking kid! You are playing mommy just as I predicted you would!" Jo followed her in.

"What do you want me to do?" asked Andie, frustrated and annoyed.

"Apparently, it is too fucking late! You are up to your eyeballs in this family's bullshit! It must be good to be fucking rich because you can pay for anything you want, even a mom-for-hire!" Jo suddenly realized she had gone too far and continued in a softer voice. "I am sorry, love. I am just afraid you will get so entangled with the

Lindberg's you will be reluctant to move forward with your real career and your own life after you graduate. I just don't want you to get hurt, and I want you to promise me, you will quit this job as soon as you are done with school. I want you to be able to make the decision that is right for you when the time comes."

"I promise. And you are right, I did fall in love with Christian, and he does bring out my maternal instincts, but I am determined to get my license as soon as I can. And so far I am on track with my time line. You have nothing to worry about."

"Are you two done with your domestic dispute?" called out Jersey.

Andie smiled, grateful to change the subject. "All done. Shall we get ready, ladies?"

"It's about time. And put on something slutty!" chuckled Jersey.

* * *

There are a few things one must remember when attending a pool party. First and foremost, a pool party is not your average day by the pool, therefore it calls for full makeup and hair, high heels and a sexy two piece. Second: hydrate.

"Poor Nick," laughed Jersey, looking Andie up and down. "He won't know what hit him."

"How do you know him, anyway?" asked Jo.

"My girlfriend dated him in high school."

"What does he do?" casually inquired Andie.

"Not really sure, but he does well, obviously," replied Jersey. "Something with IT . . ."

Andie nodded. "Cool, where is he based?"

"Austin."

"What about his friends?" asked Jo. "Do you know them?"

Jersey shrugged her shoulders. "Some of them."

"How about that Corey guy?" Jo specified.

"Nope. Never met him, but he is cute. I liked his friend, though. Whatever the fuck his name was."

"It's a beautiful thing we have different taste in men," concluded Andie as they walked out to the pool deck.

Marquee Dayclub inside the Cosmopolitan got a well-deserved reputation as one of the best day clubs in Vegas since its very inception. A massive, multilevel complex with two pools and multiple bars, always packed to the max, the club seduced the in-crowd with the promise of all-day fun with its variety of dance music and high-tech effects, generously sprinkled with eye candy. A lineup of globally renowned DJs and entertainers were hired for the sole purpose of keeping the clubgoers' senses pumping. Set a few feet above the main deck, along the perimeter were the cabanas, ultimate pool party luxury, with their private glass infinity plunge pools and lavish couches, with a bird's-eye view of both Las Vegas and the raging party scene in the club below.

"Not too shabby," approved Andie.

"Hola, chicas!" Nick greeted them with a smile.

"Looking hot! Help yourselves to the cocktails." He pointed at the table brimming with chilled bottles.

Andie and Jo, minus Jersey, who had located her guy, jumped into the plunge pool to fight off the skin-scorching heat.

"Do we know his name yet?" asked Andie nodding toward Jersey and her playmate.

"I think its Vick or something like that," Jo replied indifferently.

"Have you seen Corey?" Andie's eyes searched for a handsome guy with black short cropped hair and a powerful build.

Jo shrugged her shoulders. "Yeah, he is talking to some bimbos over there. He seems to be in a bad mood." She answered sounding just a tad annoyed.

"Why are you saying that?"

Jo shook her golden mane dismissively. "I don't know, he just looks broody and unfriendly today. Whatever."

Jersey slipped into the pool, drink in hand. "Why are you drinking water?" she asked Andie.

"Need to rehydrate."

"Are you hungover?"

"Not too bad. A little bit tired. It's friggin' hot." Andie climbed out and stretched on the couch in the shade in front of the fan. Nick materialized beside her and handed her a flute of cold champagne.

"Are you having a good birthday weekend?" Andie asked as she took a sip.

"The best. And look, I met you!"

"Aww, well, I am glad you are having fun."

"When are you flying back?" inquired Nick, playing with her fingers.

"Tomorrow afternoon. You?"

"In the morning. Let me take you out for dinner tonight."

"I would love to, but chances are I am going to crash early. I'm pretty tired, and after drinking in the sun this afternoon, I will probably be dead to the world."

"Bummer, but I understand. Can I come visit you in Miami?"

"That would be nice," replied Andie, dismissing the possibility as improbable, but not unwelcomed.

"Don't think I won't come," threatened Nick with a smile and got up to play the host.

As the afternoon drew to a close, the crowd at the club started to dwindle.

"What do you wanna do?" Andie asked her girl-friends. "I am kinda ready to get out of here."

Jersey nodded her agreement. "Let's change and grab some food. I am jonesing for a burger or something else greasy and unhealthy."

They located Nick to say their good-byes. He wrapped his arms around Andie, tucked a lock of her hair behind her ear, and kissed her neck. "I will see you in Miami, princess."

* * *

The burger joint had a crowd of people in front of it

waiting for a table. Impatient, Jersey moaned and threw her hands up in an exaggerated gesture. Jo nudged her and pointed at a table inside where Vick and Corey were waving in an attempt to gain their attention.

"We just sat down," explained Vick as the girls approached right on time for the waitress to take everyone's orders. "We have not even ordered drinks yet."

"Thank God you are here," said Corey with a chuckle. "Otherwise I would be stuck eating dinner alone with this knuckle head."

They sank their teeth into a satisfying mixture of grease and carbs, chased by cold drinks. The silence of a food coma followed after their excited chatter.

Corey pulled out a credit card to pay the bill. "This dumbass lost his wallet last night. So I feel like a fucking sugar mama," he explained with annoyance in his voice.

Vick laughed. "It's a good thing I forgot my driver's license in the room. If not, I would have to live here forever."

They walked outside.

"Thank you, honey," Vick cooed and kissed Corey on the cheek.

"Ugh!" Corey pushed his friend away, rubbing his face.

"Do you want to grab another drink?" offered Vick. "Corey is paying, so don't say no!"

They strolled down to the Chandelier at the Cosmopolitan, a stunning three-story bar encased inside a cascade of sparkling crystals.

One round of drinks turned into the next. Jersey and Vick giggled, whispering to each other, while Andie and Jo chatted with Corey, who still looked somewhat irritated. In an attempt to loosen him up, Jo ordered a round of shots.

"To Vegas!" saluted Jersey, raising her glass. "I've always wanted to get married here!"

"Fuck yeah!" agreed Vick, slamming his shot glass on the table. "That's the way to do it!"

"Great!" joked Jo. "Tinkerbell and I will be your maidens of honor!"

Vick and Jersey exchanged glances and laughed. "Fuck, babe!" Vick exclaimed. "Let's do this!"

"Are you serious?" chuckled Andie.

"That's so tran!" Jersey broke down in laughter.

"C'mon!" Vick urged. "You only live once! How many people can say that they got married in Vegas?!"

Jo's magic fingers were hard at work. "There is a chapel about ten minutes' drive from here. It has good reviews and does drive-by weddings."

"Perfect!" Vick signaled the waitress and handed Corey the bill.

They walked out of the bar and strolled past the noisy casino floor to the brightly lit entrance. As they waited in the taxi line, Corey grew increasingly annoyed.

"What is your fucking problem?" snapped Jo, fed up with his attitude.

"Fuck this shit! This is idiotic! They will sober up tomorrow and I will be stuck with paying for annulling this shit! I am not having any part of it!" He threw his hands in the air and stormed away.

"Come on, Melissa," Jo grabbed Jersey by her sleeve giving Corey a death stare. "We have not had a bachelorette party yet."

Andie pulled Jo to the side. "Hey, I am hitting the wall. I need to crash. See you back at the hotel."

"Okay, honey." Jo gave her a kiss. "Get some rest."

* * *

Andie opened her eyes, still disoriented from deep sleep. She looked around the dark room, Jersey was breathing peacefully in the bed next to hers, but Jo was missing. Andie glanced at her phone: 9:30 a.m. Careful not to wake Jersey up, she dressed and sneaked out to get coffee for them both. When she returned, Jersey was awake and hungry.

"Where is Jo?" asked Andie, handing her friend a Starbucks cup.

"She left with Corey," Jersey squeezed out as she chugged down a bottle of water. "Let's go down and get some breakfast and mimosas. I have a bitch of a hangover."

Andie nodded. "I will let Jo know where we're at."

They got a table in the far corner of the restaurant, away from screaming kids. The moment they ordered drinks, Jo stomped in, hidden behind her shades and an Oklahoma State baseball hat. She sank into the chair and dramatically tossed her glasses aside.

"How was last night?" smiled Andie.

"Amazeballs!" moaned Jo.

"Jo got some cock!" sang Jersey in a voice reminiscent of Pee-wee Herman.

Jo gulped Andie's mimosa and threw her hands on the table. "Fuck me! He has the most beautiful cock! It's like a unicorn! I found the unicorn of penises!"

"Mazel tov!" Jersey exploded with laughter.

"No! My fucking luck! He is leaving for Iraq for three months in a few weeks!"

"Iraq?" Andie echoed. "Is he in the military?"

"Are we still at war with them?" questioned Jersey.

"I don't fucking know," Jo moaned. "He is a private contractor. They provide security for dignitaries and shit! I can't believe I just found the unicorn of penises, and he is moving to Bumfuck, Iraq, for three months!"

"Three months is not forever," reasoned Jersey.

"I don't do long distance!" insisted Jo.

They did not talk much on the flight back, each of them were spent, deep in their own thoughts, reliving the weekend. What a magical trip it had been: one potential Prince Charming, one almost happily ever after, and one unicorn! Who says there are no fairy tales!

Chapter 12

With only a few lights on, the mansion looked dark and eerie from the window of the cab. Andie secretly hoped to find Erik in the kitchen so she could tell him all about the trip. She had grown to enjoy their midnight chats and was pleased to see him in his usual spot with a bowl of cereal, watching Shark Tank.

He smiled when he saw her walk in. "Welcome back. Did you have fun?"

"Oh my God! You won't believe it!"

Erik laughed as she proceeded with her story. "I wish I could be a fly on the wall!"

"I got a text from Susie," Andie said after she finished. "Her birthday is July 7th. She wants to do something that weekend."

Erik shook his head. "I will be in Paris."

"It's good to be the king! What're you doing in Paris?"

"I am going to Hong Kong for a few weeks and will stop in Paris for the weekend."

Not sure why, Andie felt a faint jolt of disappointment. "Are you coming back to Miami or New York?"

"Miami. I put down an offer on the place in Apogee.

The closing is at the end of the month. I want to be here, in case something goes wrong."

"Wow! Congrats! That's the best building in South Beach! So you are planning to spend more time here, then?"

"It seems like it."

"It must be beautiful. And the view must be sick!"

"It is. I will have you over for a housewarming," Erik promised with a smile.

"I will bring a plant," teased Andie.

"Deal."

"Are you moving in when you come back?"

"No. I will need to remodel it. I hired the designer who did my penthouse in New York. It's a gut job: travertine floors and Onyx bathrooms. . . ."

Andie yawned. Erik got up and put the dishes in the sink. "Get some rest. You must be exhausted. Christian missed you."

She smiled with warmth. "I've missed him, too. Good night."

Andie was too tired to unpack; she would have to leave that for tomorrow. Tonight, she would simply brush her teeth and clean her face before climbing into bed. From her phone she checked on Christian's room; the boy was peacefully asleep. She took a deep breath and settled under the covers. This place was starting to feel like home.

* * *

"Did you see the text from Susie?" asked Andie when Jo called a few days later.

"Yeah, I did. I won't be here though."

"Why? Where are you going?"

"DC. Corey is deploying to Iraq. I'm flying over to spend a weekend with him before he leaves."

"Holy unicorn!"

"Yeah, we've been texting and Skyping every day! Ugh! This sucks balls because I really like him. Just my luck!"

"Wow, okay. You didn't have enough guys in Miami, so you had to find yourself a Captain America!"

Jo laughed. "Yeah, no shit!"

* * *

"May I get you a drink before we take off, Mr. Lindberg?" asked a flight attendant as Erik turned his phone to the flight mode.

"Scotch."

The woman fixed him a Macallan and prepared the cabin for departure. Erik looked out the window as he once again left the lights of evening Miami behind. He pulled out his laptop and opened several files, intending to do a few hours' work before going to bed. He stared at the profit and loss spreadsheet for a potential investment, but his mind drew a blank. He lost himself in his thoughts about the upcoming weekend in Paris with Beatrix.

They would attend a notorious Madam O party

Saturday night, and Erik was planning to enjoy himself. Oscar, better known as Madam O, knew how to do things right—just enough mystery, flair, and sex. Beautiful people in beautiful settings—he delivered fantasies wrapped in pretty packages. No expense spared or detail overlooked, and the assurance of privacy had won him an affluent clientele. He hosted his soirees worldwide on mega yachts and in castles, with the members of the exclusive club flying from all over to participate in the extravaganzas produced by his outrageous and creative imagination.

The last time Erik and Beatrix had attended such an event, he had invited Natalie to join them. The three of them had spent an insane weekend in Saint Tropez. This time, it was just him and Beatrix. Natalie had been unresponsive since he had seen her last time, and Erik did not care enough to inquire why.

Uninvited, Andie popped into his thoughts. Taking her to one of these parties would be fun. His imagination ran wild with the thought—a vision of the girl in sexy lingerie sensually dancing with another woman, kissing, being caressed, his hands sliding up her body . . . the mental picture gave him a major hard-on. He had long suspected there was an uninhibited side to her and guessed she would not be appalled by the scene. A beautiful, smart, sweet, naughty, good girl—a bummer she was his nephew's nanny. Erik shook off thoughts of her; there's plenty of fish in the sea not to have to shit where you eat.

He must have dozed off because he opened his eyes, startled, at a light touch on his shoulder.

"Mr. Lindberg, would you like to retire to your bed?" the flight attendant asked, and gently helped him up.

Erik stumbled into the bedroom, only to wake up as the wheels of the plane touched the ground in Paris.

Ever since he could remember, the family had stayed at Four Seasons. Typically, he preferred something more modern and less pretentious, but somehow, he did not mind the hotel's opulence in the City of Lights. The first time he had visited Paris, he had been about five years old. He had flown in with his mother and Patrick, and their father had joined them a day or so later. They had stayed in the Royal Suite, with its elegant decor and lovely inner terrace. Accompanied by a private guide, they had visited the Louvre, d'Orsay, and Notre-Dame; they'd walked Jardin des Tuileries and Luxembourg. In the evenings, they had dined with both of their parents at elegant restaurants—the part Erik hated, since he had been expected to sit still and behave "like a little gentleman." "Children are to be seen, not heard," was Evelyn's motto. After a few days, Rick had flown back to New York, and Evelyn, with the two boys, had continued on to the Riviera for the season.

Erik's heart still turned upside down whenever he thought of his brother. He tried to use the techniques his shrink had recommended to deal with the pain. It worked—sometimes. The closer it got to the third anniversary of the accident, the more often Erik thought of

Patrick. He agonized that it was unfair Christian had to grow up not knowing his parents, while he was alive and well.

Pushing down the depressing thoughts, Erik stepped out of the airplane and handed his luggage to the driver.

The perfectly suited man grinned. "Monsieur, I have you in Paris in a New York minute!"

He had not lied; minutes later, Erik strolled into the elegant white marble lobby of Four Seasons, which was adorned with red roses and fragrant peonies.

"Bienvenue à nouveau, Monsieur Lindberg," said a girl at the check-in desk with a friendly smile. *"Nous vous proposons votre suite habituelle."* Welcome back, Mr. Lindberg. We have your usual suite ready.

"Merci, mademoiselle!" Thank you, miss!

She presented him with a large envelope. *"Oh, monsieur, vous avez une lettre."* Oh, sir, you have a letter.

Erik recognized the black pearl stationary from the desk of Madam O. Inside, he found a digital key and two black velvet eye masks. As usual, on Saturday, a car would pick them up from the hotel to take them to an undisclosed location.

Erik walked into the stylish white and gold living room of the penthouse suite and opened the glass doors to the terrace. He allowed himself a moment to take in the 360-degree view of the city, with the Eiffel Tower right in front of him and airy, ghostly Sacré-Coeur looming behind on the distant hill of Montmartre. He would see Beatrix tomorrow. Today he would simply wander the streets of the city until it was time to meet a friend at a small tavern away from the tourists. A nightcap at the hotel bar, listening to the live piano would conclude the relaxing day.

He requested breakfast in his room and, determined to avoid the city full of crowds, spent the afternoon in his suite, admiring the view of which he never grew tired. In a lazy haze, he lounged around until the butler informed him that the driver was waiting outside. The black Maybach drove him to Beatrix's Champs Élysées flat for a glass of Dom Perignon.

Beatrix opened the door dressed in a black satin bustier adorned with hand-embroidered lace, a garter embellished with the same double-frastaglio motif, silk stockings, and five-inch-high-heeled "fuck-me" stilettoes with red soles.

"*Ma chére*, you are exquisite." Erik kissed her. "I'm afraid we won't make it to the party."

"It is good to see you, my Erik," she murmured as she handed him the baccarat flute and donned a silver silk trench coat.

They sipped champagne in the back seat during their ride. After about an hour's drive, they arrived at a secluded chateaux outside the city, its entrance barred by a massive ornate gate. Erik pressed his digital key to the receiver, and the gate opened, allowing them to proceed. Erik pulled back Beatrix's shiny black hair and tied on the soft velvet mask.

Through the heavy, richly carved wooden doors,

they stepped into the candlelit grand hall with its stone vaulted ceilings, massive fireplace, and walls decorated with fourteenth-century tapestries. The sound of a gothic chant enhanced the atmosphere of suspense and sharpened the sense of mystery.

A young hostess, her face covered by a mask, bare-foot, dressed in a long black velvet skirt with slits on both sides running up to her waist and crystal-adorned pasties over her nipples, waited to greet them. She held out a silver tray with aged scotch for Erik, a glass of Dom Perignon for Beatrix, a pair of silk handcuffs, and a feather tickler.

"May I take your coats?" A man with an envy-worthy physique, wearing tuxedo pants and a bow tie, freed Beatrix from her coat.

The hostess extended her hand, inviting them to proceed. They walked into the next hall, greeted by softer music and a romantic ambiance. Whimsical, baroque-style couches, occupied by beautifully undressed bodies engaged in sensual play, decorated the chamber. In the middle of the room stood an oversized bed adorned in red silk, where multiple couples were wholly immersed in the bliss of group sex.

Erik and Beatrix followed the hostess into the large ballroom where the main party had already started. Several hundred couples, eager to break the shackles of conformity, rebelling against the very principles of monogamy, delighted in their night of fantasy and bonding.

Madam O himself greeted them at the entrance. He was taller than average with the olive complexion of a southerner, though no one knew exactly from where he came. He wore heavy black eyeliner around his eyes ala Egyptian pharaoh and combed his black hair slick back. Dressed in a flowing garment the color of royal purple, he graciously played the role of the host. "Here are my favorite guests! You truly are the most beautiful pair!" His English was perfect, with a slight accent of vague origin. He smiled, exchanging kisses with Beatrix and a handshake with Erik. "I hope everything is to your liking. As usual, your requests have been catered to your specifications. Just use your key for any special requirements. This young lady will be your hostess for the evening. Please let her know anything you might desire. And of course, I am always at your service." He bowed.

The hostess showed them to a table on the perimeter of the dance floor, preset with scotch, Dom Perignon, strawberries, and dark chocolates fashioned in the shapes of male and female bodies.

"The downstairs hall has been set up as a play den," she informed them. "But of course, your suite is also ready for you. Your luggage has been taken to your room."

Erik soaked up the scene around him. In the four corners of the ballroom, on swings, and dressed in elaborate costumes, acrobats performed their routines, while go-go dancers and fire-breathers worked multiple stages throughout the expansive space.

Beatrix took a sip of ice-cold champagne and murmured into Erik's ear. "As usual, an exquisite affair. Beautiful people . . ."

Erik smiled. "Are you in the mood for a prowl, *ma chére?*"

"Mmmm," purred the woman and stood up.

She swayed to the music, giving in to her sexuality and the seduction of the night. Erik watched her dance with a couple who had been seated at the table next to theirs. A man with wavy dark hair and a powerful build caressed her neck and ran his hand up her inner thigh, sliding it between her legs, stimulating her with his fingers. His date, dressed in a lacy bodysuit, kissed Beatrix on the lips, freeing her nipples from the restraints of the corset.

Beatrix pulled back, leaving the couple to enjoy each other, and sat on Erik's lap. She kissed him on the lips, laughing, and reached for her glass. Her dance partner, blond and petite, sat down on his other knee and pulled both of them into a kiss. Erik fondled her breasts, playing with her golden hair. He pulled her head back, nibbling on her neck as she moaned at his caress.

The music and lights changed, announcing the beginning of the show. Dressed in black silk pants with a bare torso a violinist took the stage as an accompaniment to the DJ's EDM mix, his body swaying to the rhythm with emotion and passion. A group of dancers covered in body painted costumes performed a fantasy interpretation of "A Midsummer Night's Dream," a seductive combination of erotic and modern dance. Beatrix slid down from Erik's lap onto the couch and nestled by his side. He put his arm around her, running his fingers up and down her arm.

When the music returned to a dance beat, Beatrix gave Erik a kiss and got up. "I want to go walk around."

"You want me to come with you?"

"No, *mon amour.*"

He smiled, watching her gracefully glide away. When she returned, she was followed by an exotic-looking jewel with light chocolate skin and green eyes.

"Erik, this is Innes," Beatrix said, introducing her companion.

"Nice to meet you, Innes."

"Nice to meet you, too, Erik," answered the girl with a strong French accent. "You very handsome. And she—beautiful." She beamed and put her arms around Beatrix's waist.

Innes took a sip from the glass Erik handed her. "I like this party," she said with a smile, caressing the woman's shoulder.

"You are lovely," Erik said as he gently lifted the girl's chin to face him.

"Do you want to kiss me?" she asked.

"Would you like me to?"

"Yes."

Erik covered her mouth with his lips, kissing her deliberately slowly, softly caressing her with his tongue. Innes's body grew tighter, her lips more demanding; he felt her shiver under his touch. She gently pushed away, took a sip of champagne, and smiled at Beatrix.

"I here with my friends, but I am alone," volunteered Innes. "You both very sexy."

"Can we keep her?" asked Beatrix, caressing the girl's back.

Erik smiled. "I will follow your lead, ladies."

Beatrix invited Innes to join them upstairs in their suite. Erik called their hostess and gave her the key. The young woman led them out of the grand hall and up the curved stone stairs to the second floor. Doorways to private suites lined both sides of the corridor. A few doors were wide open, welcoming others to join in, some stood open with a velvet rope across, indicating an invitation to watch but not partake, and others were shut for privacy.

They looked into the first room; a woman lay spread on the bed, her hands and feet tied to the posts, several men surrounded her, caressing her flesh as they waited their turn. She cried out with every vigorous thrust.

The next door, open to participants, housed a large group. It was hard to tell where one body ended and another began. Moans and laughter filled the room as the guests delighted in each other's intertwined bodies.

The hostess opened the door to their room and motioned for them to enter. The fire was lit and the table, surrounded by carved antique wood chairs, was set with bottles of Dom Perignon and Macallan. Mounted on the wall, embedded in a gilded frame large screen

TV played an erotic movie by Andrew Blake, artistically filmed in black and white.

Erik shut the door and popped open the bottle of champagne. Innes took the velvet mask off her eyes and unfastened her leather corset, letting it fall onto the stone floor, revealing her delicate figure. She walked over to Beatrix and untied the straps of the woman's lingerie. Innes put her hand through Beatrix's hair, running her tongue down her neck. Beatrix's hands caressed the girl's breasts while she inhaled her sweet scent. Innes pulled Beatrix to the bed and pushed her down on the pillows. With her lips, Innes moved down the woman's body, making her way to her inner thighs. Beatrix opened her legs and gasped at the touch of the girl's tongue. She arched her back, moaning, as Innes worked her skillful mouth.

Erik put down his glass and walked over to the bed. He approached Innes from behind while she made Beatrix lose her senses. He slapped her round butt and dug his fingers into the girl's silky skin, penetrating her with forceful thrusts. As Beatrix came, Erik flipped Innes on her back, throwing her legs over his shoulders, pushing deep inside her. Innes moaned while Beatrix sucked on her nipples, crying out as Erik made her come. Spent, they lay in bed, Beatrix's head resting on Erik's shoulder, while his fingers played with her hair. Innes sat up and stretched. "I go. I want to meet my friends. You two fun." She sprung out of bed, put her outfit back on and kissed Erik and Beatrix good-bye. "I leave my number.

Call me sometime." She winked at them and slipped out of the room.

Erik pulled Beatrix closer, wrapped her in his arms, and fell asleep.

He woke up before she did and got out of the bed so as to not disturb her. By the time he had taken a shower and shaved, she started to wake. He pulled the towel off his hips and joined her back in bed. She reached down, caressing and hardening him, and opened her legs, inviting him in. He slid inside her, enjoying the fruits of her body, inhaling her familiar scent, knowingly hitting the spots that pleased her. She murmured into his ear while he rested in her arms and washed him down with a soapy cloth when they took a shower afterward.

* * *

The black Maybach drove them back to Paris. The day was mild and overcast, and tiny droplets of rain stuck to the outside of the tinted window. Beatrix sat ensconced in the back seat next to Erik with her hand casually resting on his knee.

"Have you spoken to Natalie?" she asked lazily.

"Not in a while. Why do you ask?"

"We spoke a few weeks ago." Not receiving a response from Erik, she continued, "You've been dating her for a few years, no?"

"No. We have never dated. We see each other when it is convenient for both of us. But there is no dating."

"Why not? She is pretty. You don't like her?"

"Where is this coming from?" Erik asked, raising his eyebrow.

"I think she wants a relationship with you."

"You sure it is what *she* wants and not *you*?"

Beatrix laughed. "Erik, I was married since I was a young girl for almost twenty years. Now, I have fun. I may want it one day. But now, no. But I think Natalie wants it now. With you."

Erik lifted her fingers to his lips. "Not going to happen, *ma chére*."

"Pity," sighed Beatrix. "She is fun to be around."

"She is," agreed Erik.

Chapter 13

Miami was the last place in the world Erik wanted to be right now. He had tried to change the date of the closing on his condo to the beginning of August, but the seller proved to be difficult. The realtor had received a backup offer at a higher price and tried to wiggle out of the contract. Not willing to take his chances and lose the apartment, and foreseeing possible complications, reluctantly, Erik flew back.

To mirror his frame of mind, it seemed like everyone around, including even-keeled Phillippe, was in a dark mood. Mrs. Lindberg spent all of her time either in her room or in the study, working with Lucy on the charity gala she chaired.

Since his return, Erik became a ghostly figure, snarling at anyone who had the poor judgment to address him and drank more heavily than usual. Andie made the mistake of approaching him and found herself on the receiving end of his foul temper.

From then on, she tried to keep Christian out of everyone's way and to create some sense of normalcy while she figured out what the hell was going on. It seemed she was the only person in the house—or in the world, for that matter—who cared about the child's existence. Over the past couple of days, the heaviness started to wear on her as well. Even so, there were French language lessons, music classes, and playdates to keep up with.

The piano instructor arrived late on Thursday afternoon, and Christian plodded after her with an exaggeratedly somber expression on his face. *The misfortune of one is the other's bliss,* Andie told herself as she picked up a book, made herself a strong cup of coffee, and walked out on the veranda. *It's going to rain again,* she thought. A light breeze from the Bay had made being outside bearable. The coffee in her cup smelled inviting, and she relished the sip she took.

The house lay quite; Christian repeatedly playing arpeggios and the instructor's voice occasionally correcting him were the only sounds that cut the silence.

Evidently, Lucy came up with the same idea because the door onto the deck flew open and the young woman walked out with a cup of her own.

"Oh, hi, love. I can hear Christian is getting better." She pointed toward the sounds coming out of the grand room. She reclined on a wicker sofa, kicked off her shoes, and stretched out her legs.

"How's planning coming along?" asked Andie, more to be polite than with any interest.

"It's coming. Still a lot to do. Mrs. Lindberg likes everything to be a certain way, so you know . . ."

Andie nodded. "Is that why she is in such a foul mood? It's like everybody has been so depressed this past week."

There was a look of surprise in Lucy's eyes. "It's the three-year anniversary of the accident tomorrow. You did not know?" she added, seeing Andie's astonishment.

Andie floundered. "Are they doing anything? Going to the cemetery? Church? How . . . what do I do with Christian?"

Lucy shook her head. "They never do anything. Mrs. Lindberg is going to Naples in a few hours for the weekend. Phillippe and I are off."

"What? What about Christian?"

"I don't think he knows. I think tomorrow is just another day for him. There is nothing you need to do differently." Lucy took a last sip and got up. "I've got to get back. Have to finish some stuff up before I leave."

Still in shock, Andie stared into her cup. That bit of information surely explained things. But what the fuck was wrong with these people?! How's it that no one had mentioned anything to her so she could plan accordingly? How selfish could that woman be to leave her grandchild on the anniversary of his parents' death?

The music stopped, and, a few moments later, Christian broke free and ran outside, looking for her. "Andie, did you hear me? I did so good!"

"You did very well. I am proud of you!" She kissed the top of his head, hiding her distress.

The piano teacher trailed behind him. A tall, skinny

woman in her mid-forties, she gave Andie the chills and reminded her of her own failure in this discipline.

"Miss Ellis, we are done for today. He needs to practice the sonata. I wrote it all down in his book. Next week's schedule as usual?"

"Yes. Thank you, Mrs. Martinez," replied Andie as she walked the woman out to her car.

"Can I play video games now?" pleaded Christian when she returned.

Andie nodded. "You have thirty minutes."

"Only thirty minutes?!"

"Don't push it. Your time starts now."

Christian zoomed past her, eager not to waste the precious minutes. Andie hoped to buy time to collect herself but was called into the study. Seated behind her desk in front of the computer, Evelyn waved Andie in when the girl appeared in the doorway.

"I believe Lucy mentioned to you about tomorrow." Andie opened her mouth to speak but changed her mind, allowing the woman to finish. "I will be away in Naples. As far as Christian is concerned, tomorrow is just a normal day."

"He is getting older," Andie protested. "He will be asking questions soon; he already asks me to tell him about his parents. It might be a good excuse to have the conversation with him. Maybe to look at some pictures—"

"He knows his parents are dead. He does not need to know how and when. I want to keep it that way. As I said, for Christian tomorrow is just another day," stated Evelyn matter-of-factly. Andie started to speak, but Evelyn interrupted her with a hand gesture. "Andie, there will be no further discussion on the subject. I believe he has a playdate tomorrow?"

"Yes," the girl answered submissively.

"Great! Have fun."

Andie left the room furious. She marched back into the kitchen and bumped into Phillippe.

"Andie, perfect timing! I am off for a few days." He opened the fridge and pointed to the perfectly stacked containers. "Here is lunch for tomorrow and the next day; here is dinner." Phillippe picked up one of the containers. "I've made his favorite."

"Perfect! Meatballs and mashed potatoes will surely make up for everything," she snapped.

"Don't get bitchy, it does not suit you."

"What's wrong with you people?" She bolted out of the kitchen and slammed the door, fighting the tears that burned her eyes, her heart breaking for the little boy upstairs.

Phillippe followed her into her room. "We do not slam the doors in this house," he said, quietly but firmly. "I understand you might be frustrated, but there are a lot of people in this house who are dealing with a lot of shit right now."

Andie wiped off the tears that had managed to escape and were now rolling down her cheeks, realizing she'd acted like a brat. "I'm sorry."

Phillippe nodded and left the room.

Andie calmed herself down and trotted up the stairs into the family room, where Christian had been playing Nintendo.

Andie picked the second controller. "Play you?"

"Really?!" The boy switched the game from the single-player mode.

Erik, wearing his favorite worn jeans and a blank stare, appeared in the doorway. Andie lifted her eyes from the game, expecting him to say something, but he just looked down at her and the child and walked out of the room.

I don't get paid enough for this shit, she thought. Andie wished she could talk to Jo but knew the reaction her friend would have: she was "getting too emotionally involved."

Christian, happy about Andie's lax gaming policies for the day, was in the middle of his winning streak when Mrs. Lindberg came to bid them good-bye. Phillippe had already left, and the house again resembled a sleeping giant, with only the family room showing signs of life.

Andie looked at the clock. "Are you getting hungry? Should we get some dinner? Phillippe made your favorite."

"Can we go to McDonald's?" Christian tried his luck, doubling down on what already had been an unusual day.

"Sure, why not?" Andie shrugged her shoulders. "Want to ask Javier to drive us?"

"No, can we go in your car?"

"Okay."

"You think Jo will want to come with us?" suggested the boy.

Andie smiled. "I doubt that McDonald's is her first dinner choice. Come on, let's go get us some Big Macs." She poked him in the ribs.

Giggling, Christian hopped off the couch and skipped behind her all the way to the car.

* * *

"I love, love McDonald's!" Christian announced as he brushed his teeth after dinner. "Why can't we eat it all of the time?" he continued, getting under the covers. "Like every day!"

Andie picked two books. "Which one?"

Christian pointed to the one in her right hand. Andie sat down in the chair by his bed and started the story. Seeing him drift away after she'd read a few pages, she tiptoed out, grateful the day was over.

She walked into her room and looked around for her iPad. She retraced her steps and ran back up to the family room. Unsuccessful, she realized she must have left it in the library and trotted down the dark stairs on the other side of the house. Light shone from under the door. Andie figured Erik was still in his office, so she knocked.

"Yeah?"

Andie poked inside. "Hey, uh . . . sorry, I forgot my tablet. Can I grab it real quick?"

Erik gestured her in. He lay stretched out on the couch in front of the TV. A half-empty bottle of Patron and a bucket of ice sat on the coffee table. He did not turn his head when she walked in and kept staring at the screen.

Andie hoped to find her iPad and get out quickly without agitating him. She pranced up the stairs into the library loft to find her tablet on the window bench where she had left it the day before and rushed back down.

Andie looked at Erik, guessing he was not paying any attention to the program. She took a deep breath, wrestling with the thought that she could not leave him to fight his demons alone, not today.

"What are you watching?"

Without turning his head, Erik shrugged his shoulders and hit the INFO button on the remote. A movie name came onto the screen.

"Good movie?" she asked.

Erik handed her the remote. "You can put on whatever you like."

"Do you want company?"

Erik shrugged his shoulders again, took a gulp out of the tumbler in his hand, and crunched on an ice cube.

"Can I pour myself a drink?" asked Andie.

"Be my guest." He handed her a bucket. "Get me some ice while you're at it."

Andie took the bucket and walked over to the fridge hidden in the counter. She scooped some ice, fixed herself a gin and tonic, and returned to the couch. Erik moved over to give her space. He looked beat, she noticed, unshaved, with a glassy stare. She guessed he had been drinking all day.

Erik sat up, added a handful of ice and a pour of tequila to his glass, and took another sip. Andie picked up the remote, flipped through the channels, and found *Shark Tank*—the show she knew he liked. She glanced again at the man next to her. The knot in her stomach grew tighter; the invincible charismatic Erik, with his mocking eyes and charming smile, looked like a shadow of his usual self.

Feeling her stare, Erik turned to face her. At that moment he looked as innocent and helpless as Christian, his hair messy, the blond locks bunched over his forehead. Instinctively, Andie reached over and gently fixed a stray tress away from his eyes. A look of surprise at the unwarranted gesture of affection ran across the man's face. He took another swig from his tumbler, crunching on an ice cube, and turned back to the screen.

"Do you want to talk about it?" whispered Andie.

He shook his head "no." She did not believe him.

"Do you want me to leave?" she asked.

Erik thought for a second and turned his head to look at her. "Stay. Fix yourself another drink," he added, seeing her almost empty glass. "Is he asleep?"

Andie nodded and followed Erik's instructions.

"What were they like?" she asked when she sat back down.

"He was better than me. In everything."

"And Lori?"

Erik put his hand through his hair. "Mom never liked her. I think because they were too much alike. She hated it when Patrick proposed. She never said anything, of course . . . you know my mom. She never fucking says anything! But we all knew. Lori knew, too."

Shocked that Erik was actually willing to talk, she encouraged him to continue. "How did they meet?"

"Sean's then-girlfriend introduced them, at some party we went to. She was not someone I would have picked, but we knew right away my brother was serious about her."

"Why wouldn't you have picked her?"

Erik took a deep breath thinking of how to answer. "She was not warm. A bit too uptight for me. Like mom in a way. Patrick was happy though." He reclined, resting his head on the back of the couch, and reminisced . . .

* * *

Lori chuckled at Patrick and Erik, who were laughing at Sean's silly joke. The party was still going strong, but it was almost two a.m., and Lori was tired. Four months pregnant with their second child, she was the only sober guest and the designated driver.

"Okay, there, you peanut gallery," she scolded them affectionately. "Get into the car."

The brothers looked at each other and burst into another spell of laughter, but obediently followed her into the driveway nonetheless. Erik climbed into the back seat and buckled up. He pulled out his iPhone and sexted his girlfriend, Liz; they had been having troubles lately.

Lori drove over the bridge and hopped onto the Alton Road overpass.

"Oh my god! What is he doing?!"

Erik heard Lori's scream and looked up. A car was speeding straight at them on the one-way, one lane bridge. A deafening noise, a rain of shattered glass, and blackness.

Erik opened his eyes and tried to move. A sharp pain pierced his body and restricted his motion. There was an IV coming out of his arm. He reached over with his left hand and tried to pull it out. The monitor must have sounded an alert because several people dressed in scrubs poured into the room. They adjusted the needle and checked his vitals. A few minutes later, a doctor strode in, his face stoic and unemotional, his eyes fixed on the patient.

"What time is it?" asked Erik, not recognizing his own voice.

"Noon," answered the man, not shifting his gaze. "What is your name?"

Erik cleared his throat. "Erik. Erik Lindberg."

The doctor nodded his approval. "Do you know what happened to you?"

Erik paused for a few moments. He remembered the three of them laughing in the car, and then the headlights coming at them, Lori's scream, the sound of screeching tires, then everything went black.

Erik's eyes shot up to meet the doctors' gaze, which was still fixed on his face. "Lori . . ." he muttered "The baby . . . did she lose the baby . . . ?"

Erik's eyes frantically moved around the room, looking for answers. The faces around him were dispassionately concerned. Not receiving an answer, Erik came to a nauseating realization. "Lori? Where is my brother?!" he demanded and sat up, trying to get out of bed. "I need to be with my brother now!" A burst of pain in his rib cage slowed him down enough for the nurses to restrain him.

"You have two broken ribs and a concussion," the doctor informed him. "You are lucky to be alive."

"Where the fuck is my brother?" demanded Erik.

He looked at the people surrounding him and caught a glimpse of a young nurse in the corner of the room. A momentary lapse of control in her facial expression had given Erik the devastating answer. He heard a scream. Raw. Animalistic. He realized the sound was coming from him. The nurse rushed over and injected something into his IV tube. He felt numbness spread through his body, and, again, the nothingness.

When Erik opened his eyes again, it was dark outside. He scanned the room, and in the corner, he saw his mother. She had heard him move and approached the bed. *She has aged twenty years,* he thought.

A few days later, when all of the tests were completed and all of the boxes checked, Erik was released from the hospital. For several weeks, he moved like a shadow around the family house, not brave enough to enter the South Beach penthouse he and Patrick had shared before Patrick married Lori.

As soon as he was cleared by the doctors, Erik left for New York. It was a relief to be out of Miami and in his place, overlooking Central Park, but the relief was short-lived. The two brothers had been co-founders and managing partners of a private equity fund and now Erik had to face day-to-day life alone.

For six months he could not bring himself to clear Patrick's desk, but finally, Jeanne, his loyal assistant, had insisted she would do that. She had also suggested he see a shrink. He had laughed her out of his office. No shrink, just drinking—and some coke . . . occasionally. The problem was, those things made him feel worse. He was spinning out of control. More drinking, and coke . . . to numb the reality.

That Christmas, Jeanne had given him an ultimatum: he either saw the shrink or watched her walk out. She refused to be a witness to a slow but deliberate suicide mission. Finally, Erik went to see the guy she had found for him.

The doctor helped re-awaken his instinct of self-preservation and the will to move forward. Not right away, but with time. Erik saw him every day at first, then every week, and about a year into the therapy, Erik had finally seen the sun rise over Central Park outside his New York penthouse for the first time since the accident. . . .

* * *

Andie listened to Erik without an interruption. His words more a stream of consciousness than a cohesive memory. She fed him some water while he was not paying attention, but she took large gulps of her gin and tonic. She felt sick in her stomach as she tried to process the details of the accident and the aftermath. A heartbreaking tragedy, the closest she had ever touched.

Erik stopped speaking and now stared at the screen. She looked at the clock. It was 1:30 a.m.

"Come on." She got up. "Let's get you to sleep."

Erik raised his eyebrows.

"Come on, come on." She pulled him off the couch.

"Are you tucking me in?" he chuckled.

"Whatever it takes to get you to bed—don't you even!" she warned him anticipating his remark.

She walked him up to his bedroom and helped him into bed. She grabbed a bottle of water from the minifridge and set it on the side table.

"You need anything else?" she asked softly, brushing his hair with her fingers.

Erik shook his head "no."

Andie turned to leave, but Erik caught her wrist. "Thank you," he said quietly, and touched the palm of her hand to his lips.

"Good night." Andie kissed him on the forehead the way she did every night with Christian.

She tiptoed over to the child's room and poked her head in. The boy was sound asleep. When Andie finally crashed, she was both emotionally and physically drained. She lay in bed, awake, going over the past six months of her own life and Erik's story again and again. Her own woes seemed so petty and insignificant now. Finally, she drifted off to a restless sleep, best described as Goya's painting, *The Sleep of Reason Produces Monsters. Andie's restless mind brought forward her memory of the fight with JC. She felt a stab of pain and her breath got sharp and shallow as she saw JC, his face contorted with anger. Only it was not JC's face, it was Erik's. Then it was Erik smiling at her. The feeling of warmth spread over her body. She felt him touch her face with his fingers. Next thing she knew, she stood in the middle of the road looking at the blood-soaked asphalt. She heard Christian's voice calling for help. Horrified she woke up, her hair glued to her damp skin, droplets of sweat trickling down her temples.*

Chapter 14

"I've bought the tickets for the next weekend as we discussed," announced Nick, calling from Austin.

"That's great!" Andie tried to sound excited. "Where are you staying?"

"SLS."

"Nice, they have an awesome pool party on the weekends."

"That's what I've heard. I reserved a cabana for Sunday. You're off, right?"

"Uh-huh."

"Okay, can't wait to see you!"

Andie hung up the phone and walked into the kitchen.

"So, he got the tickets?" asked Phillippe, tying thyme, rosemary, bay leaf, sage and parsley with a kitchen string to create a garni for cassoulet.

"Yeah," she sat down across from him.

"You don't sound too excited," he noted and threw cloves and peppercorns into a pan to toast them for a few seconds.

"I know. I don't know . . . I don't even know if I like him. I met him twice, and both times we were drinking.

What if I don't like him? And he is flying over . . . does he expect me to sleep with him? I feel pressured—"

"Pressured to do what?" Erik walked into the kitchen and grabbed an apple. He took a sizable bite, leaned against the wall, and attentively stared at Andie, intentionally making her uncomfortable.

"A guy she has been sexting with is flying over next weekend," explained Phillippe and pulled a stick of butter out of the fridge. "Staying at SLS."

"We have not been sexting!" protested Andie.

"Ah, the one she hooked up with in Vegas," acknowledged Erik, ignoring her. "The one you told me about? From Austin, was he?"

Phillippe nodded.

"Hey!" interrupted Andie. "First of all, no one hooked up with anyone—"

"Not what I've heard," teased Erik. "Jo, for example, rode a unicorn!"

"Second," she continued, "you two ladies need to get your own lives, instead of gossiping about mine!"

"Oh, but yours is so much more exciting!" Erik responded with a grin.

"You two suck!"

Phillippe and Erik burst into laughter.

"But seriously." Erik made an effort to keep a straight face. "Pressured to do what?"

"She wonders if the boy expects her to sleep with him," answered Phillippe, still focused on his dinner creation.

Erik got up, threw the apple core into the garbage,

and made himself a cup of coffee. He poured sugar in and turned around to his audience. "The guy is flying all the way from Austin to South Beach for the weekend and staying at SLS? Yes, he expects you to sleep with him."

"Ugh!" growled Andie "You two are no help!" She got up and marched out of the kitchen.

"I disagree. I thought I was being very helpful." Erik shrugged his shoulders. "Have you seen a picture?" he asked Phillippe and took a sip from his cup.

Phillippe nodded his approval. "Not a bad-looking guy."

"Good for her," Erik said with a good-natured smirk and strode back to his office.

Phillippe shook his head and smiled to himself. It felt good that life in the house had finally returned to normal. Proof of it being the dinner party he was cooking for. Also, Erik being home meant the younger crowd would be around. It meant Sean and Matt, and now Matt's girlfriend, Susie. The house started to fill with joyful energy again. Like old times.

And like clockwork, Dr. Knight arrived first. He joined Evelyn in the grand room while Phillippe served the drinks.

"How are you doing, my dear?" asked Dr. Knight as he settled into the chair.

"I am well, James, thank you." Evelyn sipped her martini out of a frosty glass.

"And Christian?"

"Better . . . much better."

"So, I daresay, the experiment has worked, no? The girl is good for him?"

"They get along."

Clair walked into the room with a radiant smile. "Is my son here yet?" she asked, exchanging kisses.

Evelyn nodded. "Sean is with Erik in his office. You need to see him?"

"No. He did not answer his phone, and I was not sure if he is meeting me here or picking me up. Who else is coming tonight?"

"Bianca, and Matt with his girlfriend."

"Lovely gal, no?" offered Dr. Knight. "What was her name? I met her at your fund-raiser for that senator—"

As soon as he had uttered the question, Erik and Sean, accompanied by Matt and Susie, strolled into the room. Erik walked behind the bar to fix his friends drinks.

"I was just saying, it was lovely to meet you a few months ago at the fund-raiser." Dr. Knight smiled at Susie. "Now, where is my chess partner?" he asked, rubbing his hands together.

"I believe he is battling the dinosaurs." Erik tasted a drink he had fixed.

"Video games?" frowned Dr. Knight.

Erik shook his head "no." "Upstairs looks like Jurassic Park. From the sound of it, Andie is making him clean up the mess."

"How funny. Are they joining us tonight?" inquired the man.

"They are," confirmed Evelyn.

The doorbell rang, and Bianca floated into the room, as usual dressed all in white. Elegant gold bracelets adorned her wrists and made a light clinking noise every time she moved.

"Am I the last one again?" she chortled. "I am always the last one. I can never leave the gallery on time. I was in the middle of a meeting with my curator. He is fabulous! We are finalizing the list of the installations for Art Basel this December . . . it's beyond!" She waved her hand.

"What would you like to drink?" asked Erik. "Would you like a glass of wine or can I make you a martini?"

"Oh, thank you, sweetie pie. I think I will join your mother in a martini."

Andie and a grumpy Christian materialized in the entranceway. Christian, unhappy he had to change and get cleaned up for dinner, unwillingly greeted the guests. Erik poured Andie a glass of Albariño and handed Bianca her martini.

"Would you care for a quick game of chess before dinner, young man?" asked Dr. Knight.

Christian shook his head and squeezed onto the chair next to Andie.

"Are you a crank-a-saurus?" Andie smiled and swept his blond strands with the tips of her fingers.

Christian shook his head again. "Can I have your phone?"

"Here," she whispered into his ear and handed him a

game. "Stay for a few minutes like a good boy, and I will see if I can get you out of the dinner thing. Maybe set you up with a movie upstairs?"

The boy nodded and rested his head on her shoulder.

"Are we doing anything this weekend?" asked Sean, scrolling through his phone.

"We can." Matt shrugged his shoulders. "Do you guys want to get a table somewhere? Susie's friend is coming down from LA. We will have to take her out anyway."

Erik chimed in. "Not a bad idea."

"Are you off this weekend, Andie? Want to join us?" Sean tried his luck.

"She has a hot date this weekend," answered Erik on her behalf.

If looks could kill, Erik, at the very least, would have been critically wounded by Andie's glare. But since they can't, he offered a toothy grin in response.

"Oh yes? Who is the lucky fellow?" perked up Dr. Knight.

"Someone she had met on her girl's trip," offered Erik. "He is flying all the way from Austin for the weekend," he continued, despite Andie's obvious discomfort.

"That's a lovely gesture, no?" said Dr. Knight.

"I am sorry. I don't think discussing my personal life is an appropriate dinner conversation."

"Indeed," affirmed Evelyn. She was now on her second martini, and Andie took the opportunity to put in her request.

"It looks like Christian is not in a social mood tonight," she said quietly. "He had a long day. Would it be okay if I bring him his dinner upstairs instead?"

Evelyn nodded and took another sip of her drink. Andie winked at the boy, and he sprung up and trotted behind her.

"Excuse us," Andie said with a smile. "Christian will say good night to everyone now. He will have his dinner and a movie upstairs."

The boy shyly waved to everyone and followed her out.

* * *

"Which movie do you want to watch?" asked Andie, turning on the TV.

"Can I watch *Cars*?"

"Again?"

The boy nodded eagerly.

"Sure."

It was not often Christian got to enjoy a dinner in front of the TV. Engrossed in the cartoon, he occasionally picked up his toy cars and made the speeding sound. *Vrooom! Vrrrr . . . eh-eh-eh!*

Andie settled in the far corner of the room and dialed Jo.

"I thought it was the dinner night!" her friend greeted her on the other end of the line.

"It is." Andie confirmed. "Christian is not in the mood for company, so I got us out of it. He is watching *Cars*."

"Bummer. You usually like those."

"I know. I don't mind it tonight, though. Erik overheard my conversation with Phillippe about Nick coming, so he has been going out of his way to embarrass me."

"Ass. Where's Nick staying?"

"SLS. He's reserved the cabana for Sunday, so don't make any plans. We will do a pool party. Is Jersey in town, do you know?"

"I think so. What are you two doing Saturday night?"

"Dunno. Gotta come up with something fun. Is there anything going on?"

"We might go to E11EVEN. Not sure you want to take him there on the first date. Why? Don't you want some alone time with him?"

"Not really. Maybe . . . I guess I want to have an option."

"Makes sense."

Andie heard Christian calling her. "Okay, love. Got to go. I will see you Sunday for sure and will let you know about Saturday."

"Kiss, kiss."

* * *

Nick was shorter than she remembered. And the bits of chemistry they had enjoyed in Vegas dissipated under the Florida sun. Nonetheless, he was sweet, and Andie knew, Erik was right—he did expect to get laid.

"What do you want to do?" he asked after they'd finished dinner.

"It's up to you. Do you want to meet up with the girls?"

"Sure. What are they up to tonight?"

"A friend is having a birthday party at the E11EVEN. Do you want to go?"

Nick looked at her in surprise. "You want to take me to a strip club? I mean, of course, I don't mind. Just never had my date suggest it before."

When they arrived at midnight, the 24/7 ultraclub had just started to come to life. A new concept in Miami's entertainment arena, E11EVEN was a sophisticated playground catering to the needs for naughty fun in a most luxurious setting. Stars like Drake and Jason Derulo often took the stage for live performances alongside popular DJs and impressive, Cirque du Soleil–like shows.

They scouted around the floor, looking for Andie's friends. The incandescent lights, the cacophony of the sounds, provocative go-go dancers, the titillating and exuberant atmosphere—all had the desired effect on Nick. By the time they reached the table, his head was spinning from the stimulation.

"I did not think you'd make it," said Jo, hugging her friend. "The date is not going well?"

"It's fine. I need to get him laid, preferably not by me."

"Hmmm, sneaky. I like it!"

Andie looked around; she knew almost everyone at the table. She glanced at Nick; friendly and social, he chatted with the guys, sending her an occasional smile.

Andie pulled Jo to follow her. "Let's find him a girl."

They strode around the floor, stepping by multiple stages and occasionally slipping single dollar bills into the strings of dancers. When they returned to the table, a girl with a seductive body and long dark hair accompanied them.

"Hey, Nick," called out Jo, "we got something for you."

The girl approached the young man and pushed him down onto the couch. At the start of a new song, she inserted herself between his legs, moving her hips and sliding up and down. She took off her bra and buried his face in her breasts, then turned around, grinding her inhumanly tight derriere against his crotch. She directed his hands, pressing them against her body, caressing herself with his fingers.

When the music changed, she sat down on his knees, playing with his hair and unbuttoned his shirt. She whispered into his ear, and a confused look came across Nick's face. He searched for Andie, but when his eyes met hers, she merely smiled and nodded.

"You sure?" he mouthed.

"Yeah," she replied, and smiled back.

The girl pulled Nick to his feet, and they disappeared to a VIP section of the club for a private performance. When Nick returned some thirty minutes later, wearing a goofy grin, Andie finally relaxed and called a passing, short-haired girl to get a lap-dance for herself.

Chapter 15

Erik leaned back in the oversized leather chair at his desk and interlocked his fingers behind his head. His eyes traveled up to the library loft, Andie's favorite spot to study or to hide away from everyone and read. She was the only person who ever used the upstairs. His father would have been happy to see someone enjoying his favorite pet project. He would have liked her, a lot, Erik thought.

He took a deep breath and tried to concentrate on the projections spreadsheet that lay open in front of him. This deal was going nowhere fast. He hated to break it to Sean, but he was out. Frustrated, Erik ran his fingers through his hair and looked out to the backyard where Christian played in the pool and Andie tanned by his side. *What a body!*

Erik shook his head. He needed to get out of Florida. He had handed the condo reno over to his designer, and now that Sean's deal was as good as dead, nothing held him here.

New York Fashion Week was coming up the first week of September, and he had invitations to the best shows and after-parties. He texted Natalie to see if she wanted to be his date, but to no avail. She was acting strange, and Erik wondered if Beatrix had been right about her. Did their relationship hit the expiration date? He texted another friend he occasionally hooked up with and set down the phone. He heard Andie's yelp and looked outside. Christian threw a bucket of water at her and was now being chased around the lawn. Erik smiled. Another reason to leave; lately, he found Andie occupying his mind much too often for his comfort. In the current situation, that meant nothing but trouble. Not to worry; he had it under control. But he needed a distraction.

"I am going to New York on Thursday," he announced later that evening as he fixed Evelyn a martini and poured wine for Andie and himself.

"Can I come?" pleaded Christian, jumping up and down.

"Not this time, buddy."

"It is actually not a bad idea, Erik," Evelyn pointed out. "His classes have just started. Andie is not in the middle of exams. He has never been to New York, and the weather is lovely this time of year."

"Yes! And I want to go to FAO Schwartz!" The boy said getting ever more eager.

"Oh, honey, I think it has closed," said Andie.

"No, it's not! I want to go to New York anyway! Can I come, Uncle Erik? Please!"

"It's not a good time."

"I really think you should reconsider," insisted Evelyn. "I would like Andie to take him to the Met, and maybe get them tickets to a show. They could spend the weekend, and you could fly them back here Monday morning."

"Is it all against one?" chuckled Erik. "Andie?"

"'Fraid so," Andie shook her head with a smile. "Selfishly, I love New York. So, can't help you here."

"Fine." Erik threw his hands in the air defeated. "I'll let the housekeeper know to prepare for two guests."

Elated, Christian bounced around the room, thrilled about his big trip and flying on the plane. Andie bit her lower lip to hide her smile. If she could, she would have jumped up and down along with Christian.

* * *

Between packing and a general sense of anticipation, the next few days flew by in the blink of an eye. Javier drove them to the airport where the Lindberg jet awaited, ready to take off. Seeing the plane, Christian shrieked with joy and hoofed up the steps into the cabin. He jumped into the large leather seat, then immediately hopped off and ran down into the bedroom and back. Andie had never flown on a private jet either, so as much as she pretended to look cool, she beamed with excitement.

Erik smiled watching them. He knew he had become jaded and took for granted many aspects of his life. The first time he'd flown on a private jet, he was as young as or maybe even younger than Christian was now. He was well aware that most people in the world did not live the way he did. He had traveled to the most amazing places around the globe, stayed at the most exquisite hotels, and attended the most exclusive parties. He dated gorgeous women, many of whom were socialites and models who had expected all of those things. Unlike him, and many around him, Andie had not lost her childlike sense of wonder, and he envied that, admired it even. Being around her and seeing life through her eyes, he felt he experienced things for the first time himself. The desire to show her his world, to help her fly higher, to become stronger, came over him. He pushed it back down from whence it came.

"Can I get you something to drink, Mr. Lindberg? Miss?"

Erik nodded. "Please pour us some champagne. It is their first time. We need to celebrate!" Erik caught Christian, whom he ran back from the bedroom and sat him down in the seat next to his. "What do you want to drink, buddy?"

"Champagne!" answered the boy.

"Okay." Andie smiled and turned to the flight attendant. "Do you have apple juice?"

"Of course!"

* * *

Time had never flown as fast as it did during that flight onboard the Lindberg jet. On their ride from the airport to Manhattan the traffic noise, tall buildings, and the energy of the metropolis all reminded Andie of how much she missed traveling. Seeing New York for the first time, with its steel bridges and towering skyline, Christian craned to look out the window as they drove into the city.

They arrived at an imposing pre–World War II building about a block from the Metropolitan Museum of Modern Art. Andie took Christian's hand and followed Erik into the elegant lobby.

"Welcome back, Mr. Lindberg." The doorman ushered them in and called the valets to take care of the luggage.

"Thank you, Carlos. This is Andie and my nephew, Christian. They will be staying with me for a few days. Please tend to them if they need anything."

"Certainly. Welcome to New York, miss, sir."

They walked into an elevator manned by an operator who took them to the sixteenth floor.

Christian pulled on Andie's hand and loudly whispered, "Did you hear? He called me sir!" She smiled in response and patted his head.

"Did you know, miss," offered the operator, "Jacqueline Kennedy Onassis lived here on the fifteenth floor."

The elevator came to a halt and they stepped out onto a brightly lit landing. Erik held open the imposing door, and they walked into a spacious entrance hall with impressively high ceilings.

"Wow, this is cool!" Christian took off to explore every room.

"Make yourselves comfortable," offered Erik.

Andie wandered around the apartment. It was tastefully decorated with modern finishes and artwork by contemporary artists. The entrance hall led into a large living room with floor-to-ceiling windows and French doors that opened to a private terrace with stunning views of Central Park. In the formal dining room, a Chihuly chandelier hung over the massive glass-top table, its curved base upholstered in cream leather with decorative stitching. The kitchen, a crisp, all-white space with lacquered cabinets, a large central island, and an oversized wine fridge, led to a cozy breakfast nook decorated in warm colors to offset the starkness of the ultramodern space. The other side of the kitchen housed the butler's pantry and the maid's room, discreetly hidden behind sliding doors. Erik's office, designed in a mid-century modern style, was an inviting space with floating bookshelves, a comfortable couch, and a fireplace. His bedroom, with doors to a terrace and a wood-burning fireplace, was tucked away at the far end of the apartment. Down a separate hallway were two more bedrooms.

Erik opened the fridge. "Take a look," he called out to Andie. "Alicia stocked it up for you. I have dinner plans tonight, but if you'd like, I will take you two out for lunch tomorrow. Oh, I will be out tomorrow night as well. It's Fashion Week," he added with a smile.

"You have passes to the fashion shows?" gasped Andie.

"And the after-party." Erik winked.

"I hate you! Need a date?" she joked.

Erik looked down at his phone and chuckled. "I might. Feeling no love."

"Well, I will be here!" Andie smiled, cartoonishly batting her long eyelashes.

Christian came running down the corridor and slammed into Andie, almost knocking the girl off her feet, leaving it to Erik to catch them both.

"Okay, settle down! What do you want to do?" Andie asked the boy. "Want to go to the park?"

Christian nodded.

Erik pulled out his wallet and handed Andie his Black Amex. "Have fun, kids. Don't wait up."

"Can we have pizza for dinner?" begged Christian.

"Sure," agreed Andie.

"Oh, here is a good pizza delivery." Erik pulled a stack of menus out of the kitchen drawer and handed one to Andie. "Save a slice or two for me." He winked at Christian.

* * *

Andie and Christian walked out of the building and crossed the street to Central Park. The mild September sun showered the city with a late-afternoon glow, setting the sky ablaze, while a warm breeze played with the leaves on the centuries-old trees. New Yorkers and tourists poured outdoors to enjoy the last days of summer. Christian's eyes widen as he saw a sprawling lake where several boys played with remote controlled motorized boats. They were kind enough to let him race one of them and the child squealed with joy. Andie chased after him around the Rumble, Central Park's woodland, until they came across a bronze statue of Alice in Wonderland and her friends.

Wandering around the winding pathways, Andie contemplated, that in his privileged, yet dysfunctional life, Christian had never seen wide-open spaces with ponds and walkways like New York's Central Park. His world revolved around the mansion, the school, and the house in Palm Beach. He had never been outside of South Florida. When his parents were alive, he was too young, and after their death, everyone dealt with their own grief, with little attention paid to his upbringing. On one hand, Christian was afforded everything he needed—food to eat, a palace to live in—on the other hand, there was no warmth, no one who could kiss away his tears. There were, however, hordes of teachers and tutors and shrinks.

Andie thought back to her own childhood, the vacations with her parents, road trips, family night board games, and all of the silliness and laughter that went with it. When her mother worked on choreographing a show, Andie would tag along to the rehearsals and opening night parties, meeting all the crazy and artistic members of the cast. Her family was not rich, but her childhood memories were. She bitterly missed her parents, despite speaking to them almost every day. She planned to visit them over Christmas; it could not come soon enough. Thinking of Christian's situation made her angry—angry at Evelyn, angry at Erik. What had happened to this family was tragic, but the tragedy did not have to spill into Christian's childhood. Selfish! Andie resented how endlessly selfish Evelyn was. She had tried not to judge, but it was hard not to.

They returned to the apartment and ordered the much anticipated pizza. Erik had not lied; the pizza was divine—well worth the calories! Stuffed and happy, they watched *Hotel Transylvania* until Christian felt asleep by Andie's side on the couch, tired out after an eventful and memorable day. She carried him into bed, tucked him in, and lovingly brushed his hair off his forehead. She fell asleep immediately, as soon as her head hit the pillow, and did not hear Erik come back.

It was still dawn when Andie woke up to the smell of coffee. She poked her head into the adjoining room where Christian peacefully breathed in the bed. She put on a pair of cozy velour track pants and a long-sleeved tee and tiptoed out to the kitchen. Erik, wearing pajama bottoms and a tank, stood gazing out of the floor-to-ceiling windows, nursing his coffee.

"You're up early," he said quietly without turning around.

"So are you. Is everything okay?" Andie poured herself a cup and reached over to refill his.

"Yeah. Just can't sleep . . . oh, thanks." He turned around and handed her his mug.

His eyes were bright blue against the early morning sky, she noticed, and his hair was still messy from sleep.

Instinctively, she was about to reach out to fix it, but restrained herself.

Erik noticed her hesitant gesture. "What?"

"Nothing. You look pretty cute in the morning."

"Well, thank you."

Andie hopped on the kitchen counter, cuddling her cup in both hands. Erik leaned on the granite island and took a sip.

"Something is wrong," insisted Andie, picking up on his vibe.

"My aunt Gertrude has passed away."

"Oh my God, Erik, I am so sorry!"

"Don't be. We were not close."

"Where did she live?"

"Stockholm. My great-grandparents' mansion."

"Did she have any kids?"

"Yes. I have a cousin. Again, we are not close."

"You are a weird family."

"You can say that again," chuckled Erik.

"Will you have to go to the funeral?"

"Yes. I will drop you off in Miami on Sunday and then fly over to Stockholm. There are things I need to tend to."

"Will Mrs. Lindberg go?"

"No. They did not get along."

"As I said, weird!"

Erik nodded. "You are not wrong there. Don't let it ruin your day, Andie. I am fine. As I said, we did not have a relationship. It is more of a logistical and legal pain in the ass. I am not looking forward to the quality time with the attorneys and the accountants. My great-grandparents put in their will that the estate can only be divided after both my father and Gertrude are gone. I have to tend to my and Christian's interests."

"And your cousin?"

"Uh, yes. I am not looking forward to the quality time with him either." Erik ran his hand through his hair.

"He's just lost his mother—"

Erik stopped her. "Andie, don't. This is not the person or situation to waste your compassion on. I'm sorry I mentioned it."

"How long will you stay there?"

"As little time as I possibly can. Which is still longer than I would like to."

"Was she married?"

"Yeah, at one point. I don't remember what exactly had happened. I think he ran off with someone. My dad hated the guy."

"I'm starting to see a pattern. Have your parents ever liked anyone?"

"My mom likes you," Erik said with a smile.

"Aww, thanks. Though I think she merely tolerates me."

"Don't pay any attention. It's just the way she is."

"It must have been so much fun growing up—" said Andie sarcastically. Her eyes shot to Erik. "I am sorry, I did not mean it that way."

"You did, and you are right."

"From what I've heard of your father, he was quite dominant?"

"He was arrogant, there's no question about it. He was brought up by his grandfather, who, from what I've heard, was kinda cold, stoic—you know, a Viking." Erik smiled. "But he adored my dad. He was brought up to know he was better than everyone else."

"Like you," teased Andie.

Erik smiled and bowed his head. "Like me. Dad used to take us to his business meetings sometimes so we could learn. And I am a fast learner. I observed my dad and realized early that everyone has a price."

"'A man who knows the price of everything and the value of nothing,'" interjected Andie, quoting Oscar Wilde. "It's a horrible thing to say and a twisted way to think—"

"It's the truth, Andie. When I realized that, it was easy to buy people. Money is corruptive, especially for a young man."

"It's sad you think that way, but it is complete bullshit. You can't buy people—some people, maybe, but not everyone has a price."

"Everyone does, believe me. If you can't find it, you have been negotiating in the wrong currency."

"What do you mean?"

"The price is not always monetary."

"I detest that! You could not buy *me*."

"I could," stated Erik with quiet confidence.

"Really?! So what is my price?" she challenged him.

"I don't want to think about it. I might not be able to resist the temptation."

His cold, matter-of-fact attitude about the matter sent chills down her spine.

"Hey, buddy!" Erik smiled at the sleepy-looking Christian, who walked out of the guest room in his Buzz Lightyear pajamas. He patted the boy on the head, messing up his hair. "What do you have planned for today?"

"We are going to the Met," Andie answered for him and jumped off the counter to fix a cup of juice for the child.

"Oh, man, I am sorry. Brace yourself," chuckled Erik. "Better you than me."

"I take it you don't want to join us," Andie said, a mischievous smile on her lips.

"Nope. But come up after you are done. I will take you out for lunch." Erik winked at Christian and strode to his office.

She watched him walk away. Her smile faded. In the sun-filled room, she felt she had peeked inside something dark and cold.

Chapter 16

Andie looked forward to their visit to the Met, though she fully realized Christian would hate it. Mrs. Lindberg had insisted they go, and Andie was there to oblige. Tomorrow she would take him to the zoo, but today he would just have to suffer through the museum. They walked about a block up from the apartment and entered the imposing building. Andie tried to entertain Christian with the legends of Greek gods and heroes while walking around the collections of classical antiquities. Ancient Egyptian artifacts piqued his interest. They lingered in front of the fragments of the reliefs with their distinctly rigid style. Christian loitered in front of a statue of jackal-headed Anubis, the ancient god of the dead. Fascinated, he stared at the sarcophagi carved to depict bodies they once contained, with their ritualistic beards and head pieces. At the end of their visit, Andie took him to look at the antique weapons and armor from around the world. That was good enough for the first visit, she decided.

"Are you hungry?" Andie asked Christian as they headed outside.

"Okay."

"All right, let's text Uncle Erik and see if he is ready to go to lunch."

They met him in the lobby of his building and together walked to Madison Avenue. Christian was fascinated with the wide, noisy streets that ran up and down as far as his eye could see. He excitedly babbled to Erik about the Egyptian mummies and shiny suits of decorated armor he had just seen.

"That went better than I expected," Erik congratulated Andie as they walked into the Ristorante Morini.

The hostess seated them window side on the first floor. Christian, a meatball connoisseur, sampled the plate in front of him and announced that he liked Phillippe's cooking better. As they leisurely strolled back to the apartment, Andie was stopped in her tracks by the storefront of the Christian Louboutin Boutique.

Erik laughed. "Oh, yes, of course—the mothership."

Andie grinned in response.

"Go, go inside." Erik softly pushed her toward the door. "Have you ever been to one?"

Andie hesitated, intimidated by the look of the glamorous store. "It's okay."

"Check it out!" Erik rang the bell and pushed her in when the lock buzzed.

They stepped down a few steps into a small, sumptuously designed showroom. Andie wistfully looked at the seductive, red-soled objects of her desire. She would get herself a pair as a graduation present, she vowed.

Erik picked up a slender, spike-heeled sandal—a sexy masterpiece of black leather with a thin ankle strap and a satin front band encrusted in crystal shards of various sizes. He smiled, seeing Andie's eyes sparkle brighter than the crystals on the shoe.

"You should try them on," he suggested.

Andie shook her head. "Oh, no, I really should not—"

"Can I get you the right size?" inquired the consultant.

"Please," answered Erik. "What is your size, Andie? 38, 39?"

"38."

The woman disappeared behind the curtain and came back holding a brown box with the scrolled Christian Louboutin signature. She opened it and handed Andie the shoes, one at a time. Andie sat down on the bright pink velvet couch, ornately embellished with geometric designs, and slid her foot into the wearable masterpiece.

Twenty-two hundred dollars, she thought ruefully. She wouldn't be buying this pair as a graduation present.

"What do you think, buddy?" Erik asked Christian. "Do you like them?"

"Yeah, they look like Cinderella's shoes."

Andie smiled. "Cinderella wore glass slippers. These are stilettos."

"Get it right, man." Erik winked at the boy. "You will need to know these things."

Andie stood up and checked herself out in the large mirror. Her eyes traveled up; having a serendipitous moment, she saw the reflection of Erik standing behind. She shook off the mirage. Erik Lindberg was off limits.

"Wow, they look great. Do you like?" asked Erik.

"This is our latest collection," explained the saleswoman.

"They are beautiful," admitted Andie.

Erik gave the woman his credit card.

Andie stopped him. "Erik, thank you, but I cannot let you do that!"

"Of course, you can," argued Erik. "Consider it a belated bonus after your ninety-day review."

"Oh, no! Not after our morning conversation, it is not—"

"It's just shoes, Andie. Nothing else. So, please, allow me the pleasure of buying a friend her first pair of Louboutins," insisted Erik. "A beautiful woman must own at least one pair. And she should never buy one for herself," he added with a smirk.

The saleswoman packed the shoes into a bag and handed them to Andie. "Enjoy."

"Thank you." Andie kissed Erik on the cheek. "You should not have, but I am not strong enough to resist."

"It is my pleasure. Truly."

"Erik, hey!" Andie heard the voice behind her as soon as they stepped onto the street.

Erik turned around. "Hi, beautiful," he smiled.

In front of them stood a tall young woman with silky hair and ebony skin. Andie could swear she recognized her from some designer ads.

"And who is this?" asked the model.

"This is my nephew, Christian, and Andrea. She takes care of him."

The woman dismissively nodded her hello. "Are you going to my show tonight?"

"I intend to!" replied Erik.

"Great. See you at the after-party."

"Yes, you will. Are you working the runway?"

"Sure am." She winked. "Ta-ta!" She wiggled her fingers good-bye and strutted away.

Erik looked at his phone.

"Still no love?" asked Andie.

Erik chuckled and shook his head. "Nope, you will just have to be my date!" he joked, but as he finished the sentence, he realized he felt excited by the prospect.

"Sounds great," Andie replied facetiously. "Christian, you don't mind watching yourself tonight, do you?" She gave him a playful wink to let him know she was kidding.

Erik shrugged his shoulders. "Alicia is coming to cook you dinner. I can ask her to sleep over. We won't leave until around eight, anyway."

"You know I can cook, right?"

"I did not, but this is not the point we are discussing right now, is it?"

"Okay, even if we presume Christian is cared for, I don't think I will look good next to you in jeans."

"You are correct. It is a black-tie affair."

"My point exactly. I don't have a fairy godmother, you know."

A sly smile spread across Erik's face. "Maybe not. But I just might."

They walked into the apartment and were greeted by Alicia. "May I speak to you?" Erik waved her to follow him into the kitchen.

Andie looked at Christian, her heart jumping with hope and anticipation. "Would you mind if Alicia stayed with you tonight?"

Christian shrugged his shoulders, then squinted one eye. "I guess. . . . Can I have ice cream after dinner, then?"

"We are not trading favors now, are we? But you can watch a movie, as long as you are in bed by nine. Deal?"

"I guess. I still want ice cream."

"Let's have it together tomorrow when we go to the zoo. That way we can get different flavors and try them both," suggested Andie.

"I guess." Christian was not sure if he was getting duped, but ice cream tomorrow was better than no ice cream at all.

Erik, phone in hand, strode out of the kitchen, followed by Alicia, who gave Andie a disapproving look. Erik scrolled through his contact list and dialed a number, putting it on speaker as it rang.

"Rachel's phone," answered a young male's voice on the other end of the line. "You are on speaker."

"What do you need, Erik?" inquired a woman in the distance. "I am busy!"

"Hi, Rachel," Erik said, raising his voice a bit. "I know it is a crazy time for you. Thank you for taking my call—"

"What do you need Erik? Actually, don't answer that. Is it for the show tonight?"

"Yes."

"Tickets?"

"No, I have the tickets. I need an outfit."

"Give the details to Diego, I will send something over in a few hours."

Erik thanked the woman, and Diego's voice became louder. "Please give me her measurements, Mr. Lindberg."

Erik sized Andie up. "Size two? About five eight?" he asked and answered at the same time. Andie nodded.

"Bust?"

Erik glanced at Andie's breasts. "I'd say a C-cup." He answered matter-of-factly.

Andie blushed and gave Erik an evil look but nodded her affirmation.

"Thank you. Should not be too hard. I will pull a few things and bring them over. Please give me your address."

Erik dictated the address and hung up the phone. "And this is how it's done." He proudly grinned. Once again, it was good to be "the King."

As promised, a few hours later, the doorbell rang, and Diego appeared in the hallway accompanied by the bellman, with a cart loaded with multiple garment bags. The thin young man, with quick dark eyes and a funky haircut, evaluated Andie and smiled. "Doll, I think you will like what I've picked for you."

"Are you ready for a fashion show, buddy?" Erik winked, and Christian nodded in response.

The butterflies inside Andie's stomach flapped their wings, dancing. She was well aware that this whole situation was utterly inappropriate, but once again, she just couldn't resist. Knowing Erik, she anticipated it would be a VIP night all the way, which was tremendously exciting. So was the prospect of being his date.

In the bedroom Diego pulled the dresses out of their bags and assessed them, then the girl. "Here, doll, try this one." He handed her a navy blue, high-low, strapless number. He helped her put it on and nodded, indicating she was ready to show it to the audience.

Andie stepped out into the living room where Erik, cocktail in hand, and Christian, with a cup of juice, sat on the couch waiting for her debut.

"It's pretty," Erik acknowledged. "Try another one."

Next, Diego dressed Andie in a red flowy piece with a key-hole front and a halter top.

"Eh." Erik shrugged his shoulders unimpressed.

"Eh," Christian mimicked his uncle.

Andie smiled. "Tough crowd."

"Try this one," suggested Diego when Andie returned to the room.

Andie put on a silk rose-stained dress with lingerie-inspired lace trim around a V-cut front that continued to a low back crisscrossed with spaghetti straps. A high slit ran up the side, exposing Andie's leg.

"Ding, ding, ding! We have our winner!" announced Diego, pleased with what he saw. "I don't think you need to try anything else. Just do simple hair, nude lips, and smoky eyes."

"Thank you. It's beautiful," Andie agreed.

"On you, doll. Not everyone could pull it off. I don't think you should show it to him. Surprise him tonight," suggested Diego.

"Oh, no," protested Andie, "it's not that type of relationship."

"Don't matter, my beauty."

"What happened?" asked Erik when Andie walked back into the living room in her jeans and T-shirt.

"We have the dress," announced Diego.

"Am I not to see it until later?" Erik asked with a raised eyebrow.

"Exactly," confirmed Diego.

"I like surprises," agreed Erik and exited the room, followed by Christian.

"Have a good night, doll." Diego smiled. "I will be backstage for the show but might see you later at the after-party."

"That would be great." Andie gave him a hug.

"And hey, if I may say so, you should make this 'that type of relationship.' You two would make the hottest couple."

As soon as Diego left, Andie walked into the kitchen to check on dinner for Christian. Alicia's face did not leave room for interpretation about how she felt. Andie could not blame her. She was well aware that all of this was so wrong, but—

"Ready for your bath?" asked Andie after Christian finished his meal.

Fresh from the tub, clean and rosy-cheeked, with wet, messy hair, the child got into his favorite pajamas.

"Go let your uncle know which movie you want to watch, and he will put it on for you. I will go get ready, okay?"

The boy nodded and skipped up the corridor to find Erik.

Andie took a long shower, and, as Diego suggested, brushed her long golden hair straight. She put a light pink gloss on her full lips and applied smoky makeup to her eyes. The dress gloved her body, teasing the onlooker with its high slit, the heels made her long legs go on forever.

Erik, dressed in a tuxedo, sipped a tequila he had fixed for himself and turned around as he heard the clicking of Andie's stilettoes. He stared at her for a few seconds without a smile or a word.

"Ready to go?" he asked finally.

Wary of his reaction, she asked, "What do you think?"

"You look beautiful," he answered dispassionately.

Christian jumped off the couch and threw his arms

around her. "You look like a princess. And if you are a princess, I am a prince!"

Andie smiled. "Of course you are! Remember our deal. As soon as the movie is over, you go straight to bed!" She kissed the child and wiped her gloss off his cheek.

Erik fist-bumped his nephew. "Be good, bud. See you in the morning. Alicia, we are leaving." He called out and opened the door for Andie.

The black Maybach waited downstairs to take them to the show. Erik held the door open and helped Andie inside. He popped a bottle of champagne and poured them a glass. He seemed lost in his thoughts, and silently, so as not to intrude, Andie looked out the window. They crossed the city and arrived at a funky-looking building. Erik protectively put his hand around Andie's waist and steered her through the crowds. A waiter approached them with a tray, offering hors d'oeuvres.

Andie looked around, taking in every moment, every outfit, wowed at recognizing the faces she had seen on TV and in magazines. She tried to imprint all of the details into her memory so she could give a play-by-play account to Jo when she next spoke to her. She sipped her drink, struggling to ignore the sensation Erik's proximity stirred in her body.

They walked around the massive hall, occasionally shaking hands and exchanging kisses. Erik steered them to a high-top table to set down their glasses and take a breather.

"Thank you for inviting me," said Andie, catching Erik's glance. In her heels, she was just a tad shorter than him.

"The pleasure is mine."

He felt proud to have her on his arm; it was a new feeling, a good feeling. Graceful and elegant, she stood out even in this room full of beautiful women. He knew many of those women, some intimately, others socially, the rest by reputation; most of them had neither a brain nor a soul.

He looked at Andie again. "You really do look pretty tonight."

The doors into the hall flew open, revealing the runway, the music got louder indicating the show was about to start. They proceeded inside. Confidently, Erik walked the girl to the first row where they took their seats. The runway was dimly lit, the walls draped in white, and Azuma's funky flower creations decorated the space.

Andie looked around. She recognized Anna Wintour who was seated across from them hidden behind her sunglasses. Like a kid in a candy store, she tried to remain cool, but her eyes were shining and her fingers fidgeting. Erik gently took one of her hands in his. Surprised, Andie glanced at him, meeting his calm and smiling gaze.

"Breathe," he said softly.

Caught off guard, Andie grinned and bit her lip.

Model after model, dressed in high fashion for the

upcoming season, teased the audience with elevated creations. The designer's newest collection full of electric colors and metallic accents pumped up the volume on everyday style. Andie tried to absorb every detail, picturing how she would incorporate this higher knowledge into her own wardrobe.

The after-party was held a few blocks away at a raw, industrial-looking space with a killer view of the city lights. The atmosphere was lively and the music loud. In the distance, Andie recognized the girl they had run into earlier, she was sharing a laugh with a slender, short-haired woman. Andie could swear they were talking about them, but brushed the thought off as her own paranoia.

It seemed Erik knew half of the people in the crowded room, and Andie was not surprised when they stopped again to greet another friend.

"Marc!" Erik extended his hand.

"Oh, Erik. Hi. Good to see you." Marc awkwardly returned the handshake.

"You too. What are you up to these days?"

Andie noticed the man looked uncomfortable.

"Not much," Marc replied.

The slender, short-haired woman that Andie had noticed a few moments earlier appeared behind Marc and took the drink out of his hand. "Hello, Erik."

"Natalie. Long time."

The woman sized Andie up and down. "Fornicating with the help, I see. How cliché."

Erik clenched his jaw, his eyes darkened. He instinctively put his hand around Andie's waist and slowly moved his glare from the woman to Marc.

"Enjoy my leftovers, bro." Not waiting for the response, Erik turned around and walked away, protectively holding Andie.

Andie chuckled under her breath. "Man, you like them bitchy!"

"Apparently so."

"An ex?"

Erik shook his head. "Just a fuck buddy." He took her hand. "Come, I want to show you something."

They climbed up a flight of stairs and walked out onto the rooftop with its 360-degree view of the city. Andie spun around and laughed. "Wow. Breathtaking!"

There were only a few people on the deck. Erik smiled and took a sip of his tequila. They set their drinks on the railing, and Andie leaned over and looked down at the lights and the roofs of the surrounding buildings. Erik watched while her gaze wandered. She turned her face and carelessly met his eyes. A magnetic force pulled them toward each other and impelled their lips into the kiss. But just like magnets of the same charge, they immediately pushed apart.

"I'm sorry!" they muttered at the same time.

Trying to steady her breath and shaking hands, Andie turned away to face the city.

Erik wiped her gloss off his lips and took a generous gulp of tequila. "Ready to go?"

Andie nodded.

Again, they rode back in silence and quietly walked into the apartment. They stopped just past the threshold and looked at each other.

"Thank you for the lovely evening, Andie," Erik said quietly.

She kissed him on the cheek. "Good night."

Erik marched into his bedroom and threw his tux onto the chair. He put on a pair of pajama pants and a sweater, walked out to the dark kitchen, poured himself a generous portion of whiskey, and pulled out a cigar. Then he opened up the sliding glass doors and stepped out onto the terrace. The muted noises of the city that never sleeps vowed to keep him company. He settled into the lounge chair, stretched out his legs, lit the cigar, and breathed in the aromatic smoke.

What the fuck just happened? The idea was to fly to New York to put some distance between him and the girl. How did he end up getting talked into bringing the two of them along? Did he foolishly hope that if he spent more time with her, she would start getting on his nerves just like everyone else did? Well, that backfired. It felt natural and comfortable to be around her. He did not need to search for the right words or force their conversations. He could speak to her freely on any subject and expect an intelligent response. In fact, he shared with her more than he had ever shared with anyone else, even Sean or Patrick. She did not hesitate to challenge him when she felt he was wrong and stimulated him in more ways than one. And the evening . . . Erik imagined her again in that dress. When she walked into the room, he was at a loss for words. He remembered her scent and her lips. She had the softest lips. . . .

His body responded accordingly. He looked down at his hard-on.

"*Et tu, Brute?*"

Chapter 17

The trip to Stockholm was as unpleasant as anticipated. After a week of family infighting, Erik flew
back to Florida to check the progress on the remod-
eling of his apartment. The floors were laid and most
of the dirty jobs were finished, so he decided it would
be wiser to stay at his place. He wouldn't be staying
for long, after all, only a few nights, before he flew
to Hong Kong on Sunday. He set up a makeshift
bedroom-slash-office with bare essentials and did not
bother to unpack. His first night back, Erik drove over
to the house to have dinner with his mother to discuss
family affairs. While there, he packed for his upcoming
trip. After that, there was no reason to go back to the
mansion until his return.

Evelyn could not understand why Erik decided to
stay at the half-finished apartment, but she was used to
not questioning her son.

* * *

Andie fixed herself a gin and tonic and sat down on the
blue suede couch. Jo stood in the bathroom in front of

the mirror holding a flat iron in her hand and a lock of hair with her teeth. She released the strand, smoothed it out with the hot tool, and carefully laid it to frame her face.

"You never told me about New York," said Jo.

She unpinned another handful of hair, secured a small portion with her teeth, then flattened it piece by piece.

"It was fricking awesome!"

"Looked like it! The pictures you sent me looked amazing! I need the details, girl!"

Jo teased her mane with her fingers and spritzed it with hairspray. Satisfied, she walked out of the bathroom and crashed in the chair. Andie told her all of the awesome details—omitting the kiss. They would never speak of it. It had been a mistake.

"That's great, love! Glad you had a good time. And, man, Erik is so effing hot! If it weren't for Corey, I would be all over him like trash on white!"

Andie laughed. "Yep, the boy's smokin'."

"So why aren't you?"

"Why aren't I what?" Andie did not like where the conversation was heading.

"All over him?! He is hot, he is rich, and you—" Jo searched for the right adjective. "Well, you are Tinkerbell—magic pussy dust and all!"

Andie giggled and shook her head. "Exactly. He is hot, he is rich. For how long can I keep his attention? A month? Two? He sleeps with the most beautiful women in the world—"

"Yet, he did not have a date for the party," pointed out Jo.

"Exception to the rule. I just don't see it going anywhere besides a quick fling."

"So, what's wrong with a month or two? What's wrong with a fling? You don't have to try a glass slipper on every Cinderfellow you meet. It does not have to be a 'happily ever after.' You are really young. A fling with a guy like that is a good thing! He is a perfect 'Mr. Right-Now.'"

Andie carefully searched for the right words. A frown appeared on her forehead as she attempted to make sense of the situation. "I was devastated when JC broke up with me. I've barely picked up the pieces. Erik is more dangerous. Besides, I am not in a position to have a fling with him. I live in his house and take care of his nephew, remember? What do I do? Fuck him at night and run down to my room in the morning to change? And then, when things go sour in a month or two—because you know they will—what am I to do then? Pretend nothing has happened when we are all sitting at one of Evelyn's dinners? I would have to quit, and that would really screw with Christian's head. I am responsible for that child." She reasoned, trying to take the emotions out of the equation.

"That was quite a tirade," chuckled Jo. "Obviously, you've never thought about it."

"Oh, shut up!" Andie stuck out her tongue and got up from the couch. "Can I put my phone in your purse? I have my credit card and ID there."

"Of course, love. Hope Jersey is on time."

They Ubered to downtown Miami to Sugar, the latest hotspot atop the East Hotel. Jersey was waiting for them outside. Since its opening, Sugar presented a challenge to get into without a hookup. Luckily, Jersey had one.

The girls took the elevator to the fortieth floor and walked out into the Asian-inspired rooftop lounge, a perfect balance of yin and yang, with its bare masculine concrete columns and the delicate feminine garden, nestled atop the sprawling business district. They secured their spot by the bar and ordered a round of craft cocktails.

Andie was excited to finally have an evening with her girls. The last time the three of them were out together was in Vegas, over two months ago. A lot had happened since then. She had become so entangled in the Lindberg's world, she hardly had any time to step out of it and simply be.

Jo's phone made a chirping sound; she smiled and quickly typed the response. She continued exchanging messages for a few minutes, but finally set her phone down. "Sorry, it was Corey messaging me."

"What is he doing up?" asked Andie. "What time is it in Iraq?"

"Are you sexting?" probed Jersey with a devilish smirk.

Jo smiled back. "Totally!"

"When is he back?" inquired Jersey.

"Mid-November. He is here through Christmas and New Year's. So that'll be nice."

"Great. Will he come to visit you?" asked Andie.

"Actually," replied Jo, "he is coming straight here to stay with me. We will go meet his family over Thanksgiving and we will spend Christmas with mine."

"Oh, wow!" gasped Andie.

"I hear you," chuckled Jo. "I found this sick resort in Cancun, so we are taking a trip there before Christmas and will spend the rest of the time here."

"Oh, that will be perfect. The weather should be amazing then!" approved Jersey.

The phone made a noise again, and Jo picked it up to look. "Corey says 'Hi.' He wants to buy us a round of drinks." She waved to the bartender and gave him a separate credit card for the round of cocktails. "He added me to his account," she explained.

"This is what I call a one-night stand gone wrong," joked Andie.

"Yeah, exactly," giggled Jo. "His password for me is 'ExpensiveWife.'"

"Ha ha, at least he knows what he is getting into!" laughed Jersey.

"He sure does! Where are we going after this?" asked Jo.

"LIV?" suggested Jersey.

"I don't want to deal with it. Getting in is a huge pain," Andie pointed out.

"Yeah," agreed Jo. "Uncle Paul is in Greece, so he won't be there."

"How about Faena?" proposed Jersey. "A client of mine just started working there. We will get VIP treatment there."

"It's incredible." Jo shook her head. "You have hook-ups everywhere."

"Everywhere that counts," Jersey proudly agreed, sent a quick text to her contact, and asked for the check.

They rode over the bridge, leaving behind Port-Miami with its elegant white cruise ships on one side and the islands with their multimillion dollar mansions on the other. After a fifteen-minute ride through streets brimming with nightlife, the car pulled over in front of Faena. They walked into the "Cathedral," the hotel's entrance area decorated with awe-inspiring floor-to-ceiling murals by Juan Gatti that were themed around the quests of conquistadors to El Dorado and the Fountain of Youth. Motifs of love, nature, and science were painted in vibrant greens, golds, and reds. Fat golden columns and mosaic tile inlays added to the sensory indulgent experience. The girls felt like they were suddenly transported into the Land of Oz. They strolled down the lobby and out to the garden where the "Gone but Not Forgotten" statue by English artist Damien Hirsh, a skeleton of a colossal mammoth plated in twenty-four-karat gold encased in hurricane-proof glass, dominated the landscape.

After taking mandatory pictures with the nine-foot

mammoth-in-residence, they descended the stairs into the plush basement with gold leave ceilings that is Saxony Bar.

* * *

Erik rested his eyes and scrolled through the presentation he had been working on one last time. It was almost ready. He just needed to get a few more numbers from his team to finish it. He clicked back to his spreadsheet with the revenue projections and plugged in some new assumptions. The deal still made sense. He glanced at the time in the bottom right corner of the screen; it was almost 2 a.m. An Iron Man movie was playing in the background. Erik set aside his laptop and turned up the volume. He would finish his work on the plane tomorrow. Tonight his brain was fried. The phone rang; he saw an unfamiliar Miami number and looked away, intending not to answer, but, at the last moment, he changed his mind.

"Hello?"

Andie's voice came through the speaker. "Erik, hey, where are you? Are you guys out?"

"Andie? What's wrong? Where are you?"

"I am at Faena. Are you out somewhere?" She sounded distressed.

"No, I am at the condo. What's wrong?"

"Oh, I am so sorry. If I knew . . . I thought . . . I did not mean to wake you—"

"I was not sleeping. Answer my question!" he demanded.

"I've lost the girls. My phone and credit card are in Jo's purse, and she is not answering her phone. I asked a guy outside to borrow his phone . . . I am not sure what to do . . . thought if you were out—"

"Just have a valet hail you a taxi and come here to the apartment. I will text Jo and let her know."

"I don't—"

"I will meet you downstairs," he interrupted her.

"Okay. Thanks."

"See you in a few."

Erik got out of bed, put on a pair of jeans, and headed downstairs. Several minutes later, a yellow cab pulled in and Andie got out, wearing a skintight minidress and a guilty smile.

"Andie, Andie, Andie." Erik paid the driver and shook his head.

"I am so sorry—"

"Don't be. It was smart of you to call. Come." He took her by the elbow and guided her through the lobby. "It's a construction zone," warned Erik as he opened the door to the apartment and invited her in. It was, with the newly laid floors still covered, an unfinished kitchen, and empty rooms.

Andie walked out onto the balcony that opened up to the downtown skyline and PortMiami, a sleeping Fisher Island, and the dark waters of the Bay flowing into the ocean. "Wow, what a view!"

"As you see," Erik gestured toward the bare space behind them, "the best I can offer you is the left side of the bed."

"Why do you stay here and not at the house? This is still pretty raw." She surveyed the sparse surroundings.

"I had to be here most of the time to oversee the renovation anyway. Besides, I am only in town for a few days."

"When are you leaving?"

"Tomorrow?"

"Where to? Hong Kong?"

"Yes, then San Paolo."

"Quite a trek. For how long will you be gone?" asked Andie, trying to sound casual.

"A couple of weeks maybe."

"I am sorry again about this . . ."

"It's okay."

Andie took a deep, frustrated breath.

"Yes?" asked Erik, raising his eyebrow.

"Ugh . . . it's just . . . I've always been the responsible one who had it together. And lately, I have been making one mistake after another, constantly dropping the ball. I work for you, so you should never see what a mess I have been, but somehow you are the one who ends up picking me up—"

"Is that a complaint or a thank-you?"

"I am sorry. It's a thank-you, of course . . . it just sucks that you are who you are."

"Okay. Whatever that means. Don't think any more

tonight. It's a new day tomorrow; you will feel better. Here." Erik handed her a T-shirt and a pair of boxers. "Bathroom," he pointed to the door.

Andie took a shower to wash off the night. She walked out, dressed in Erik's boxers and T-shirt, and hesitantly crawled into bed. She curled into a ball and closed her eyes, trying not to think of the predicament into which she had put both of them.

Erik looked down at the girl in his bed. The universe surely had a sense of humor. He took a deep breath and flipped through the channels. He was willing to watch *Golden Girls* if that would help to keep him from thinking about the girl, the one he wanted, sleeping next to him.

He chuckled to himself, there was a first time for everything. *Sex is highly overrated. Not!*

Chapter 18

There's a lot of commotion today, Andie thought as she jogged alongside the Indian Creek golf course toward the mansion. Attracted by the mild October weather, the Lindberg's neighbors zoomed past her riding in their cart and eager to tee off. She ran past the clubhouse and squinted her eyes against the morning sun in an attempt to catch a glimpse of a VIP who came out to play a round of golf.

"I think it is former president Clinton," said Phillippe when she asked him.

He was cooking breakfast for Mrs. Lindberg and jokingly slapped Andie's hand when she stole a strawberry off his cutting board. She popped it in her mouth and sat at the island when her phone rang.

"Hello?"

"Hi, Andie. It's JC."

Andie's heart jumped into her throat. The expression on her face caused Phillippe to stop what he was doing and stare at her. She got up and walked out onto the patio, struggling to regain control over her faculties.

"Hey, are you there? Can you hear me?" asked JC, responding to the silence on the other end of the line.

"Uh, yes. Hi." She answered, relieved her tone did not betray her emotions.

"How have you been?" His voice was smooth, with just a hint of his sexy Spanish accent.

"I am doing well, thank you. You?"

"Very well. How's school?"

"It's good. I have one more semester left after this one."

"Great! I am so proud of you!"

"Thank you."

JC paused and cleared his throat. "Listen, I have, ah, two tickets to *Jersey Boys*. I know how much you love the show, so I thought maybe you would like to come . . . with me? Next Friday?" he added, waiting for an answer.

Andie took a calming breath; her heart was beating so vigorously it hurt. "Yeah . . . sure. That sounds good."

"Great! That's great. . . . It's at the Arsht Center."

"Okay."

"Okay. I'll call you next week to firm up, but it will be great to see you."

"Yeah, you too." She pressed the END button and, for a few seconds, dumbfoundedly stared at the wallpaper on her screen, then got up and walked back into the kitchen.

"Who was that?" Phillippe tried to sound casual, though he was burning with curiosity.

"JC."

"JC? JC?" He searched his memory bank. "Oh! As in your ex JC?"

"One and the same. I am sorry . . . I have to clear my head. I will be right back. I will get Christian up in a moment."

* * *

The week crawled along agonizingly slowly. A slew of contradicting emotions swarmed inside Andie's head and made the situation at hand evermore confusing. She had gone through her stages of grief and had arrived at acceptance, or so she thought. Now that JC so thoughtlessly reemerged, she did not know how to feel. Since their breakup, in her mind she had had plenty of time to build their relationship into something that was the best thing that had ever happened to her. All the fights and resentment grew blurry, while all the happy times exaggeratedly blissful. She did not excuse his behavior leading up to the breakup, come to think of it, she still felt angry at him, but shouldn't she at least hear what he had to say?

JC called back on Wednesday.

"Do you want to meet for a drink beforehand?" he asked.

"I won't be able to get out in time for drinks—"

"Dinner then? I took the liberty to make a reservation at the Bazaar."

"Sure . . . yeah, that sounds good," Andie agreed.

The next phone call she made was to Jo. The question of the day: "What are you going to wear?"

"No clue! Something pretty, but not too sexy. I seriously need to go shopping," Andie said, flipping through the dresses in her closet.

After a lengthy video chat and a few costume changes, they decided on a knee-length, deep blue, form-fitting dress with bell sleeves. A perfect choice for a Saturday night date.

JC arrived early. A long line of cars and an army of valets in front of the theater, a sophisticated audience, and excited chatter—all signs pointed to a sold-out performance. He paced back and forth in front of the entrance, not knowing what to expect from the reunion. Had she missed him? Was she as beautiful as he remembered? Did they still have chemistry? After a few months of intoxication with his freedom, he started to miss her bitterly. The more he tried to date others to get her out of his system, the more he wanted her back. He anxiously looked at his watch. The Andie he knew would never be late. Finally, he saw her get out of a car, and he ran down the steps to greet her.

"It's really good to see you, Andie. You look great." He leaned in to kiss her on the cheek and lingered to take in her scent and her nearness.

"Thanks. You too."

He looked great, indeed, Andie thought. Dressed in a light blue Armani suit with a dark blue shirt casually opened around his neck, with his crazy black hair and the slightly crooked smile he looked as sexy as ever. *Fucker!*

The familiar sounds of the musical brought a smile to Andie's face, the distinct voice of Frankie Valli, the melodies, the songs she knew by heart spread a feeling of joy and warmth through her soul.

JC looked at her as the final curtain fell. "As good as always?"

Andie nodded and, still smiling, followed him outside. They drove across the causeway through the Venetian Islands into South Beach. Andie looked out the window at scenery she had seen hundreds of times, scattered thoughts roaming through her mind. JC took her hand, giving her that same feeling of contentment and ease they had once shared. When they arrived at the tall art deco building of the SLS Hotel, JC opened her car door and helped her up the steps. The Bazaar, a brainchild of the James Beard award-winning Chef José Andrés, is located on the ground floor of the chic hotel.

The hostess greeted them with a pleasant smile. "Good evening, do you have a reservation with us tonight?"

"Yes, it's under Juan Cortes," answered JC.

"Certainly! Right this way, please."

They were led into an intimate dining room with a massive chandelier made entirely out of seashells and got seated at a small table facing each other. JC ordered a bottle of wine he knew she'd like and raised his glass. "So, tell me, what have you been up to?"

Andie casually shrugged her shoulders. "Nothing crazy. School, work—"

"Where do you work now?"

Andie explained that she was a nanny, which afforded her the opportunity to continue her studies and put some of what she had learned into practice with Christian and his family.

"Okay, that's good. Killing two birds with one stone." She nodded.

"I am glad you've agreed to see me," said JC, after a brief pause. "I was not sure if you would. . . ."

Despite a jolt in her stomach, Andie calmly looked at him without offering a response.

"I had time to think," he continued, "a lot of time to think. . . ." He chuckled. "I am sorry I hurt you. It was never my intention." He paused, hoping for any type of acknowledgment. Realizing she was not going to offer it, he continued, "It's just that things started to move so fast, I freaked out. I started to panic, I felt I was missing out on something . . . you know what I mean?"

"No."

JC chuckled and shook his head; he hadn't expected she would make it easy. He knew her better than that. He reached across the table and took her hand. "What I am trying to say is, the only thing that I've missed out on is you."

Andie looked away, hoping to hide the mélange of emotions flooding over her. Her heart hammered mercilessly against her rib cage, she felt the blood in her temples throb, the massive lump in her throat made it difficult to breathe or swallow.

"I don't expect to pick up where we've left off—"

"We did not leave off at a good place."

"That too. So maybe we can try again and start somewhere from the middle?"

Andie looked into JC's eyes with a calm she did not feel. "JC, we broke up over six months ago, and the last few months that we were together were hell. This is not a movie. You cannot cut out the bad parts and arrive straight at the happy place. A lot of things have changed, including you and me."

"I know you still have feelings for me. I can see it."

"I do," affirmed Andie. "I just don't know what they are."

"I am sorry I hurt you. I did not mean to—"

"But you *did* mean to!" exclaimed Andie. "You cannot have said the things that you said without meaning to hurt. But I do believe you are sorry."

"That's a start. Can we build on that?"

"I don't know," Andie answered quietly.

"Can we try? I know I screwed up, and I really want to fix it. Let's start at the beginning if you want. We can take it slow and see if there is anything left."

Andie nodded. "Yeah."

JC reached over and kissed her hand. "Thank you."

After dinner, they stepped out to the veranda bar and walked down the steps, following the sounds coming from Hyde Beach. The ten-foot-tall duck sculpture by

Philippe Starck welcomed them into a whimsical garden with baroque style full-length mirrors and trees adorned with hanging lights.

At night the pool deck with its private hideaway cabanas turned into an indoor-outdoor club. Philippe Starck once described it as "a sexy hell where beautiful bad girls and bad boys are dancing on the chairs, on tables, drowned in the music, in the heat, in the sweat."

A sophisticated version of an enclosed tiki bar, clad in warm wood with leather couches, houses a DJ spinning an artful mix of EDM, top 20, and revamped classics. There is no dance floor; it is not needed. People dance wherever they find themselves, their tables, by the bar, at the cabanas, and on the deck; everyone moves to the music, intoxicated by the cocktails and the night.

JC was close, so close their bodies almost touched. Andie inhaled the smell of his cologne, felt his breath on her skin. With the back of his hand, he stroked her arm, then ran his fingers up to her face, cupping it with his palms, his lips now caressing hers. The earth did not move from under her, and when their lips parted, Andie's feet were still firmly planted on the ground.

JC did not risk suggesting a nightcap. They would take it slow, if that was what she wanted. They had plenty of time ahead of them.

* * *

Over the weeks that followed, JC continued with sweet text messages and casual calls. He tried not to be pushy, yet he methodically reestablished his presence in her life. They had jumped headfirst into the whirlpool of their relationship before; this time, Andie proceeded with caution. When her schedule allowed it, they met for dinner or coffee.

The last time, her relationship with JC had taken priority over the rest of her life, including her friends. She was not about to make the same mistake twice; her life came first. Furthermore, Andie felt more and more confused. Ever since she had first met JC, all she'd wanted was to build their life together, but since their breakup, her picture of what that perfect life looked like had been altered. Therefore, no thoughts of the future, past the weekend plans, were allowed.

JC was not thrilled with Andie's living arrangements. Her staying in someone else's house, taking care of someone else's kid, and not having much time available for their newly established relationship was far from ideal. He bit his tongue and chose to bide his time, but in his mind the situation had a shelf life, and its expiration date was fast approaching. As soon as he felt their relationship was strong enough, he would put an end to this nonsense. She needed to concentrate on her school, her future career, and their life together. He had his time to play around for the past six months, but he quickly learned it was more fun when they played together. Andie was smart, caring, and open-minded—not to mention beautiful. Now that he realized he missed her and made a mistake, he was determined to correct it and close the deal once and for all.

Three weeks into it, however, the charm of teenage courtship started to wear off on JC. Finally, both of them had the weekend off at the same time, and Andie agreed to stay over. She came down to his South Beach condo just as the sun was setting over the city. Dispassionately, she looked around. Nothing had changed in his apartment since she had been there last. Still, the place felt foreign. As a matter of fact, she realized, it had never felt like home.

"Look what I've made for you!" He smiled and handed her a lychee martini, the kind she used to love.

He cooked a romantic dinner, and they sat on the balcony and listened to music, enjoying the warmth of the fall evening and the ocean breeze. The conversation was natural and familiar, and so was the sex. Andie wondered if she would have to fake an orgasm or if she could get away without the theatrics.

She woke up early but lay in bed with her eyes closed, listening to his peaceful breathing. Eventually, she slid from under the sheets and quietly dressed. She looked down at the sleeping JC. She felt nothing.

Andie walked out to the kitchen, made herself a cup of coffee, and stepped onto the balcony. This was the beginning of a new day.

Chapter 19

Erik woke up as the wheels of the plane touched down on the runway in Miami. He massaged the inner corners of his eyes in an attempt to shake off fatigue, looked out the window at the night-darkened landing strip, and stretched his limbs. The plane stopped at a private hanger where Javier awaited with the car.

"*¿Como estuvo el viaje, Señor Erik?*" *How was your trip, Mr. Erik?* asked the man as he loaded Erik's suitcases into the trunk of the Maybach.

"*Exitoso. Gracias. ¿Mi mama, esta en casa?*" *Fine. Thank you. Is my mom home?*

"*Si, señor. Pero ya ceno.*" *Yes, sir. But she already ate.*

"*Me parece bien.*" *That's okay.*

After rush hour, the drive to the mansion was quick enough. Javier parked the car, then brought the luggage up to Erik's room. While Erik took a shower and changed, Consuelo unpacked and hung his clothes. Refreshed, he went down to the informal dining room where Evelyn was waiting for him at the table. As soon as they exchanged greetings, she asked Phillippe through the house intercom system to bring the dinner.

Erik poured himself a large glass of red wine and sat back in a chair at the head of the table.

"How was your trip?" asked Evelyn.

"Can't complain. Anything new here since we've spoken?"

"Thankfully not. I began to plan the Thanksgiving party."

A tradition Evelyn had started nearly thirty years earlier, the Thanksgiving eve soiree to kick off the holiday season was a first-class affair. The list of several hundred guests included both old and new money, politicians, socialites, and promising penniless artists and entertainers. If someone was invited once, they had an invitation for life. This was Evelyn's favorite event to plan and the main reason she had hired an assistant years ago, a position that for the past few years had been held by Lucy.

"How many people this year?"

Evelyn smiled. "We are still working on the list, but it's getting out of control."

"Gets bigger every year."

"I've heard the senator and his wife will be in Miami at that time. Not sure if I should include them."

Erik recalled his little episode with Vicky and smiled. "It's up to you. Do you still like him?"

Evelyn nodded. "I do. I thought he was charming, and she was lovely."

"She *was* lovely," Erik agreed. "But I thought he was a douchebag."

"Erik! Mind your language!"

"Forgive me. An asshole."

"Erik—"

"When are you sending out the invitations?"

"They need to go out next week. Shall I invite Matt's girlfriend? Are they still an item?"

Erik smiled at his mother's use of modern vocabulary. "Indeed they are. I think Matt might pop the question before the year's end!"

"That's quite wonderful. And Sean? He still does not have a lady friend?"

"No lady friend for Sean."

"What a pity. Such a handsome and charming boy. I hate to see him alone. Both of you."

"Thank you for your care, Mother, but we are doing all right."

Evelyn nodded, acknowledging that the topic was closed for discussion.

"Will you invite Andie?" asked Erik casually.

"I think I will. I have grown quite fond of her. She is a lovely girl. There will be a few eligible men . . . maybe she will meet someone. I would like to see her with someone appropriate."

"I thought you did not like to 'entertain gentlemen callers,'" Erik said, pointing out one of Evelyn's conditions when hiring staff for the house.

"Not if it is someone from our circle."

"How liberal of you."

"Oh, stop it! Don't call me that word!"

Erik smiled. "I am sorry, I did not mean to insult you."

Evelyn patted her son's hand. "Do you want a dessert, dear?"

"No thanks, Mom."

"Okay, then. I will retire now, if you don't mind."

"Of course. Good night, Mom."

"Good night." Evelyn paused for a second as if she wanted to say something else, instead she changed her mind and left the room.

Erik got up and strode into the kitchen where Phillippe had just finished loading the dishwasher. He warmly smiled at Erik. "Welcome back."

"Thank you."

"Tea?"

Erik nodded. "Yes, please. I also brought you some for your collection. It's upstairs. I don't feel like getting it right now."

"Thank you. How was the trip? Got everything done that was needed?"

"For the most part. You know how it is. It's a battle."

"Are we winning?"

"Ha! We will at the end."

"All that counts, right?"

Phillippe brewed two cups, put one in front of Erik, and sat down across from him.

"So, what's new in the zoo?" Erik asked. "How's your boyfriend?"

"We are okay. We both feel a little burned out. I think we will try to take a quick trip, just to get away for a few days before the holiday season starts. Before the party. Besides, it's our anniversary."

"Happy anniversary! Where are you thinking of going?"

"Somewhere close. Maybe San Juan or Cartagena."

"Sounds nice," Erik approved. "Take the jet. I'll be here for a few weeks, so I won't need it."

"Seriously?" exclaimed Phillippe.

"Of course. You deserve a break."

Phillippe beamed. "That would be amazing! Thank you!"

"What else is happening?"

"I think Lucy has started seeing someone. She bolts out the door every evening." Phillippe chuckled. "Oh, and it looks like Andie got back with her ex."

Surprised, Erik lifted his eyebrow. "Who are you talking about?"

"The one—you know, the broken heart, blah, blah blah . . . before she started to work here?"

"Why do you think so?"

"He called her one day, out of the blue," Phillippe explained. "They went out. It looks like they've decided to try it again. I am pretty sure they've hooked up."

"Hmmm, I'm surprised she would take him back. Obviously, the guy isn't a brain surgeon, since he let that one slip away." Sensing an uncomfortable pause, Erik looked at Phillippe. "What?"

"Actually," chuckled Phillippe, "a heart surgeon, from what I hear."

"You're fucking kidding me."

Phillippe shook his head.

After they finished their tea and Erik retired, Phillippe turned off the lights and crossed over to his apartment over the garage. He could not wait to talk to Greg. Bummer—his boyfriend was somewhere over the Atlantic Ocean, hard at work as a flight attendant, and when he landed, it would be deep night in Miami. It was fabulous, just fabulous, that Erik had offered them the use of the Lindberg jet. "Fabulous"—Phillippe hated that word! Such a cliché to assume all gay men over-used the adjective. But in this situation, "fabulous" was entirely appropriate.

For the tenth time, Phillippe searched the internet and checked out the hotels and the restaurant scene. He had decided they would go to Cartagena. Surprisingly, Greg had never been there, and Phillippe had always wanted to take him. The place was so romantic, such a foody destination. *It will be fabulous.*

Phillippe shut down his laptop, put on silk paja-mas, and climbed into his Tempur-Pedic bed with six hundred–count Egyptian satin sheets. Simply because the apartment was over the garage did not give him an excuse to live like a slob. He closed his eyes and thought of Greg. They had been together for almost ten years. Neither of them had thought the relationship would last that long. As a flight attendant, Greg was often gone, and Phillippe spent most nights at the apartment at the mansion. As a matter of fact, when they had first met, Phillippe had lived here permanently. Only when their relationship developed had the two men decided they needed a home and a life of their own. They bought a small cottage near the beach in Hollywood, about twenty miles north of Miami. It was perfect for the two of them.

Phillippe felt lucky to have Greg as his partner. Greg had been there for him during those horrible years. First Mr. Lindberg, then Patrick and his young wife—Phillippe's heart still ached at the thought. He had been connected to this family for so many years! He still remembered how he'd first met them.

As a young man, Phillippe had worked as a chef at a restaurant in Palm Beach. One evening, a wealthy patron asked to speak to the chef. Phillippe came out to the dining room where the Lindbergs were entertaining their friends. Rick had enjoyed his dinner and drunk quite a bit of wine, so he was in a complimentary mood. He was surprised to see the chef was a young man in his mid-twenties. Feeling generous with his time, Rick had engaged Phillippe in conversation, and when he and Evelyn finally left the restaurant, he was pleased with the evening. They returned a few weeks later and subsequently frequented the restaurant whenever they were in Palm Beach. Every time, Rick called Phillippe out for a chat; he had grown fond of the young chef and was displeased to hear that Phillippe was planning to leave to open his own place.

"Most restaurants fail within the first year, Phillippe," advised Rick. "It is not a sound investment of capital or time."

"I know, sir. But no one in Palm Beach cooks the food I do! I am sick of cooking what I am told. You will see, sir. It is a whole new concept."

"And the money?"

"I have saved. Also, my grandmother recently passed away and left me a small sum. I think that should be enough."

"Whatever you think you need, double it," warned Rick.

"I can make it work," insisted Phillippe. "I know that in my gut!"

Rick nodded and took a sip of his scotch. "Good luck. You have a customer in me."

Halfway through the project, Phillippe ran out of money. The place was almost ready to open; all he needed were a few finishing touches, and to hire the staff and purchase inventory. Oh, and to keep the lights on. Phillippe gathered all the courage he could summon, grabbed his business plan, pictures of the progress, menu ideas, and asked Rick for an audience.

Rick was not surprised to receive the call. As a matter of fact, he had expected it for quite some time. He listened to Phillippe's spiel and glanced over the plans and the photos.

He stared at the obviously nervous young man in front of him. "I am a disciplined investor, Phillippe, and

I think the restaurant business is a rotten investment. I also do not invest in projects that are less than fifty million dollars. I would not be able to keep track of my finances if I did. You are a hardworking kid and a talented chef, I don't doubt that—"

"Sir, I am! If you give me a chance, I will prove it to you! I know I can do this!"

"As I've said, this is not an investment for me—"

"Sir—"

"But I am at a point in my life when I am entitled to a hobby. I think everyone deserves a chance to make a mistake. This will be an expensive one for you. All important lessons are. I will not invest, but I will lend you the money. However, you must promise me, if you don't make it within the first year, you will cut your losses and move on."

"Thank you, sir! I promise!" Phillippe knew he would not fail.

On opening day, Phillippe felt he was on the top of the world. His dream, his life goal, had come to fruition! He realized how lucky he was that Rick had given him a chance—a chance most people would never get! In his heart, he knew he would make Rick proud, and he would be loyal to him forever—not for the money, but for the kindness.

Rick and Evelyn often came to the restaurant for dinner. Sometimes, they were joined by their two teenage sons. Every few months, Rick would invite Phillippe into his office to hear about his running of the business.

Phillippe was grateful for the mentorship; he never took for granted how valuable Rick's time was.

A year later, the restaurant closed its doors. Phillippe was devastated. As Rick had predicted, the young chef lost everything. Rick called him into his office for the last time.

"What now?" Rick asked.

"Sir, I will pay you back every penny! I promise! I will work day and night until I do." Phillippe professed with conviction.

"I know you will. The money I don't worry about. The money I have. What do you *want* to do next?"

Phillippe took a deep breath. Cooking was the only thing he knew. The thought of going back to cook in someone else's kitchen brought tears to his eyes.

Rick silently watched the young man experience a range of emotions in front of him.

"I will find a job at a restaurant," answered Phillippe finally.

"Good." Rick nodded. "Let me know where you end up."

Phillippe swallowed what felt like a rock; the hopelessness of his situation settled deep in his gut. Rick continued to observe him while sipping his scotch.

"It is all I know," mumbled Phillippe, more to himself than to Rick.

"Is it?"

Phillippe nodded. "I have always worked in the kitchen. I don't know anything else."

"Too bad. That means the last year was wasted on you."

Puzzled, Phillippe stared at the man in front of him.

"Let's recap, shall we?" started Rick. "You did the market research and found the real estate for your restaurant. You headed the construction project and designed the place practically yourself. You ran the business, and I must say, you ran it fairly well. You managed a dozen or so people. You made the difficult decision of cutting your losses on time. You consolidated and closed the business."

"But I failed."

"Not every loss is a failure."

"Thank you, sir."

"I will make you an offer, Phillippe. Don't answer me today. I want you to come run my household. You are a fine chef, and you have a good head on your shoulders. My wife is heavily involved in the community and regularly entertains. A lot of people would sample your food, that's for sure. I want the answer in a week."

With that, the audience was over.

Phillippe enjoyed working for the Lindbergs more than he had expected. Instantly, he was thrust into the enchanted and unfamiliar world of the mega-rich. Rick had not lied; Evelyn did entertain *a lot*. Phillippe cooked his heart out, with the knowledge his food was appreciated. Surprisingly, he also enjoyed managing the household. He had accepted many responsibilities besides the kitchen. Evelyn had been all too happy to take that weight off her shoulders. But of course, the most amazing thing was a change in his lifestyle. There were summers in the Hamptons, long vacations in the French Rivera and the Greek Isles, Christmases at the Florida mansion, and skiing in Aspen. There were expensive holiday gifts and flights aboard the private jet. The world he became part of turned out to be more glamorous than he could ever imagine.

The death of his mentor from a heart attack shook Phillippe to the core. Then life as they knew it came to a sudden stop with the death of Patrick and Lori.

"I want you to come run my household. . . ."

That was over twenty years ago, thought Phillippe, unable to sleep.

Chapter 20

Halloween in Miami is not child's play. Halloween in Miami is an excuse for a girl to put on a sexy outfit and attend yet another fabulous party—as if a Miami girl needed an excuse. It is a far cry from days of trick-or-treating, dressed up as one's favorite princess. Halloween is a justification to "slut it up"—as if a Miami girl needed a justification! The boys love Halloween as well. There is eye candy everywhere, no trick-or-treating required. Only the amateurs celebrate Halloween on October 31; true Miamians party the whole week. And any decent party ought to start with a pre-party!

Day one of Halloween week at the SoHo House had proven to be a success. Day two would require a full costume change. Jo, channeling Little Bo Peep, walked into the room with a bottle of champagne. Her blond hair was set in tight curls and covered by a miniature bonnet. Every time she moved, the blue bows that topped her white stockings peeked from under a short, ruffled skirt; a white and blue corset accentuated her slender figure and pushed up her boobs.

Jersey, a smoldering she-devil incarnate, finished gluing on fake eyelashes and passed her glass over for a refill. Dressed—or more appropriately, undressed—in a sequined red leotard and red wig with silver horns, she asked rhetorically, "How do I look?"

"Looking fabulous, girl!" acknowledged Jo.

Andie took a step back from the full-length mirror. She put her perfectly manicured fingers through her hair, then shook it into place. Today she was a pirate. A black mini skirt with gold detailing, encircled by a wide shiny belt, barely covered the lace trim of her fishnet stockings. A dark blue velvet and lace bra, topped with a matching cropped jacket, exposed her flat stomach. Five-inch heels finished the look.

"Damn, your boobs look amaze-balls!" approved Jo.

Jersey danced over and cupped Andie's breasts. "Am-azi-ing!" she sang.

Andie laughed and picked up her glass.

"Okay," Jersey said, laying out their night, "let's stop by a party that the owner of my salon is throwing, and after that we will head out to the club around midnight."

"Sounds like a plan," agreed Jo. "I'll call Uber."

* * *

Erik walked out of the house and climbed into the back seat of the limo.

"Where to, sir?" inquired the driver.

"We are picking someone up at this address first," Erik handed the man his phone with the directions.

"then to Star Island for a few hours. Afterward, we will have you take us over to LIV around midnight. Wait for me to call you."

"No problem, sir."

Erik opened a bottle of Dom Perignon and poured himself a glass. Fifteen minutes later, the car stopped in front of an oceanfront condo in North Miami Beach.

He texted *here* and got out to greet his date. A beautiful young woman with luscious dark hair strode out of the lobby, clad in a black latex Catwoman bodysuit.

"Jessica," grinned Erik.

"Hello, handsome." Jessica smiled and threw her hands around his neck.

"Mmmm. . . ." Erik ran his fingers down her back, cupped her butt, and kissed her on the lips.

Jessica took a step back and looked him over. Not quite Halloween material, he wore silver gray pants and a tailored white Hugo Boss shirt with the sleeves rolled up.

"Well, and what are you supposed to be?" she asked him.

Erik shrugged his shoulders and smiled. "A boring guy?"

"No matter. You still look sexy."

The driver opened the door and helped them in. Next stop, Star Island, where a waterfront estate had been decked out as a haunted mansion. Erik and Jessica followed other guests through the lushly landscaped grounds to the expansive yard with its unobstructed views of downtown and PortMiami. A DJ booth had been set on a platform floating in the middle of the infinity-edge pool, with Biscayne Bay as its backdrop. Multiple bars, inside and outside, fully stocked with top-shelf liquor, were ready to serve up a good time. The waitstaff, clad in Grecian togas, passed whimsical hors d'oeuvres and cocktails with a splash of grenadine to simulate blood.

Erik looked around and spotted Matt and Susie getting their drinks at the inside bar. They noticed him and walked over.

"Nice to see you two dressed up for the occasion," Erik looked at his friend, who was dressed in black jeans and a black T-shirt with a Batman sign, and Susie in full Batgirl gear. "You fit right in." He pointed to Jessica in her Catwoman suit.

Newly arrived, Sean approached them with a broad smile. "Dudes, dudettes! Matt, what's up, bro? Couple's costumes? Are you seriously wearing a couple's costume?!"

"Oh, shut up, man! What are you supposed to be, a stockbroker on a casual Friday?" teased Matt.

"I'm with Erik," responded Sean. "And Jessica, did you conspire with those two?"

"Yes, it was a well-coordinated effort," Jessica chuckled.

"Man, oh man, Erik, we are the minority!" exclaimed Sean.

"Yep," Erik said with a smirk. "The endangered species."

"Boring?" nudged Susie.

"Single," retorted Erik.

Jessica frowned. She was about to change that.

"But enough about you," Sean interjected with a grin. "The party's started, and I am still sober!"

"Well, we can't have that!" teased Susie.

After correcting the unacceptable situation with drinks in hand, they looked around for their host and found him surrounded by a group of guests. Dressed as Caesar, the man was showing off his new toys.

"Hey, guys! I'm glad you could make it!" he shouted.

Sean shook his hand. "What's up, man? Great party!"

"Thanks. You got drinks? Good!" "Caesar" waved for them to follow him. "Come, I wanna show you my garage. Erik, have you seen the new Lambo? Man, it is swe-e-et. Come, I want to show you!"

Unwillingly, Erik followed the group. He had always found such displays of excess to be in poor taste but felt obliged to humor their host.

They proceeded into the brightly lit garage, which housed a meticulously exhibited collection of luxury cars. The brand-new Lamborghini occupied the most valuable real estate.

"Man, come, come! Look at this beauty!" their host urged. "Erik, what'd ya say? Sweet, right?"

"Very nice," complimented Erik with little conviction. Feeling more and more annoyed, he started to regret his decision to stop by.

"Hey, did you see my Aston Martin?" "Caesar" continued with his show-and-tell, pointing at a dark blue Vanquish. "Is it the same one you have?"

"It is," confirmed Erik.

"Yeah, that's what I said when I bought it! If it is good enough for Erik Lindberg, it is good enough for me. But seriously, man, get yourself a Lambo! You won't regret it! Sweet, really sweet!"

"I am too tall for it. Excuse me, I am afraid my date feels neglected. Congrats on the Lambo." Erik took Jessica by the elbow and hurried out.

Susie laughed. "OMG! This guy was so far up your ass, I swear I could see his head popping out of your chest!"

"I thought he was nice," Jessica contested.

"Is that Jonathan over there, by the pool?" Matt pointed at a tall man who stood talking to the DJ.

"This party just went from bad to worse," noted Sean.

Erik ran his fingers through his hair. "I am done. I am getting the fuck out of here."

"Why, who's Jonathan?" asked Susie.

"Erik's favorite cousin," replied Matt.

"You don't want to say 'hi'?" asked Jessica; Matt's sarcasm lost on her.

"Not if he was the last person in the world," Erik replied. "Let's go."

"Wait, let me grab a roady," protested Sean.

"Come on, Sean," Erik commanded, "there's plenty of booze in the limo."

They hurried out onto the driveway as Erik texted the driver to pick them up.

"LIV?" the driver checked as soon as the door closed behind his passengers.

"The one and only," affirmed Susie.

The entrance to the club resembled a zombie apocalypse; a mob of characters were trying to penetrate what seemed like an impregnable stronghold.

"Oh, please tell me we don't have to deal with this mess," pleaded Susie.

"Come," Erik said, and wrapped his arm around her, leading them toward the side door, reserved for the celebrities and VIPs.

Sean grabbed Erik's arm and pointed in the direction of the club's main entrance. "Wait! Is that Jo over there?"

"Oh, yeah!" exclaimed Susie. "I see Andie and Jersey, too. Erik, we can invite them to our table, right? Will the club let us bring in more people?"

"As long as we spend the money," Erik replied, "they will let us bring an army. Sean, can you go grab the girls?"

Sean did not wait for Erik to ask again and, with Matt in tow, was already on his way to pull the damsels out of the distress. He tagged Jo's arm and waved them over.

"Oh, thank God!" exclaimed Jo. "I could not deal with this shit-show anymore! We were about to leave!"

"I'm glad Sean saw you!" Erik exchanged kisses with the three of them. "Jo, looking hot in your Little Bo Peep outfit! You can herd me anytime!"

Flattered, Jo grinned and tapped her staff on the ground. "Come, my little sheep, let's get this party started!"

Sean could not take his eyes off Andie. "You look sexy as hell!" he murmured into her ear.

Her beautiful eyes smiled at him. He could not get enough of her, her seductive body, her tanned, silky skin—he would try again. He would talk to her tomorrow at dinner at the Lindbergs', and, hopefully, she wouldn't blow him off this time.

They entered the club and the VIP hostess escorted them to the table Erik had reserved. The epicenter of premeditated insanity, LIV had the party going strong. A lineup of celebrity DJs and a horde of professional dancers kept the senses heightened and adrenaline pumping, all fueled by a cocktail of legal and illegal substances.

With much ado, model-looking girls in sexy outfits brought champagne and tequila bottles decorated with sparklers, followed by ice buckets full of mixers. The drinks began to flow and bodies to move to the beat as the ever changing explosive energy of the club overtook them: dancing—no more a matter of choice, but a necessity.

Meanwhile, Jessica firmly planted herself in Erik's sight. She had no interest in making friends with these random chicks; she was annoyed enough that Erik had invited them to join. She was here for one reason and one reason only: this was her chance to hook him, and she was not going to miss it.

Erik fixed himself a tequila and sat back, watching Jessica dance in front of him, her rocking body moving in a slow sensuous motion. She turned her back to him, swaying her hips to the rhythm, rubbing celestially against him in a private lap dance.

Andie, tired from dancing, climbed atop the back of the couch between Matt and Sean. Unable to sit still she continued to move, sipping champagne. Susie jumped up next to her and pulled her to her feet. Unsteady, as their high heels dug into the soft cushion of the couch, they giggled trying to keep balanced in their attempt to dance.

Sean looked up at Andie. "Your stockings are uneven." He ran his fingers up her leg, grabbed the top of her right stocking, and pulled it up slightly to even it out with the other. "Here, that's better."

Andie laughed, not reprimanding his frivolity, and sunk next to him, sipping from the flute. Champagne! She loved champagne!

Across the table, Erik had not taken his eyes off the two of them. He watched as his best friend's hand caressed the girl's bare back, then Sean leaned over and whispered something in her ear, and Andie laughed again, her beautiful eyes sparkling, her full, sensual lips smiling and whispering back to Sean. Erik swallowed a mouthful of tequila. Jessica leaned over, putting her breasts in his face; he glanced up and patted her butt. She slid next to him, slowly kissed his neck and stroking the inside of his leg.

Erik watched as Sean's hand moved higher up Andie's inner thigh. She did not seem to be paying attention, sipping her drink, chuckling with Susie, and swaying her body to the music. Sean brushed a strand of hair off Andie's face and paused, his hand in caressing her neck, leaning ever closer to her.

Erik softly pushed Jessica off, got up, and walked around the table. Without saying a word, he reached across Matt and Susie and caught Andie by her elbow. She raised her eyes at him surprised. Erik pulled her over, forcing her to stand up. She wobbled, struggling to keep her balance. Erik lifted her up, carried her over the others, and steadied her on the ground. He clutched her hand and steered her to follow him. She complied as if in a daze. Erik was unsure what he was doing and, most important, why. He felt agitated, his jaws tightly clenched, blood throbbing in his temples. Holding her tightly, Erik pushed through the crowd to the second floor. He saw an opening on the viewing balcony and, shoving people out of his way, pressed toward it. He thrust Andie into an empty spot and put his hands on the railings, encircling her, shielding her from the assault of the crowd.

She savored his closeness, the heat of his body, his breath on her cheek. She leaned against him, feeling his heart pound violently in his chest; he wrapped his arms around her waist and drew her closer as they melted into each other. The club, with its madness, had shifted to the background. Careful not to interrupt the unexpected intimacy, she turned her face slightly, brushed against his cheek, his lips so close to hers she could smell tequila on his breath.

Someone bumped into them, throwing Erik off balance. A fight was brewing.

"Come." Erik navigated Andie away. "Ready to go?" he asked as they got closer to the exit.

She nodded. They stepped out of the club into the bright lights of the lobby, where the heart-pumping music became a muffled noise behind them. Erik called the driver, and a few moments later the limo pulled over in front of the hotel entrance to pick them up. Once inside, Erik turned on the radio and reclined, unwinding from the frantic night. The ultimate crowd-pleaser, "Billy Jean," came on the air. Enthralled by the song, Andie moved to the familiar rhythm, singing along, perfectly off-key, imaginary microphone in hand. Amused, Erik watched her in disbelief; how could she look so innocently authentic and so damn fuckable at the same time?

The limo dropped them off at the side entrance of the mansion, and they quietly walked into the kitchen.

Erik opened the fridge. "Are you hungry?"

Andie nodded, took plates out of the cupboard, and set them on the counter. She turned around to grab the forks but bumped into Erik and lost her balance. As he caught her, Andie lifted her eyes, clinging to his shoulders to regain her stance. A lightning bolt pierced through her body as she met his burning glare. Erik pushed her against the fridge. She shuddered, feeling the ice-cold steel against her skin. He pressed his body against hers, pinning her down, their lips locked with a hunger that had been unfed far too long. Unlike New York, this kiss was neither soft nor gentle, but demanding, almost angry, full of pent-up energy exploding in a violent outburst.

Erik swung Andie around and sat her up on top of the counter. She wrapped her long legs around his waist as he pulled her closer. He dug his fingers into her thighs, then ran them up her back and ripped off her jacket. He gripped her long hair in his fist, masterfully unhooked her bra and flung it to the floor.

Erik cupped her breasts, feeling their softness, squeezing her nipples with his fingers. He pulled his shirt over his head, and Andie dug her nails into his sculpted chest. She gasped as Erik drew her nipple into his mouth, twirling it with his tongue, then he found her lips again and pulled her into a deep kiss. Erik's hands explored her body, caressing her breasts, his lips demanded her response—

The sound of a ringing phone ruthlessly cut the silence and brought them back to reality. Erik sensed Andie's body jolt and stiffen. She pulled back, gently pushed him away, and jumped off the counter.

Erik locked his arms around her. "No, no, Andie . . . please!"

"Erik, I am sorry, I am so sorry . . ." She freed herself from his embrace, picked up her clothes, and disappeared out of the kitchen.

Initially, Erik started after her but stopped himself. He cursed under his breath, ran his fingers through his hair, and pulled the phone out of his back pocket—a missed call from Sean. Erik swore again. The phone made one more attempt at reaching him by announcing the arrival of a text. Erik looked down. A message from Sean was concise: *WTF!?*

Erik picked up his shirt and stumbled upstairs to his room. He threw his clothes on the floor and turned on the shower. Walking around with blue balls like an adolescent was getting old.

Chapter 21

Andie sprang out of bed. Oh fuck! She needed to talk to Erik pronto, before Evelyn's dinner tonight.

In the kitchen, Phillippe was humming the newest Taylor Swift song as he prepped for the evening. Andie threw him a quick "good morning" and ran upstairs to look for Erik.

She found him stretched out on the couch in the family room, watching the news. He sat up when she walked in.

"How are you feeling?" he asked softly, gesturing for her to sit beside him.

"Okay. Tired. You?"

"Same." Erik fixed his gaze on the girl.

Andie sat down and nervously lifted her eyes to face the man in front of her. It did not look like he was going to start first. She collected herself and searched for the right words. "Erik, about what happened last night . . ."

"Yes?"

"It didn't . . . I mean, I am sorry. It never should have happened, it was irresponsible of me. Totally my fault . . . and . . . I am sorry. We are both adults. . . ."

Erik raised his eyebrow, mildly amused. "So, in your opinion, what has happened?"

"It was totally a lapse of judgment. . . . Please don't think it meant anything to me—"

"Really?"

"I am sorry—"

"Stop saying that!" he interrupted.

"I don't know what else to say! It should have never happened, but that's life and shit happens, and we are both adults!"

"Are you serious right now?" Erik sat up fully, no longer entertained. "Is that what you've convinced yourself happened—we got fucked up and messed around?"

"Erik, I am sorry, I did not mean it like that—"

"How *did* you mean it, Andie?"

"I don't know! I am sorry! What do you want me to do or say? Can we just pretend it never happened?"

Erik looked at her and said coldly, "*Shit* did not *just happen* last night, so don't lie to yourself."

Andie took a frustrated breath. "As I said, I am sorry. I just wanted to clear the air between us and let you know you don't have to worry about me."

She stood up, ready to leave. Erik caught her wrist and pulled her back down.

"Well, thank you for that. It is very understanding of you," he chuckled. "But I do have something to worry about. I like you. And I know you like me, even though you have done a superb job convincing yourself otherwise." He touched her cheek with the back of his hand.

"Look at me, Andie. Can we give it a go? Let me take you out on a proper date. Let's see what happens."

"See what happens?!" she exclaimed, "I am not in the position to see what happens! I take care of your nephew, remember? If things go sour, it will be a mess! I would have to quit! How would I explain that to Christian? He would think I don't care about him or that he did something wrong! It will really screw with him—"

"What if things don't go sour?"

"And how do you imagine that would play out? I have sex with you upstairs and run downstairs to change in the morning before I wake up Christian and take him to school? I live in your house! I work for your family!"

"It's not like things like this have never happened before," reasoned Erik.

"Yes," retorted Andie in agitation, "And that is what makes this so cliché. Besides, I still have almost a year left of school. I can't lose a place to live and my job at the same time. I will never put myself in that situation again! I've watched you jump everything that moves over the past six months—all of your relationships are ephemeral! What would make us different?"

"You make us different." He said softly, "You are right, I do date a lot of women, that's how I know when something is special. And I think this could be. I really wish you would let us try."

"I don't have that luxury."

"Wow, you really have it all figured out!" exclaimed Erik. "Looks like you have given it a good deal of thought and have already made up your mind that things would not work out. It's too fucking bad I don't have a say in it."

Andie got up. "I am sorry, Erik."

Erik nodded and stated coldly. "Your boyfriend screwed you over, and now you are projecting that shit on me and expecting that I would do the same. You gave him a second chance, though. But won't even give me a first one!"

Trembling, Andie rushed out of the room.

Erik looked over at the house intercom and saw a green light. "Phillippe, could you please bring me a cup of coffee? And don't pretend you weren't listening."

* * *

Andie curled up in her bed and cursed herself over and over again for her weakness and stupidity. Erik Lindberg was not the man for her—JC was! But it was now clear she did not have the same feelings for JC anymore. Her mind brought her back to the night before, and her whole body started to ache for Erik. She roared and punched her pillow in frustration.

* * *

As the afternoon neared its end, Erik got dressed for dinner and walked down to the library. He turned on the TV and sat at the desk in front of his computer. There were a few e-mails in his inbox, nothing that could not wait until Monday, but he answered them anyway. His assistant, Jeanne, had sent the details about the Global Business Leaders conference in London where he had been asked to speak.

The phone rang. Erik smiled seeing the familiar number. "*Ma chére*, just the person to brighten my day!"

"My Erik, I miss you. I have not seen you for so long!" sang Beatrix.

"I will be in London in a few weeks. I can hop over La Manche to see you."[3]

"Oh, don't bother, darling. I am overdue for a London trip. I will meet you there. When do you say you come?"

Hearing her voice with that delectable French accent was music to his ears. "Last week of November. I will be preoccupied Thursday and Friday afternoon, but I will extend my stay so we can spend the weekend together. I am staying at the Ritz. Shall I have my assistant reserve you a room?"

"No, I prefer Dorchester. I stay there."

"As you wish," agreed Erik. "I will have Jeanne make a dinner reservation at Alain Ducasse for Friday night?"

"That will be lovely! Can't wait to see you."

"You, too, *ma chére*."

"Kiss kiss, my Erik."

Erik hung up the phone; at least something pleasant had come out of this day. He heard footsteps approaching from the corridor, and a few seconds later, the door flew open and a grim-looking Sean stomped into the room. Erik got up and extended his hand for a shake.

"Fuck you!" barked Sean, his hands in the pockets.

Erik nodded and walked over to the bar. He poured two glasses of scotch and handed one to his friend. Sean took a large sip and sat down on the couch in front of the TV.

He took another sip. "Fuck you, you fucking fuck!"

"Okay, I guess I deserve that," chuckled Erik.

"You bet you do, you asshole!"

"Are you done?"

"Not even close! I have been asking her out for months, and you just turn around and fuck her!"

"I did not fuck her," Erik said grimly.

"Why the hell not?!"

"You interrupted."

"Good! Did you at least mess around?"

Erik nodded.

"So, what now?" asked Sean in a calmer voice. "You two are dating, or it's a one-off kinda thing?"

"It's a one-off kinda thing," answered Erik.

"What the fuck is wrong with you, man? Andie's awesome. None of the bimbos you screw around with even come close."

"I agree," Erik replied. "She blew me off."

Sean looked at his friend in surprise.

Erik chuckled bitterly. "Oh, she gave me the whole 'we are both adults, let's pretend it never happened' speech."

"You kidding? Oh, that's cold! Even for her. Did she give you the reason?"

"Oh, yeah! She gave me the whole list. With bullet points."

"Ouch, dude! Are you okay? You look kinda upset."

Erik shrugged it off. "I'll live. There are plenty of fish."

"Yeah? So, how many did you catch so far?"

"None that I've wanted to keep."

Sean tried to change the subject. "Jessica was pretty pissed last night. Have you called her?"

"Nope."

"Are you planning to?"

"Nope."

Sean sneered. "You are an ass."

"That seems to be the consensus," confirmed Erik.

Consuelo knocked on the door. "Señores, Señora ask you come have drinks with guests. Señor Sean, your mother here."

They both got up to follow Consuelo and join the rest of the party. It was a beautiful November evening; all of the doors in the grand room were open, inviting the fresh breeze to roam through the spacious hall. They walked out onto the veranda where Evelyn was serving drinks.

"Hi, Mom," Sean greeted Clair with a kiss on the cheek.

Christian, deeply engaged in a battle of chess with Dr. Knight, sat on the floor. Andie relaxed next to him in the lounge chair and nursed a glass of white wine.

"I was saying," continued Dr. Knight, "I love Halloween. Did you fellows go out?"

Sean nodded. "Yeah, we hit a few parties last night."

"Did you dress up? I dressed up as the Phantom of the Opera. I went to a splendid party on Fisher Island!"

Sean shook his head. "No, we did not dress up. The girls did."

"I dressed up as Batman!" interrupted Christian.

"You and Matt both," snuffed Sean.

"Oh, yeah?" Dr. Knight said approvingly. "And his gal-friend, did she go with you?"

Sean nodded. "Yeah, Susie came."

"Nice gal, no? Did she dress up as a Batgirl or Catwoman?" Dr. Knight inquired.

"Batgirl," answered Erik.

"Erik's date was Catwoman," volunteered Sean.

"Nice, nice, very nice. Andie, did you dress up?"

Andie nodded unwillingly, not happy about being pulled into a conversation she had no desire to be a part of. "A pirate."

"Argh!" exclaimed Dr. Knight, covering one eye with his hand and making a severe face. "Did you find any buried treasure, mate?" he shouted, for some reason in a Scottish accent.

"Oh, she made out with plenty of booty," Sean confirmed sarcastically.

Andie was grateful when a car pulled into the driveway, drawing attention away from her. Bianca, in a white flowing dress, walked across the front yard onto the veranda, bringing with her the sweet scent of jasmine and the jingling sound of delicate gold bangles.

"What lovely weather we finally have!" she exclaimed, exchanging kisses with her friends.

Erik got up. "What can I get you to drink, Bianca?"

"Oh, thank you, yes! White wine, please. The same one Andie is drinking."

Erik walked over to the bar and returned with a chilled glass.

"Thank you, sweetie pie. Thank you!" Bianca took a sip and sat down in the chair Erik offered.

"How's your apartment coming along?" asked Clair.

"Great. Pretty much done," answered Erik. "Just received the final bill from the decorator. The furniture is being delivered Monday and Tuesday. I will be fully moved in come midweek."

"You will have to throw a housewarming party! We are all dying to see it!" exclaimed Dr. Knight.

"You should do a home cleansing!" suggested Bianca. "I can bring some crystals and sage to clean the energy of the old owners and all of the people that came in and out of there."

"Thank you, Bianca," Erik said with a smile. "I will let you know."

"The dinner is ready," announced Consuelo.

The party moved inside into the informal dining room. The inviting smell of a home-cooked Sunday dinner filled the room, and an array of hearty dishes were spread in the middle of the table.

Dr. Knight rubbed his hands together. "Oh, boy! This looks scrumptious!"

Consuelo walked around the table, filling the glasses with wine. Dr. Knight passed around platters of meat and fish and helped himself to a spoonful or three of golden potatoes au gratin. "Andie, would you like some, my dear?" he offered.

Andie looked at the enticing aromatic dish, baked in heavy cream and smothered in Gruyère cheese. "No, thank you." She helped to pass the platter down the table.

"How can you refuse that?" exclaimed Dr. Knight. "It's just divine!"

Bianca laughed. "If you want to look like that, this is not the food you eat!"

"I have no self-control," Clair offered with a laugh. "I can't resist the temptation!"

"Oh, we all know Andie has ice in her veins," Sean pointed out.

Andie's heart dropped though she retained her composure. Defiantly she straightened her back and raised her chin. *Never let them see you bleed.*

"You have to enjoy life!" proclaimed Dr. Knight. "Food, wine, sex—all the human experiences are filled with temptation!"

Erik fixed his eyes on Andie. "Well, 'the only way to get rid of a temptation is to yield to it. Resist it, and your soul grows sick with longing.'[4] Doesn't it, Dr. Knight?"

Dr. Knight nodded, taking a generous bite of his food. "Absolutely! Terrible business! Makes people do crazy things—"

"Are we still talking about the potatoes?" interrupted Evelyn.

"I think we are on a whole different subject," Sean replied.

"Very profound." Dr. Knight shook his head. "From the denial of 'self' to a timeless piece of literature!"

"Doesn't every timeless piece of art come from the denial of self?" suggested Andie, sick of the innuendoes.

Dr. Knight nodded, pointing his fork at her. "Of course, my dear. You are absolutely right!"

Erik smiled coldly. "You must be working on a masterpiece, Andie."

"What are you talking about?" asked Bianca, confused.

"Potatoes," Sean said with a grin, "we are talking about potatoes."

"What about them?" Clair laughed.

"A sacrifice for the greater good," volunteered Erik. "Something that Andie desires but she fears is detrimental to her body and soul."

Andie smiled coldly, returning Erik's glare. "Oh, I don't fear—I know. 'The best prophet of the future is the past.'"

"Oh, very good, Andie! Touché! Lord Byron!" cheered Dr. Knight, "another tragic example of denial and sacrifice! He had loved Mary Chaworth and could never find happiness with any other woman!"

"He did marry later in life," Andie pointed out. "He also had a child with his sister."

"What?!" exclaimed Sean. "Oh, that's just wrong!"

Andie laughed. "You don't seem to mind incest in the *Game of Thrones*!"

"I also like the dragons. Does not mean I want to pet one in real life."

"I like dragons, too!" exclaimed Christian. "I would like to have one!"

Andie smiled, patting the boy's head. "You do have one in your room. Good job on finishing your dinner, Monkey."

Consuelo started to clear the table, and Evelyn invited everyone back to the terrace.

"Gentlemen, I brought cigars," announced Dr. Knight. "Straight from Havana."

Andie put her arm around Christian. "Say 'good night' to everyone."

Finally, this day was over!

Chapter 22

Andie stretched out her slender, naked body, wrapped in the soft satin sheets, and looked out of the floor-to-ceiling windows at the dying daylight over the mirror-flat ocean. JC sat down on the side of the bed and kissed her shoulder, his fingers playing with her hair.

"I am sorry I had to work last weekend. I know how much you love Halloween. I'll make sure I am off next year. Okay, I'm going to hop in the shower and get ready."

"Mm-hmm," Andie responded lazily.

The sound of running water and soulful singing of Seal filled the room. Andie sat up, took a deep breath, and stretched like a kitten waking up from a nap. Here was where she belonged. JC was the one she belonged with. He was the type of man she had always envisioned she would end up with—intelligent, responsible, handsome, with a great career.

Erik has just been an infatuation, the madness of the past weekend, just that—madness. She resolved to get her emotions under control. She was in a good place; one more semester in school, her relationship moving in the right direction, her life all figured out.

She imagined her future with JC. Her stomach tightened, and it was getting difficult to breathe.

"Your turn," JC interrupted her thoughts as he emerged, his body covered in droplets of water.

Andie shook off her anxiety and took a quick shower. JC set a martini on top of the vanity. She sipped it while she applied evening makeup, accentuating her eyes, and ran the curling iron through her hair, creating soft waves around her heart-shaped face.

Dressed in a tux, JC walked into the bathroom, pulled a pair of cufflinks out of the drawer, and gestured for Andie to help him. Still nude, she cuffed his shirt and fastened his bow tie.

JC caught her hand and put it on his manhood. "You have to get dressed. Otherwise, I am not responsible for my actions."

He kissed the spot where her neck met her shoulder and drove his tongue up toward her ear, drawing it into his mouth, softly biting. He saw goosebumps run up her arms, her nipples tighten.

"I will be careful not to mess up your makeup."

JC spun her around and pushed her down against the vanity. He grabbed her hair, pulled it back, and spread her legs. His finger traveled inside her, penetrating her in circular motions.

"There you go," he said, feeling her wetness. He

dropped his pants and bent her over farther, grasping her hair in his fist. "Arch your back for me, baby."

He entered her harshly, digging his fingers into her thighs. She enjoyed his roughness and turned around to kiss him when they were done. She rinsed off carefully so as not to wet her hair and slipped on a lacy La Perla thong. JC handed her a navy-blue halter-top dress with a choker neckline and helped her to zip it up.

"You look gorgeous, baby!" He smiled.

They took the car to the InterContinental Hotel in Downtown Miami to attend one of the most spectacular annual galas of the year. An army of valets scrambled to move the cars that lined the driveway. A greeter in the brightly lit lobby directed the guests to the appropriate ballroom, where a crowd of who's who hovered around, taking pictures, drinking top-shelf liquor, and socializing. This was the ultimate Miami social event at which to be seen. The men wore tuxedos, the women evening gowns showcasing their flair for high style and fashion.

Andie hated to admit that she loved the scene. A glass of champagne in hand, she walked around, checking out the items in the silent auction, saying occasional "hellos," and stopping for casual conversations with JC's colleagues and familiars.

JC felt he was finally on top—a prominent young surgeon, his woman next to him, a part of high society. A beautiful wife was good for the career, a smart one, for life. Andie was both. He needed to lock this up. A Christmas engagement, a fall wedding—she would be done with school and her internship by then. Yes, late fall next year would be the perfect time for a wedding in Miami.

He glanced at his bride-to-be. Andie was admiring a pair of chandelier diamond and blue topaz earrings at the auction table. She picked them up, watching the light playing exquisitely on the brilliant surface. JC took the piece of jewelry from her hands and held it up beside her eyes. He looked down at the silent auction bidding sheet with its fifteen hundred dollar opening bid and signed his name.

"Well, Christmas shopping is taken care of," he said, and smiled.

"You don't have to get them for me just because I looked at them."

"Who said they are for you?" he teased, wrapping his arm around her neck and kissing her forehead. "Wow, that's a beautiful woman," he said, his eyes traveling past her.

Andie did not need to turn around to know who accompanied that beautiful woman. She could sense Erik's presence in the room with every nerve in her body. She felt them coming closer, the sweet scent of Creed Millesime Imperial—Erik's cologne of choice—getting stronger.

"Andie? What a pleasant surprise!"

Andie summoned a smile and turned around. "It is good to see you. Please, meet my boyfriend."

"Erik Lindberg." Erik extended his hand.

"Juan Cortes."

The two men exchanged tense handshakes, locking eyes for a long few seconds.

"You look lovely, Andie," Erik said, shifting his gaze. "JC, it was a pleasure to meet you."

"You too." JC's stare followed Erik into the crowd. He glanced at Andie. "Your glass is empty." He smiled and headed to the bar.

The ballroom was styled after Old Hollywood glamor. A famous Miami personality emceed the program, and the awards were followed by musical performances and dancing.

JC looked down at a message on his phone, letting him know he had been outbid on the earrings and that the auction was now closed. He picked a lock of hair off Andie's face and tucked it behind her ear. "Do you mind if we go? I am pretty tired."

"Of course." She followed him out, keeping her gaze fixed ahead of her, anxious not to come across a pair of icy blue eyes.

Back at the apartment, the windows were open, and the room had filled with salty ocean air. JC threw his tux jacket on a chair, unfastened his bow tie, and poured two glasses of wine. He walked out onto the balcony, leaned over the railing, and stared into the darkness. Andie followed him outside and reclined on his wicker couch.

"I think you should quit," stated JC.

"Excuse me?" Andie raised her eyebrow and set down her glass.

"You don't need this job, and, at this point, you really should concentrate on finishing school and on doing your supervised counseling hours. Your nanny job is a distraction."

"I see," she replied coldly. "And this is the point where you tell me you will take care of me?"

"Our relationship is moving in the right direction," JC mansplained, "and I would like us to take it to the next level, but I hardly see you. We need to work on us right now, but we cannot do that if you are never here."

"I appreciate your input," Andie said, trying to keep her voice calm, "but I do have a responsibility to that family. They took me in when I needed it the most. And I am not about to drop everything and leave just because you've decided you are ready for the relationship. Christian is a fragile child and getting used to a new person would be too much stress for him right now."

"He is not *your* child, Andie. Let them worry about him. You are going to leave after you graduate in May. What difference can a few months make?" JC was annoyed he had to explain his point to her; she surely knew he was right!

"Yes and no," she replied patiently. "First of all, everyone knows I am done in May, so everyone is prepared for me to leave then. Second, I will still need to do an internship and counseling hours and study for my license, so technically I can still take care of Christian while I am jumping through all of the hoops."

"Are you kidding me?!" JC exclaimed. "And where

do I come into the picture?! You should be concentrating on taking care of our relationship and worrying about *our* children, not playing house with that guy!"

Andie nodded. "And he-e-re we go—the real reason for this shit-fit! Well, be assured, I am not playing house with anyone. Erik has his own place. I live in his mother's house, taking care of Christian, who is not his child."

"Andie, I don't fucking care!" JC shouted. "I am done with this job of yours! I want you to quit! Is it too much to ask that I don't want my future wife to be a fucking maid?"

"Oh, thank you for that!" she snarled. "First of all, I am not a maid! Second, I don't fucking remember you proposing and me saying yes!"

"Don't play coy! You know that's all you've ever wanted! You've always known where this is heading!"

"Yes," Andie yelled back, "and then you broke up with me!"

"You will never let it go, will you? Okay! I am a horrible guy! I've made a mistake, and I said sorry a thousand fucking times! What else do you want me to do?"

"Nothing! It is you who wants me to do something! I did not start this!"

"I am offering you a chance to concentrate on your career—something that you've always wanted—and to work on our relationship, another fucking thing you've always wanted! I will take care of everything else! Sounds like a fair fucking deal to me! Why are you being so obstinate?"

"Because I don't love you anymore!" Andie shouted back, only realizing what she had said after it was too late.

A long pause filled the air.

"So where do we go from here?" asked JC calmly.

"Our separate ways," responded Andie.

She got up, marched into the bedroom, grabbed her overnight bag, and walked out of the apartment. She took an elevator down to the lobby and dialed Jo.

"Are you home?" she asked.

"Yeah, what's up?"

"Are you alone?"

"Of course I'm alone!" answered Jo. "Why?"

"Can I come over?"

"Sure."

The next thing Andie knew, she was seated on the blue suede sofa, holding a large margarita. Jo held an identical glass in her hand and attentively watched her friend. Andie took a deep breath. It was time to fess up.

"You are an idiot," concluded Jo after Andie's detailed account of the previous few months.

"I thought you might say that." Andie chuckled and took a long sip.

* * *

Andie woke early feeling unexplainably light and happy. Jo was still deep asleep in bed next to her. Quietly, so as to not to wake her friend, she slipped out of bed and walked out to the kitchen. She opened the cupboard where Jo kept her Dunkin' Donuts coffee and the filters, grabbed a jug of water from the cabinet, poured it into the coffee machine, and pressed an ON button.

Brian, awakened by the smell, walked out of his room in his boxers. "Oh, hey, babe! Did not know you were staying over." He kissed her forehead and poured himself a cup.

"It was a last-minute thing," explained Andie.

"Everything okay?"

Andie smiled. "Everything is great!"

It was a familiar and comforting morning scene: Brian cooking eggs and bacon, the girls drinking coffee, giggling at the table, and flicking through gossip magazines.

Breakfast over, Andie drove back to the mansion. She walked into her room and set down her bag. An envelope with an invitation to Evelyn's Thanksgiving party waited on the bed, next to it, a jewelry box with the diamond and blue topaz chandelier earrings.

Chapter 23

The invitation to Evelyn's Thanksgiving reception came as a surprise. Andie assumed she would be attending as Christian's caretaker, but she had not expected a stand-alone, personal invite. The event stirred up a slew of emotions and predicaments. Did Erik have anything to do with it? Does Evelyn know? And, of course, at the forefront of it all, Holy crap, what am I going to wear?!

After hours killed on Rent the Runway website and a brief deliberation with Jo, she decided on a terracotta-colored, silk wrap dress with a thigh-high slit and a V-neckline, with thin spaghetti straps crisscrossing the low open back. The elegance of the dress highlighted its understated sex appeal, which made it the top contender for Evelyn's high-society bash.

A pretty dress was nice, but it did not solve the Erik dilemma. Sha had not seen him since the gala and, despite her best efforts, her heart came to life every time he crossed her mind. Which was often. There was no denying it anymore: she was in love with him, but every instinct in her body screamed that he was trouble.

On the other hand, was Jo right? Was she an idiot? Would an affair with a guy like that really be such a bad thing?

"Christian," she repeated her mantra.

But then, Erik did not live in the mansion anymore; maybe they *could* make it work. But of course, on top of it all, Erik himself had sent her mixed signals. This all would have been so much easier if she was merely in lust with the man, but what she felt for him was much different. What Erik felt for her, she very much suspected, was the first. He already held the power to torment her; Andie decided she would not hand him the power to destroy her.

* * *

Andie slipped into the dress and wrapped the thin straps around her waist, cool silk caressing her body, softly cascading to the floor. The terracotta color accentuated the glowing bronze of her sun-kissed skin and brought out the blue in her eyes. Andie looked herself over in the mirror, first her makeup, then she turned around to check out her back. She had to admit, she looked good. Andie approvingly nodded at her reflection, collected her courage, and marched outside.

The estate has been transformed into what looked like a scene from *The Great Gatsby*. The pool was covered with transparent tiles with light glowing beneath them, turning it into a luminescent dance floor. The sounds of live music and the throaty voice of a jazz singer filled the air. High-top tables, dressed with elegant, flowing linens and decorated with fall-themed centerpieces, were scattered throughout the yard. Multiple bars were set up on the perimeter, manned and fully stocked. Delicate lights adorned the trees and walkways. The front yard was converted into a play area for the kids, where magicians and superheroes were hired to entertain them for the night. Christian, in his big boy clothes, ran around with other children, delighting in the numerous fun activities and indulgent treats.

Andie spotted Evelyn, martini in hand, encircled by adoring guests. Evelyn evaluated her from afar and nodded her approval.

As for all of the large parties, the event was run from the catering hall on the northern side of the estate. Feeling out of place, surrounded by unfamiliar faces, Andie wandered over there to look for Lucy. As expected, the young woman was preoccupied with making sure every detail ran smoothly, and Phillippe was busy bossing around an army of caterers and waiters.

To Andie's relief, she saw Matt and Susie arrive and rushed over to greet them.

"Are we the first ones here again?" exclaimed Susie. She looked chic in a metallic Halston Heritage dress, simple and elegant makeup, large hoops earrings, and an asymmetric Tiffany cuff bracelet.

"You look great," Andie complimented her.

"Aww, thank you, lady. So do you. How have you been? We need to catch up after the Thanksgiving."

"For sure. What are you guys doing tomorrow?"

"Going to my parents' house. My mom cooks for days. We will need heavy machinery to move us after dinner. Are you staying with the Lindbergs?"

"Yes."

"Okay, good. Otherwise, I would tell you to come with us," offered Susie.

Matt disappeared to the bar. When he returned a few minutes later, Sean strolled in behind him.

"Look what the cat dragged in." He nodded at his friend and handed Susie her glass.

"Is Erik here yet?" queried Sean, kissing the girls.

"No, your brother from another mother has not yet arrived," teased Matt.

"Leave it up to him to be late for his own mother's party," commented Susie.

"Where is the schmuck?" Sean asked rhetorically and pulled his phone out of his pocket to check his messages.

Bianca, wearing her signature white, approached them, bringing with her the scent of jasmine and an aura of lightness.

Andie looked around. The party was at its height and the dance floor began to fill with gracefully moving couples. Andie tried to guess how many people Evelyn had invited as the yard looked packed. She recognized several of Evelyn's guests: Dr. Knight actually managed to summon up a date, and Clair, dressed in an elegant pantsuit, was talking to the senator and his wife. Andie bit back a smile, remembering the incident at the fund-raising six months earlier.

"I need to talk to the senator," announced Susie, whose attention was drawn to the man. "I want to see if he is supporting the education bill. It would be disastrous for schools like ours if it passes."

Matt shrugged his shoulders and tagged along behind his politically active girlfriend.

Bianca pointed. "Oh, there's Erik."

Dressed in a dark Brioni suit and crisp white shirt, Erik sliced through the crowd, saying hellos, shaking hands, and exchanging kisses. On his arm was an exotically beautiful woman.

"Ladies, you look lovely," Erik said with a grin when he finally made it to their table. "This is Simone," he introduced his date. "Simone, this is Bianca, Andie, and Sean."

The woman granted them a dazzling smile.

Erik waved over the waitress. "Champaign for the ladies. Man, what are you drinking?" he asked Sean, and nodded as his friend pointed to his tumbler. "And two Patrons on the rocks, extra lime. Is Matt here yet?" he asked after the waitress disappeared to fetch the drinks.

Bianca smiled. "Susie went to give the senator a piece of her mind."

"Huh, they're here, too?" smirked Erik.

Taking advantage of the distraction of chatter at the table, Erik shifted his eyes to focus on Andie. She looked hot, despite the long dress, which he usually did not care for. This one hugged her in all the right places, accentuating her body. For a brief moment, he allowed himself to picture her naked. Feeling his stare, Andie glanced back at him. Erik's gaze lingered on her lips, making her blush, then he lowered his eyes to her breasts, indulging himself in the flashback. Andie's breath caught in her throat; an unwelcome wave of awakening washed over her body, tightening her lower stomach, her nipples hardened under the thin silk. Satisfied with the effect he had elicited, Erik turned his attention back to his date.

The senator's wife, Vicky, strutted to the table with a friendly, if somewhat pretentious, smile. "Erik, it is so nice to see you again! It was so kind of your mother to invite us!"

Andie took the opportunity to sneak away. Tears threatened to escape, stinging her eyes. With much effort, she kept them in check. Needing a sense of safety and support, she scanned the crowd, searching for Susie or Lucy.

"Who are you looking for?" A voice from behind interrupted her self-pity fest. "Could it possibly be me?"

Andie turned around. A handsome man in his mid-thirties separated from the table and walked over.

"Jonathan," he introduced himself.

"Andrea."

"Charmed." He kissed her hand. "Plus one?" he inquired.

"Solo."

"What a lucky coincidence." Jonathan smiled.

He was about six feet tall, with dirty blond hair, blue eyes, and a square jaw. Small lines around his eyes appeared when he smiled, but they did not spoil him— quite the opposite. There was something feline in his manners.

"You don't look like a Miamian," he noted. "Where is home?"

"Northern California."

"A lovely place. Did you go to school there as well?"

Andie nodded; Jonathan gestured, encouraging her to elaborate.

"Stanford," she added.

"Remarkable," Jonathan said with an approving grin. "Beauty and brains. Quite a threatening combination. No wonder you are solo."

"That's not a nice thing to say."

"I don't burden myself with the socially expected niceties."

"Convenient."

"Very," agreed Jonathan, flashing a Cheshire-cat smile. "But you don't have a drink," he noted. "Can I get you something? Anything? A glass of wine? Diamond ring? Chateaux in Switzerland?"

Andie laughed. "I will settle for a drink."

"Too soon?"

Andie squinted her eyes. "Just a little."

Jonathan waved to a waiter. "So, Andrea, far away from home, solo at the party—is there a story?"

"No story."

"Oh, I don't believe that. You do not strike me as a woman with no story."

"I am sorry to disappoint you."

"You could not if you tried," Jonathan assured her.

He was a witty conversationalist. After a while, she noticed a slight accent. His English was perfect, too perfect in fact, but a slight intonation in his voice suggested the U.S. might not be his only home. *Very sexy, indeed.*

It started to get late and Christian found her in the crowd and pulled on her hand to get her attention.

"You are Christian's nanny!" Jonathan gasped as the fact dawned on him.

"I am," confirmed Andie.

"How interesting!" A smile spread across his face, creating those faint wrinkles around outer corners of his eyes.

"Andie, I am tired. Can I just go upstairs and watch TV?" pleaded the child.

"Sure," nodded Andie. "Excuse me."

"By all means!" Jonathan threw his hands in the air.

Andie walked the boy to his room and laid out his pajamas while he showered and brushed his teeth.

"I am setting the timer for one hour." She pointed at the control. "Deal?"

The boy nodded, and she tucked him in and kissed his forehead. Andie tiptoed out of the room and shut the door.

In the dark hallway, a shadowy silhouette pushed

away from the wall, and Erik stepped into the light in front of her.

She jolted, startled. "Jesus! You scared me!"

Without saying a word, he seized her in his arms and, before she could protest, covered her mouth with his.

A commotion downstairs sprang Erik to attention. For a brief moment, he loosened his grip, then grabbed her hand and pulled her across the family room into his bedroom. Andie's mind went blank as she meekly followed him. Erik shut the door behind them, spun her around, and pinned her against the wall.

"Please, stop," whispered the girl.

"No," Erik breathed out, again demanding her lips.

Caressing her body with his experienced hands, he ran his fingers up the slit in her dress. Gasping for air, Andie arched her back, responding to his touch. He wrapped his right hand around her neck, rendering her motionless, and pulled the straps of her dress off her shoulders to expose her breasts. His mouth burned her skin with every kiss, his fingers under her dress igniting her every sense, she quivered at his caress, her treacherous body unresponsive to reason.

Suddenly, Erik pushed away, banged the wall with the palm of his hand, and walked out. Andie sank onto the floor. *A complete mindfuck!*

Still shaken, she struggled to regain her composure. All she wanted was to get back to her room and pull the blanket over her head, but she suspected Evelyn would not be keen on her breaking the norms of etiquette and just disappearing. With that, Andie got back on her feet and stumbled into Erik's bathroom. She stuck her wrists under cold running water to cool down her flushed cheeks, blotted her makeup, and ran a brush through her hair. She looked around for the perfume and picked a bottle of Creed for its sweet unisex scent.

Putting on a brave face, Andie snuck out of Erik's room and hurried downstairs. She noticed the crowd had started to thin out, and Evelyn stood on the veranda, saying her farewells to the guests. She noticed Andie and waved her over.

"Stay here with me for a moment," Evelyn requested, as several more couples departed.

"Great job, mother!" congratulated Erik, walking his date over. "Your parties are getting better every year!" He pecked Evelyn on her cheek and turned to Andie. "Andie, you look lovely, by the way." He smiled, inhaling his perfume on her. He leaned over and, as if by mistake, kissed the corner of her mouth. "My scent becomes you," he whispered.

"Honey, please don't be late tomorrow," requested Evelyn. "You know how hard Phillippe works on the Thanksgiving dinner."

"Don't worry. I will come in the morning, so I can spend some time with you and Christian."

"Great. Have a good night, dear. It was nice to meet you." Evelyn nodded to Simone.

Erik wrapped his arm around the woman's waist and

strolled to their waiting car. He smiled at his date, aware Simone wouldn't be the one he would be fantasizing about during sex later that night.

As soon as Erik's silhouette disappeared, Jonathan came up to them with a cocky grin. "Aunt." He kissed Evelyn's hand. "Wonderful party, as always."

Evelyn politely smiled. "It was lovely to see you, Jonathan."

"Dinner is at the usual time tomorrow?"

"It is. Will you be joining us?" asked Evelyn, hiding her surprise.

"Yes, I will," confirmed Jonathan. "It was a pleasure to meet you, Andrea," he said as he walked away.

Evelyn turned to Andie. "Please let Phillippe know to add an extra setting for the dinner tomorrow."

"Of course." Andie understood she was dismissed.

"You really do look lovely today, Andie."

"Thank you, Mrs. Lindberg. Good night."

Andie crossed the yard and stepped into the kitchen. Phillippe was done ordering around the caterers and now sipped a glass of wine while looking over the final invoice. He smiled when he saw her come in.

"Did you enjoy yourself?"

Andie nodded. "Yes, thank you. Mrs. Lindberg has asked me to let you know to add one more for dinner tomorrow."

"Hmmm. Okay." Phillippe shrugged his shoulders. "Do you know who?"

"Her nephew, I guess."

"Jonathan?!"

"Yeah, why? You sound surprised."

"They are not close," responded Phillippe.

"Got it. Good night."

It was good the family was not close, she thought, as she might have to turn to the old and proven method of getting over by getting under.

* * *

"Phillippe, could you please bring some port for Clair and myself?" asked Evelyn through the intercom.

He got up and poured two glasses of fine aged wine. Evelyn and Clair sat outside, enjoying the stillness of the calm November night and the view of the Bay. Clair always spent a few days at the mansion over the Thanksgiving break, a tradition going back way before Phillippe's time.

Clair patted Evelyn's hand. "You did well, dear. A wonderful evening."

Evelyn smiled a tired smile. "Thank you. Luckily, I have help. I don't think I could do this by myself anymore."

"Lucy is a gem. You have good people around you now. I am happy."

Evelyn took a deep breath. "We will lose Andie soon. I can't even start thinking about the nanny situation again."

"She is a good one," Clair agreed.

Evelyn turned and looked at her friend. "What's

wrong with our sons, Clair? We put this lovely, bright girl under their noses, and nothing! They still run around with hoodlums!"

"Where did we go wrong?" Clair shook her head with a smile.

They sat in silence, nursing their port. They did not need words to feel comfortable around each other. The friendship that went back decades had formed a bond stronger than blood. On a night like this one, many years ago, when Rick was absent as usual and Clair had found out her husband was having an affair, and the two of them felt forsaken by everyone, they became closer than friends, finding comfort in each other. They had never spoken about it, but they did not need to; their closeness afforded them the luxury of silence.

* * *

Thanksgiving morning brought a spell of colder weather. Andie slipped into a Juicy velour jumpsuit and peeked her head into the kitchen. Phillippe, who for the occasion hired a sous chef, looked like a crazy professor in his laboratory. Steam poured out of different pots, pans sizzled with aromatic concoctions, the sound of the knife hitting the chopping board echoed throughout the room, and so many different smells competed with each other. Phillippe moved around, opening and closing the lids, the fridge, and the oven doors, tasting his creations. He threw a dash of salt into a bowl, and Andie imagined an evil laugh would come out of him at any moment, followed by a colorful explosion, but Phillippe only grinned and nodded when he noticed her.

"Are you going to be in the family room?" he asked.

"Aha."

"I will send you kids some hot chocolate," he said with a wink.

Christian was already up when she knocked on his door. He sat in bed playing with his tablet.

"Hey, Monkey," Andie greeted him with a kiss. "Did you brush your teeth?"

The boy nodded.

"Come, let's watch the Macy's Thanksgiving Day Parade. Phillippe will make us hot chocolate."

Christian jumped out of bed. "Can I have marshmallows, too?"

"Sure!"

"And cookies?"

Andie smiled. "Don't push it. You have to have breakfast first."

They cozied up on the couch in front of the TV as they sipped bittersweet hot chocolate and giggled.

The mansion was filled with commotion. The dining room was decorated with Thanksgiving-themed linens and tableware, yellow and orange flower centerpieces adorned the long table. The house staff, Consuelo and Javier, as well as Phillippe and his partner had all been invited to the holiday dinner along with Evelyn's guests—another tradition Evelyn had started way back when.

Sean arrived early in the afternoon and walked

straight into the library. Erik was stretched out on the couch in front of the TV, a whiskey tumbler in hand.

"Man, you started without me!" Sean chided jokingly. "What'ya drinking?"

Erik nodded at the bar cart. "There's Blue Label and Macallan."

Sean fixed himself a drink, crashed onto a large leather chair, and squinted at the game on the screen. "Who's winning? Did you have a chance to talk to Matt last night?"

"A little. Why?"

"You know he is planning to propose to Susie today?"

"You kidding me? Okay, wow, good for him."

"Yeah," chuckled Sean, "another one bites the dust."

Erik raised his drink. "To a fallen comrade!"

"Speaking of, is Simone coming for dinner?"

"Of course not. My mom would have a shit-fit. But you know who is coming? Jonathan."

"What the fuck?"

Erik chuckled. "Didn't you see him talking to Andie all night at the party?"

"Seriously, dude? You think he is coming because of her?"

"Probably. And to piss me off, of course."

"Are you still giving money to Liz?" inquired Sean.

Erik nodded.

"You got to tell Andie he is a douche."

"She might consider it a conflict of interest," Erik pointed out. "Besides I am pretty sure, I am on her shit list."

"Uh-oh what did you do now, asshole?"

"Nothing," Erik said dismissively. "I hear people. We should probably join everyone."

They walked out to the grand room where Evelyn, Clair, and Phillippe's partner, Greg, lounged, enjoying the wine and a lazy afternoon. Newly arrived Jonathan lingered by the bar in need of a drink. The men greeted each other with polite coldness.

"I am sorry about your mother," said Sean, after the men exchanged handshakes.

"Thank you," Jonathan replied, taking a sip of his whiskey.

"When did you get into town?" asked Sean, not sure what else to talk about.

"A few weeks ago."

The three of them walked out onto the front patio and sat down by the firepit.

"You've been gone a while. How long?" inquired Sean.

"About six months," answered Jonathan. "I stayed in Stockholm with my mother for the most part but was able to fit in a few short fun trips."

"Oh yeah? Where to?" asked Sean.

"Ibiza, Saint Tropez . . ."

"Nice," nodded Sean. "Are you in Miami for good?"

"For now."

They turned around when they heard Christian and Andie's voices.

Jonathan smiled. "A hot nanny. How romantic. Is

either one of you fucking her?" He scanned their faces and laughed. "What? Neither one? Gentlemen, you are losing your edge! Not that it would've mattered either way, would it?"

Erik's jaw tightened as his eyes drilled into his cousin.

"Stay away from her, dude," warned Sean.

"Sean, my friend, you should know by now, empty threats don't work on me—"

He stopped abruptly as Christian ran out to the patio and climbed onto Erik's lap. Andie followed him and sat down in the chair next to Sean.

Jonathan smiled at her. "Andrea, you are a breath of fresh air in this house. But I still would love to hear your story. On the other hand, I can probably just ask Erik to let me take a look at his PI report. Do you still have it, Erik?"

Andie felt like she got slapped on the face. Nonetheless, she was not about to give anyone the satisfaction of confronting Erik publicly. Besides, for some reason, it looked like that was exactly what Jonathan had hoped for. Instead, she got up, walked inside the house, and sunk down into the chair next to the bar.

"Oh, look at that, the old geezer is here," nodded Jonathan at Dr. Knight crossing the yard.

"Hi, fellows!" Dr. Knight smiled, coming up the steps. "Jonathan, I am sorry about your mother."

"Thank you, James."

"James, what are you drinking?" asked Erik as he strode into the house.

Dr. Knight followed him. "What are you pouring?"

"Whiskey? Macallan, Blue Label?"

"Oh, you pulled out the good stuff for the occasion! Blue Label."

Erik fixed the man a drink, then poured a glass of white wine and walked over to hand it to Andie. She drilled her eyes into him, and while Dr. Knight distracted everyone in the room with his greetings, she hissed at Erik.

"You had me investigated?"

"Would you expect me to let anyone from the street around my family without knowing anything about them?" responded Erik coldly.

"Christian, dear, would you like to play for us what you have been rehearsing?" suggested Evelyn.

The boy shook his head and slid into Andie's chair.

"Come on, Monkey, you have been working so hard on it," Andie cheered him.

"You want to do it together?" Erik patted the boy's head, walked over to the piano, and sat down on the bench.

Christian joined him and gracefully lifted his hands. The sweet sound of Beethoven's "Für Elise" filled the room.

He looks so much like his father, thought Evelyn, *and so much like Erik*. The two of her boys . . . the idyllic family she had tried and failed to create. She took a deep breath and thanked the universe for what she did have. It was Thanksgiving, after all.

Chapter 24

"Jeanne, can you hear me?" barked Erik as he settled in the back seat of the car.

"No need to yell, I can hear you perfectly," answered the calm, friendly voice on the other end.

"Okay, good. Sorry. I misplaced my conference agenda for this week. Can you resend?"

"Sure. Are you in London already?"

"Just landed." Erik could hear the clicking of the keyboard as Jeanne typed a quick message and hit SEND.

"You should have the agenda and your schedule in your inbox," she said using the British pronunciation of the word *schedule*, "I also reformatted your presentation and sent it to the coordinator at the conference, so you should be all set."

"Thanks. Have a good one."

"You too, Erik. Let me know if you need anything else."

The familiar drive into the city lulled him into a trance-like state. With an unblinking stare, he looked out the window at the wet black asphalt and the row houses on the outskirts of the capital. In the distance,

London, stripped of color as if sketched with a number-two pencil, grew more prominent against the backdrop of the gray sky.

The suburbs gave way to stately buildings and broad avenues. The car turned onto Piccadilly, drove past Green Park, naked and in hibernation, and pulled up in front of a building more Parisian than British in its exterior. White-gloved doormen opened the double doors and escorted him into the opulent lobby of the legendary Ritz Hotel.

His room was not yet ready. Through the Long Gallery aligned with the palm trees, Erik wandered into the restaurant to grab a bite to eat.

"Pardon me, sir." The maître d' stopped him. "We require our guests to wear a jacket. If you do not have one, our concierge will be delighted to loan one to you."

"That won't be necessary." Of course. He'd forgotten where he was.

Erik raised the collar of his coat and stepped out into the street. Almost immediately, his nose started to drip, assaulted by a gusty wind. The slush under his feet and biting chill cooled his desire for a walk and Erik dove into the closest restaurant. He sat down at the bar and threw his coat onto the chair next to his.

"A pint of Guinness and a burger with chips," he ordered.

A sip of stout took the edge off. Erik leaned back in his chair and looked at the news on the TV that hung over the bartender's head. The sense of anxiety had not left him for weeks, but he could not pinpoint the cause of it. Still, Erik struggled to shake it off. The foul mood haunted him all the way to London, and now that he was here, he wondered what it would take to change it. The conference he was attending would only occupy a few hours out of his day, and then he was free to do as he pleased. Finding what would please him, however, had proved to be a challenge. Nonetheless, there was one thing he looked forward to: Friday night dinner with Beatrix. Besides the obvious, he valued her friendship, and at this moment he craved the comfort of her company just as much as sex.

* * *

They agreed to meet at 8 p.m. at the bar at the Dorchester. Stepping into the lavishly decorated lobby, Erik found himself transported into the extravagant splendor of bygone years. A row of marble Corinthian columns with gilded details framed the grand entrance and the Promenade. Bedecked with French tapestries, dazzling chandeliers, and furnishings upholstered in deep green and accented in gold leaf details to stand out against the orange marble, the hotel embodied luxury and glamour. Gold, marble, and velvet echoed throughout the public spaces and into the opulent guest rooms.

Erik followed the sound of piano music into a curved bar at the end of the Promenade. Outfitted in mahogany and mirrors and topped with dancing glass flames designed by Thierry Despond, the bar was one of the most legendary spots in London.

"Club soda," Erik answered the barman who stepped forward ready to take his drink order.

Beatrix did not make him wait long, and moments after the barman set down his glass, Erik saw her glide toward him in an elegant cream-colored dress.

"You look more beautiful every time I see you," he said, standing up.

"Oh, Erik! It is so good to see you!" She kissed him, then rubbed the lipstick off his cheek with her long, manicured fingers.

They continued on to dinner at one of the hotel's restaurants—the three-Michelin-starred Alain Ducasse—and were seated at a table by the window. The sommelier handed Erik the wine list, ready to educate him and to make his recommendations.

"Chateau Lafite, 2014," Erik interrupted.

The man returned with a bottle, opened it, and set the cork on the table, then continued with the ritual of tasting. After enduring the show, Erik hoped to be left alone to enjoy his wine and company in peace. But an army of waiters and runners continued to helicopter around.

"I hate this place," confessed Erik after they ordered.

Beatrix smiled. "Yes, but I like it."

"And that's why we are here." Erik kissed her hand.

The first course of Dorset crab in caviar sauce arrived,

followed by the entrees of filet de turbot with clams and a perfectly cooked duck with turnip and orange.

"I saw Natalie a few weeks ago," Beatrix mentioned casually as they moved on to cheese and dessert. "She came to Paris. We had sex. Hope you don't mind?"

"Not at all."

"She said you had a fight."

"No fight."

"She said you were rude to her at a party."

"She was being a bitch." Erik wished she would let it go.

"She was upset. Something about you and some girl. I did not understand. A maid, she said."

Erik poured the wine, his jaw tightened. "I did not have a date for the party, so I invited Andie, Christian's nanny. Can we change the subject?"

Beatrix raised her eyebrow and observed him tentatively. "Okay." She picked up her glass and twirled it in her fingers. "Ah!" she exclaimed. "I met her! At that disco, in Miami!"

Erik nodded, getting tenser.

"Ahhh, I remember! Pretty girl."

Erik looked at Beatrix with a dry smile. "Would you like me to take you Christmas shopping tomorrow?"

She squinted at him, confused by his hostile reaction to the casual conversation, then laughed and snapped her fingers. "Oh, my Erik! You are in love! With the girl!"

"No, that is not it." Erik shook his head, took a sip

of his wine, and stared into the space in front of him for a long few moments. He put the glass down and looked at Beatrix. "That is exactly it."

She smiled and patted his hand. "Oh, my darling!"

They walked out of the restaurant and into the bar, which was now dimly lit. Erik waved over the barman.

"A glass of Dom Perignon," ordered Beatrix.

"Macallan M. A double."

The barman jumped to attention; with a seven-hundred-pound price tag for the drink, he had just been guaranteed a sizable tip.

"So," murmured Beatrix, "does this mean we don't have sex?"

Erik smiled at her. "Would you like me to take you right here on top of this bar, *ma chére*?"

Beatrix laughed and petted his hand. "Come."

* * *

The monotonous humming of the jet engines and the vast nothingness of the Atlantic Ocean had long become a constant in his life. The variable was either a movie he watched, or a slew of financial spreadsheets and legal documents he worked on while in flight.

Watching Kate Beckinsale in skintight black leather kick vampire and Lycan ass for the tenth time still entertained him. He had heard somewhere that she was a vegan or vegetarian and did not drink. That fact put a damper on his fantasy. Was no one perfect?

Erik's mind's eye turned to the last interaction he

had had with Andie at the Thanksgiving dinner. Jonathan. He hoped she would not do anything so stupid as to sleep with his cousin, though he recognized he might have pushed her to do just that. The thought made him nauseous. Jonathan was probably the only person in the world he would not be able to get over her being with. Erik had always been an "equal opportunity" kind of guy; women were entitled to have fun just as much as men, and sexuality was not something to be ashamed of. Jonathan was an exception to that rule. He and his cousin had a history—an unpleasant one. And knowing Jonathan, he would try to get Andie into bed, especially if he knew how Erik felt about her.

Oh, yes, and there was that. His feelings so masterfully exposed by Beatrix. Andie had made it clear she wanted nothing to do with him. But then, what had he offered her? Not much indeed—dinner and a maybe. Was he ready to offer more now? He thought so. Would she change her mind if he committed to a relationship? Oh, fuck! He sounded like a teenage girl!

No matter. He would have to try again. And again, if necessary. He was old enough to know how rare it was to find someone special, and he didn't want to live with regrets. He hoped he could come up with the right words when he saw her, and he prayed he had not pushed her away for good.

Chapter 25

The tree, a tall Noble fir, arrived with much ado on the first Saturday of December. It was given an enthusiastic welcome and erected in the corner of the grand room, between the piano and the entrance. While it stood there naked satiating the air with its scent, boxes of Christmas decorations emerged out of storage and were piled around the room. The next day, the effort of bedecking the house had commenced with Lindberg-like efficiency and grandeur. There were no ornaments from the local craft store or mismatched sentimental treasures. There were, however, color coordinated, perfectly placed decorations, ribbons, and wreaths. Every staircase got adorned with rich garlands with the clusters of metallic ornaments and bows affixed to them, giving the house a chic and majestic look. Textures, tones, and overall gold, silver, white, and purple color schemes played off each other and created a unified décor.

Decorating the house for Christmas was not child's play, it was a well-coordinated production. Therefore, Christian's participation and input were not required. Hoping to breathe some Christmas into this Elsa's ice palace from Disney's *Frozen,* Andie asked for and was permitted to get a tree for Christian's room. Grateful for small blessings, she took Christian on a treasure hunt through Cracker Barrel, Target, and Michaels. They decorated their tree with strings of lights and the most colorful, shiny mismatched ornaments they could find. Andie showed Cristian how to cut snowflakes and stars out of aluminum foil, and together they tied them to the branches. After they were done, the entire household made a pilgrimage to their tree and congratulated Christian on his creative masterpiece.

Andie hadn't seen much of Erik since Thanksgiving. He traveled most of December, and when he was in town and stopped by the house, she was either at school or out with Jo. She, however, had met with Jonathan a few times. Once for coffee after school and once for a drink, after Christian had gone to sleep. Always a gentlemen, witty and charming, he began to capture her interest. Sadly, like a sore muscle, her heart ached every time Erik crossed her mind. She was determined to apply an ice pack to curb that pain. Jonathan ought to be her ice pack, she decided; it seemed he would be happy to oblige. So when Jonathan invited her to a New Year's Eve party at a fabulous mansion on Star Island, Andie eagerly agreed. On one condition: she could bring Jo and Corey.

"It's a date, beautiful. Can't wait to ring in the New Year with you." Jonathan responded to her request flashing his Cheshire-cat smile. "Have a great trip! See you when you are back."

The day after Andie took her last exam, she packed her bags and set off for California to visit her parents for the holidays. She bought a few small gifts for Christian and placed them under their tree, securing the promise he would not open her presents until the night before Christmas. She looked forward to sleeping in her old room, eating her dad's famous paella, reading by the fire, going to Christmas shows, and browsing the galleries in Carmel. Her time off with parents and friends flew by too fast, and two days after Christmas, Andie returned to Florida, in time for New Year's.

Everyone knows New Year's Eve is best celebrated at a house party, away from the amateurs that come out of hibernation once a year. It is best celebrated at a multimillion-dollar mansion, with first-row seats to firework displays, with an unobstructed view of the InterContinental Hotel and its Big Orange Countdown, surrounded by a few hundred of one's closest friends.

Andie took a bottle of Veuve out of the fridge, poured two flutes, walked into a small bathroom, where Jo was finishing her makeup, and set one of the glasses on top of the sink.

"Oh, thank you, girlie. I am almost done. Is Corey ready?"

"He is," answered Corey from the living room.

Andie joined him in front of the TV and stretched out on the couch. *He looked tanned and well-rested after vacation in Cancun*, she thought.

"Did you have a good visit with your parents?" asked Andie, making a small talk with her friend's new man.

"We did! They loved Jo."

"It's because I am fabulous," Jo interjected, laughing as she paraded into the room, revealing her glamorous New Year's look.

"Jonathan is on his way to pick us up," announced Andie. She put down her phone and picked up her champagne.

"Jonathan," humphed Jo.

Andie rolled her eyes at her friend's disapproval.

"I am simply saying," continued Jo, "if you are trying to get over by getting under, you are trying to get under the wrong guy. Sleeping with Jonathan will not help you get over Erik, but it will surely complicate shit."

"I just want to have a good time tonight. The party should be amazing, and I am glad Jonathan invited us." The headlights of a car pulling into the driveway flashed into the room. "I think he's here!"

Happy he was not dragged into the touchy conversation, Corey rushed to open the door. Jonathan and a woman in her mid-thirties, festively dressed, entered the house. *She was well-groomed but not particularly pretty*, thought Andie.

"Happy New Year, everyone!" Jonathan greeted. "This is a friend of mine, Liz."

"It is nice to meet you both!" Jo effused. "This is my boyfriend, Corey. Do you guys want a drink before we go?"

"No, thank you. Let's get going, we have champagne in the limo," Jonathan prompted them. Everyone followed him to the car eager to start the celebration.

Andie was not sure whether Erik and the gang had opted for the same plans, and quite honestly, she was even less sure whether she hoped they would or not. She had mixed feelings about going with Jonathan. There was clearly some weird family history, and she knew this would provoke a reaction from Erik, but then, was that a good thing? Jo did not seem to think so. Frankly, under normal circumstances, neither would she, but contradicting emotions had been clouding her judgment lately. She felt a jolt of guilt when she saw Erik and Sean in the crowd, but she pushed the nagging feeling away and washed it down with champagne.

Jo nudged her out of her contemplation. "Come, there's Susie and Matt!"

They hadn't seen the happy couple since their Thanksgiving engagement.

One of the pleasures of the first six months of the engagement period is all of the congratulations and the excited recitations of the D-Day. Susie, blushed with joy and in an uncharacteristic high-pitched voice, recapped the moment of the Big Bang. The main subject of the conversation—her flawless three-carat, round, Cathedral pavé diamond ring. Proudly, she stood tall, all five feet four inches of her—plus five-inch heels, of course.

"That's a beautiful ring, girl!" Jo admired the brilliant perfection on Susie's French-manicured finger.

Matt laughed. "Cartier! Putting the price on love for almost two hundred years!"

"Is this something you would want?" Corey quietly asked Jo.

"No, I am more of a Tacori kinda girl. I know a jeweler who will give us a good price," Jo whispered back, exchanging conspiratorial glances with her boyfriend. She looked past him and noticed Sean and Erik collecting their drinks by the bar. *Oh, fuck, this can't be good!*

Sean saw them as well, his facial expression did not leave room for interpretation. "What the fuck? What is she doing with Jonathan? And Liz?" Sean could not contain his astonishment at the unpleasant surprise.

Erik turned around to look who his friend was referring to and immediately felt the proverbial punch in the gut. He ran his hand through his hair, struggling to suppress an overwhelming desire to knock out his cousin.

Meanwhile, Jonathan, bored with the small talk, left Andie in the care of her friends and stepped away to pay his respect to their host. Liz trailed behind him.

"Oh, hey, guys!" Jo smiled at Erik and Sean as they approached. "Happy New Year! Meet my boyfriend, Corey."

"Nice to meet you, man." Erik shook his hand. "Welcome to Florida. I trust you have the best guide?"

Corey beamed with pride. "Yeah, thanks! Jo *is* the best."

With everyone's attention on the two happy couples,

Erik turned to Andie. "Why are you doing this?" he asked, dismayed, in a half-whisper.

She opened her mouth to reply but got interrupted by Jonathan and Liz who had rejoined the group and inserted themselves between the two of them.

Liz brushed Erik's hand. "Happy New Year! It's great to see you! It's been too long."

"It's good to see you, too, Lizzy." Erik smiled only with his lips, barely acknowledging her kiss. "Excuse me." He walked away, ostensibly to find the bathroom.

"They used to date," explained Jonathan, caressing Andie's back. "My poor cousin has lusted after her forever. Liz and I are really good friends. We share a kind of bond."

Andie watched Liz disappear after Erik. She raised her glass and finished her bubbly.

"Come, let's get you another drink," Jonathan offered.

"Actually, let me sit down. These shoes are killing me."

Andie found a loveseat and, feeling deflated, sank into the ultra-chic white cushions. *Of course,* she thought, *as soon as I give him the benefit of the doubt, another woman pops up. When will you learn, you idiot? He is just a player. I hate him!* Any remorse Andie might have felt earlier in the evening for going out with Jonathan flew out the window. She will sleep with him, she decided.

"He is not a good guy, you know. Jonathan," Sean said as he appeared out of nowhere and sat down beside her.

Andie smiled a tired smile. "You are a good friend, Sean. I know you are loyal to Erik, but that's not a reason to diss Jonathan. Even though Erik hates him, it does not mean Jonathan is the bad guy here. And I don't see why everyone is so bent out of shape about me going out with him. Erik is not too worried. He is probably hooking up with Liz somewhere as we speak. Since he was sooo in love with her! Well, now is his chance to get her back. She seems willing enough!"

"Liz?" Sean looked at her confused. "Honey, I don't know what exactly Jonathan told you, but there is nothing going on between Erik and Liz. It will never happen! What did Jonathan tell you about his relationship with her, by the way?"

"Just that. Erik was pursuing her, and that Liz and Jonathan are friends. They share a *bond*, he said." She shook her head bitterly.

"Well, *bond* is one way of putting it, I guess. It's really fucked up. Andie, Liz cheated on Erik with Jonathan. You know, we all grew up together and were really close. After she learned she was pregnant, she tried to convince Erik it was his. She didn't know Erik knew all about them. Jonathan wanted nothing to do with her or the baby. He refused to take a DNA test or to give her any financial help. Erik felt bad for her and somehow responsible for what happened. He still helps her with money."

Andie felt like she was going to be sick. "Excuse me." She got up and walked away.

* * *

Erik splashed water on his face, looked in the mirror at his enraged reflection, drew a deep breath—a tool he learned at the shrink's office—and walked out of the bathroom. It took some time for his pupils to adjust to the dim light of the hallway.

"Erik . . ."

His ears recognized the voice before his eyes could see the person. "Liz," he said with a nod and marched past her in the narrow corridor.

"Erik, wait!"

He turned around, suddenly feeling tired. Of everything.

"Erik, we didn't part on the best terms—"

"You think?"

"Stop that!" reprimanded Liz. "I have blamed myself for the longest time, but then, I realized we both were to blame—"

"You slept with my cousin," Erik pointed out unemotionally.

"You became distant—for weeks!" Liz exclaimed. "You even forgot my birthday!"

Erik shook his head in disbelief. "There lies your whole essence, Liz. I had been in a major accident that killed my brother and his wife! And *you* felt forgotten because I hadn't bought you an expensive trinket?"

"I should have been more supportive. I am sorry."

"Lizzy, you have nothing to be sorry about. You are who you are—"

"I know, right?!" she interjected. "I wanted to see, since it has been a few years, maybe we can try again? We had a good thing going."

Erik smiled. He could not even be mad at her. How could one be mad at a brainless puppy who had pissed all over the bed? "Liz, Jonathan or not, there was nothing that would have kept us together. Don't take me wrong, it was a fucked up thing you've done, both of you, but it did not change the outcome. Let me ask you something, though. Why are you here? I didn't think you and Jonathan were even on speaking terms."

"Jonathan invited me to the party. I think he is making an effort. I think he wants to get to know the baby and this is his way of starting the relationship."

Wow, apparently delusions are clinical. "I wouldn't hold your breath," he said out loud.

Erik rushed out of the house and headed straight to the outdoor bar. "Patron on the rocks, extra lime."

He longed for this nightmare of an evening to end, but the party had barely started. Leaving now would mean leaving Andie in Jonathan's care—not his first choice.

Speaking of . . .

He looked around. Andie had kicked off her stilettos and now sat on the edge of the dock, dangling her feet over the water. Her upper lip was curling, a tell-tell sign that she was more than a little tipsy.

Erik grabbed a bottle of water, walked over, and parked himself next to her. "Here, drink this." She was about to protest when he interrupted her. "Your lip is curling. You will be hurting tomorrow."

The argument seemed to have convinced her. She took the bottle and gulped its contents. Erik put his hand on hers. She lifted her eyes to meet his.

"How are you doing?" he asked softly.

Andie shrugged her shoulders and turned away to stare at the water. How could she tell him how much she hated him, how much she wanted to hurt him, how much she wanted to throw herself into his arms?

"Another day in Paradise," she replied.

"I have fucked things up, haven't I?" he admitted.

She did not answer. Instead, she got to her feet, wanting to leave. Erik caught her hand and sprung up, blocking her path. He grabbed her by the shoulders.

"Andie, please don't run. Don't push me away. You are the bravest girl I know, so please be brave for me. Take a chance. I know what you feel because I feel the same way—"

"I want to have sex with you," Andie interrupted him, matter-of-factly.

Erik cleared his throat, not sure if he had understood her correctly. "Oh . . . okay," he answered, proceeding with caution in this uncharted territory.

Andie raised her left eyebrow, daring him to challenge her. Erik collected himself, desperately trying to keep a straight face.

"I am going to be a shrink," she reasoned, "and I can analyze myself. I don't want to date you, but I am smart enough to know I have a crush on you. And I think having you as a forbidden fruit only makes things worse. You are a fantasy. If I have sex with you, the mystery of it will dissipate—voila, problem solved."

Erik nodded. "Makes sense."

"What is your schedule like the next few weeks?"

Erik pulled his iPhone out of his pocket and opened the calendar. "I am around. When is good for you?" he asked in his best all-business tone, hiding a smile.

Andie thought for a few moments. "Next Saturday works. Mrs. Lindberg and Christian are away, and I am off after 7 p.m. Sorry, I know it's a weekend."

"It's okay. I'll take one for the team," Erik reassured her. "Saturday works. I am adding you to my schedule. Bring an overnight bag, just in case you don't feel like dealing with Uber."

Andie nodded and headed toward the party. "Will do."

"Andie," Erik called to her.

She pivoted. "Hmm?"

"Out of curiosity, why don't you want to date me?" he asked.

"I don't think you know how, and I don't have time to teach you." Andie spun around and walked away without giving him a second look.

Jonathan, having observed the scene from afar, turned to Liz. "You really are useless."

Chapter 26

Erik wasn't sure if Andie would keep their appointment. Neither was Andie. But when Saturday came and she had not canceled, he dared to hope. At 8 p.m., he received a call from the front desk, announcing he had a visitor. Erik opened the door, awaiting the arrival of his fascinating date. He would never have admitted to anyone, least of all to Andie, how excited and anxious he felt.

Andie walked in, quiet and uncertain, dressed in a simple short blue suede A-line skirt, a stark white button-down GAP shirt, and black, strappy high-heeled sandals. She barely wore any makeup, and her hair cascaded down her shoulders.

Not saying a word, Erik gestured to her to come in. He brought out a bottle of Dom he had been chilling in the fridge and poured two flutes. They sat down in the living room on the two white leather couches, facing each other, separated by a low coffee table.

Andie sipped her champagne, too nervous to raise her eyes to him. Erik watched her closely, trying to follow her cue. Finally, she gathered her courage, stood up, and walked over. Still not saying a word, she straddled him, encased his face in her hands, and kissed him. Deep. Sensual. Her tongue caressed his mouth. Erik stayed still, resting his hands by his sides. He let her unbutton his shirt and explore his body. She bit his lip slightly and brushed the tips of her nails across his chest. Andie pulled back and gazed into his eyes. She looked so beautiful and sexy, her pouty lips swollen and bright red from kissing.

"How do you want it to be?" Erik asked quietly. "Am I allowed to touch you?"

She blushed. "Yes."

Erik ran his fingers up the silky skin of her legs. He clutched the back of her head and drew her toward him, greedily meeting her mouth again. Turned on by her taking control, giving herself to him with confidence and no hesitation, he unzipped her skirt, pulled it over her head, and tossed it to the floor. Then he unbuttoned her shirt and threw it in the same direction, leaving her bare, wearing just her heels and a black lacy thong. Holding her, Erik stood up. Andie wrapped her long legs around his waist as he carried her into the bedroom and sat her down on the bed.

Resting on her elbows, Andie watched him undress, feeling empowered by having initiated their encounter. Slowly, recognizing he was on display and being judged, Erik peeled off his shirt and unzipped his jeans. He was not wearing underwear.

He set his knee on the bed, grabbed Andie's ankles,

and pulled her toward him. He threw her legs over his shoulders, taking a moment to admire her statuesque body. With his thumbs, Erik picked her thong and slid it off. He kissed her leg, his lips traveling up her inner thigh, up her toned stomach to her breasts. He sucked her nipple into his mouth, softly biting it, making her hurt, just a little.

Andie gasped for air, trembling. Erik slapped her breast and reached between her legs, stimulating her until she cried out, arching her back.

"Please," she muttered.

He looked into her eyes. "Please? You want me?" he whispered.

"Yes . . ."

"Yes what, Andie?"

"I want you," she exhaled.

"Sorry, did not hear you. What is it?"

She batted her fists against his shoulders and giggled, "I hate you!"

"What do you want, baby?" he insisted.

"I want you."

Erik assaulted her mouth and entered her, thrusting with the full force of his pent-up energy. Andie called out his name, driving him mad, her body responding to his every touch. He paused and collected himself, then resumed to expertly guide their motion and amplify their sensation.

She shuddered, and as she did, Erik allowed release for himself. Exhausted, he collapsed on top of her, resting his head on her chest. Andie lay quietly, affectionately playing with his hair, running her nails up and down his back. She brushed the blond locks off his forehead and kissed his face. Spent physically and emotionally, Erik rolled off onto a pillow and pulled Andie into his arms, resting her back against his chest.

He dozed off for a quarter of an hour or so, and when he awoke, he was ready for her again. He pushed her down on her stomach, propped the pillow under her hips, and roughly entered her from behind.

"Is this what you've wanted?" he asked, digging his fingers into her flesh. Impaling her harshly, he grabbed her by the back of her head, pulling on her hair, and slapped her hard, leaving a red mark on her skin. He sank his teeth into the sensitive spot on her neck, making her scream. He made her come again, leaving both of them breathless.

* * *

When Erik woke up in the morning, his bed was empty. He chuckled; if nothing else, she was consistent. Erik hopped into the shower, letting the hot water soothe his sculpted, tanned body. He poured shower gel over his chest, fragrant bubbles soaping over his skin. Finally, he walked out of the shower, shook the water off his hair, wrapped the towel over his hips, and crossed the living room to the opposite side of the apartment and into the guest bedroom.

Andie was peacefully asleep, her naked body wrapped in soft white Italian bedsheets. A silk mask covered her eyes, protecting her from the morning light.

"Okay," said Erik quietly to himself, "let's mess up this bed now."

He slipped in next to her and peeled off the sheets. He traced the arch of her neck with his tongue and gently fondled her breast. She took a deep breath, waking up with a smile, and reached up to her face to take off her eye mask. Erik stopped her. He pinned her wrists over her head and latched onto her neck. Oh, the blindfold was working for him this morning.

Holding her in place, he reached down, caressing her until he knew she was ready. With his knees, he opened her legs, leaving her exposed and aching. Erik looked down and allowed himself a private moment to admire her body, with no one, including her, to intrude or interrupt. Finally, Erik pulled off the mask and, holding eye contact, he entered her with measured thrusts until he drove her to cry out in another climax. Spent, he crashed down onto the pillow. Andie propped herself up on her elbows, butterfly-kissing his face, gently tracing his features with the tip of her fingers. He raised his gaze to meet hers. She did not need to say anything; he could read everything he needed to know in her expression. Erik kissed her hand, got up, and wrapped the towel around his waist.

"I know, you need coffee." He smiled.

Andie climbed out of bed, put on her shirt, and

followed him out to the kitchen. She mounted a chair, watching him make coffee. He turned around and smiled, her bright blue eyes and Farrah Fawcett bed-hair almost inspired him for another round. Saved by the bell, his phone sounded, demanding his attention. Erik read the text message and looked at Andie.

"Are you hungry?" He laughed. "Never mind, you are always hungry. Do you want to meet Sean for brunch?"

Andie nodded. "Uh-huh." Suddenly unsure, she looked back at Erik. "Unless you want to keep this on the down-low."

Erik shook his head and chuckled. "I can't believe you just said that." He kissed the top of her head and handed her the mug.

He typed: *Will meet you in an hour at Books & Books. I am with Andie.*

"Go get ready," Erik instructed. Knowing what she was thinking, he added, "Leave your bag here. I am not done with you."

When they got out of the Uber forty-five minutes later and strolled down Lincoln Road, to Erik, it felt so natural and peaceful to hold her hand. He did not have to feel embarrassed running into the guys she had dated before him, or into some cheesy douchebag she had fucked. He had met JC, a guy he could respect; the fact she had dated him before did not diminish his self-worth. In other words, he was in good company. That meant a lot. Especially in Miami and New York, where socialites were passed around like cocktails.

If Sean was surprised they were walking toward him holding hands, he did not let on.

"Hey, kids," he said as he got up to greet them, "Andie, you look hot, as usual."

A waitress in a black T-shirt that read I CAN'T SLEEP UNLESS I AM SURROUNDED BY BOOKS in white text came to take their drink order.

"I'll have a mimosa, please," Andie said, a smile lingering on her lips.

"Two," nodded Erik.

"Ugh, what the hell, make it all around," conceded Sean. "So, both of you look good." He smiled, staring at them. "Now that you two are dating—"

"Oh, we are not dating," Andie corrected him. "We're just hooking up. Excuse me." She got up to find the washroom.

Sean looked at his friend, a question mark written all over his face. Erik laughed and shrugged his shoulders.

"If this is what she needs to tell herself to justify being with me, I am fine with it. Besides," Erik threw his hands in the air, "if Andie wants me for her boy-toy, who am I to argue?"

Sean shook his head. "You two should stick together. You are just perfect for each other. You are both fucked up!"

The End

Acknowledgments

This debut novel took over eighteen months to write and produce. I could not have done this work without the support and help of those close to me.

With this, I would like to thank the people who helped to make this book happen:

Ellen Frazer-Jameson for the mentorship and encouragement, Stacy O'Nell of SO Photography for the beautiful pictures, talented Dimitry Chamy of 2urn for the book cover design, Carol Rosenberg for her help with the manuscript, and Gary Rosenberg for the interior layout. A special recognition to Susie K Taylor for her vivid and colorful readings of the book.

Thank you to my friends who inspire me and support me.

Endnotes

1. "Winter is coming." Reference from *Game of Thrones*.

2. "... a front seat and a back seat and a window in between." Reference from *Sabrina*, Thomas Fairchild, 1954.

3. La Manche: the French name for the English Channel.

4. "... the only way to get rid of a temptation is to yield to it. Resist it, and your soul grows sick with longing." Reference from *The Picture of Dorian Gray*, Oscar Wilde, 1890.

About the Author

Born and raised in Estonia, Elena Djakonova came to the United States at age twenty. She has always had a hunger for literature, travel, and high cuisine. Living in Miami Beach with her husband and Chihuahua, she has now brought her passions to life in her debut novel, *Glass Slippers and Champagne.*